Elysium Dreams

Hadena James

Acknowledgments

I have to give my mother the first acknowledgment, without her, none of my writings would ever see the light of day.

My best friend, Beth, who is also my first content editor and helps me keep some humor, even when the writing is at its darkest.

Then there is my life partner, Jason, who supports my writing even though he doesn't share my passion for the written word and often goes to bed without me so that I can work.

I need to give huge kudos to Kelly Nichols with EZ Book Covers for another wonderful cover that turns my thoughts into a visual feast to cloak my words.

Finally, my readers who keep Aislinn Cain and her merry band of misfits going.

Also By Hadena James

Skins

He pulled the knife from the flame. The blade was blackened by soot and had a ghastly hellish glow from the heat. He paused a few seconds to admire it. He always did. It was his most prized possession. He'd earned it.

His other prize lay on the ground. Her feet were bound at the ankles. Wrists bound behind her back and cloth shoved into her mouth with duct tape over her lips. She was going to scream. They always did. He could appreciate the muffled noises she would make.

Slowly, he walked towards her. The glow of the knife fading with each step he took. He picked up the rope that bound her ankles. Her perfect, smooth, manicured feet were in front of him. This was the starting point.

With the care a mother takes washing a newborn, he slid the knife into her skin. Her cries, muffled by the cloth and tape, filled him with a feeling of euphoria. It was a high that very few people could understand.

The knife moved easily through her skin. It seared the vessels, letting almost no blood seep from the wound. It took only a few minutes to completely remove the skin from the bottom of the first foot. He took a propane torch and reheated the knife.

When he feared it would start to melt, he turned the torch off. Just as gently, he slid the knife into the skin of her other foot. This time the cries were louder, despite the gag. Tears flowed down her cheeks.

He was an expert at this. A few gentle, but solid, movements and the skin on the bottom of the other foot came off. He turned the torch back on.

It wasn't the knife that got the torch this time. He placed it just inches from the top of her feet, the flame nearly touching them. The skin around the toes almost instantly began to blister. Her screams intensified. He knew from experience she was on the verge of passing out.

He turned the torch off. He didn't need the knife for this part. He took hold of a flap of skin that had crisped up under the heat and pulled. It peeled easily, revealing muscles, tendons, and ligaments.

The peeling did it. Her cries stopped, her head lolled to the side. He could take a break now. He sat down on the ground next to her and lit a cigar. He waited. As the ash grew longer, he flicked it at her.

After smoking the cigar, he got back up. His break was over. He attached a carabineer's hook to the rope that held her feet. The other end lay on the ground at his feet. It was already looped over the branch of the tree.

With one swift motion, he hoisted her up. Her hair brushed the ground. He attached the free end of the rope to a stake in the ground. The torch was turned back on.

The knife was reinserted into the flame. This was the part that took the most skill. He started just below the rope around her feet. The knife entered the skin at an angle, the side laying against the rope. He moved it downwards, steady and even in pressure and speed. If he went too fast or the pressure became uneven, it would mess it up.

Tenderly, he held the skin as it detached from her leg. He managed to get all the way to the knee before having to take it off. He put the skin on the ground and began again, this time on the back of the leg.

For several hours, he worked carefully. Moving with precision, he meticulously removed her skin. Sometime during removing it from her torso, she had died. He had watched the moment, felt he had seen her soul flee from her mangled corpse. She had been fun. Gently, he picked up the discarded skin. He went through it like a child carefully unwrapping a Christmas present.

Each piece was laid out on the ground, around her hanging corpse. Each one delicately selected to create a symbol on the ground, his symbol, a bow and arrow. When it was done, he snapped a quick picture with his iPhone. The sun was beginning to come up. He left the torch next to the stake, cleaned his knife with a bottle of peroxide he had brought with him, and sheathed it into its holster. He took a bottle out of his pack and dumped it on the body. His work for the night was done. It was time for him to sleep.

He hiked out of the woods, wondering how long it would take for her to be found. Two days, maybe three. The last had been found the afternoon he had finished his masterpiece. This time, the location was more remote.

It took him close to thirty minutes to follow the path out of the trees. His truck was parked a little way down the road, hidden behind a large, abandoned pump house. He found his truck keys and unlocked the doors.

The engine caught and the truck purred to life. He smiled and took a drink of water. The sun was now racing up the sky, morning was upon him. He drove off.

As he exited the park, a car pulled in. He smiled wider. He'd been wrong, she'd be found today, probably within the next hour. Good, he could begin looking for a new one.

One

Someone was flipping on the light in my bedroom. I knew this was a bad sign considering I lived alone. However, considering I lived in the Federal Guard Neighborhood, it meant that it was someone with a key to my house.

Since we had returned less than two days ago from tracking down our most recent serial killer, I was hoping the intrusion in the middle of the night was because my house was on fire. We had tracked down twelve serial killers in the time I had been a member of the Serial Crimes Tracking Unit with the US Marshals.

Our last case had taken us almost two weeks. He had been elusive to say the least, coming out only to kill a few women on random nights of horror. He'd been bold, starting the first night with four women, all shot in the head. After that, he had scaled back to only two or three a night. He had claimed fifty-three women in all before receiving his own head wound.

Frankly, I had been looking forward to a few weeks of rest and recuperation. I blearily opened my eyes. The cool, soothing, green walls greeted me first; Lucas McMichaels greeted me second. I groaned.

"Come on, we've got another and it's a priority. The press has latched onto him and is calling him 'The Flesh Hunter.' He picks a new victim the day his old victim is found. In three months, he's claimed forty-one victims. The locals were keeping it quiet until a journalist found the most recent body while taking a hike in a local wooded park."

"Great," I got out of bed and looked around the room.

"What?" Lucas asked.

"I have yet to repack my travel bag. Where are we going?"

"Alaska."

"It's March. I do not want to go to Alaska."

"Doesn't matter, we're going, pack some sweaters and hoodies." Lucas left my room.

It took me fifteen minutes to pack my bags and toss on some warm clothing. It wasn't exactly warm in Missouri. Alaska was going to be a hell of a lot colder.

Xavier, Michael, and Gabriel were in my living room. I was glad it was Lucas who had come up and woken me. Crawling into bed the previous evening, I had grabbed the two cleanest articles of sleep wear I could find: a black lacy baby-doll style top and flannel polar bear pajama pants with feet. He didn't care what I was wearing; the others would have made an inappropriate comment or two.

Gabriel was doing a good job as team leader. He made sure that the right hand always knew what the left hand was doing. This was in direct contrast to the way Alejandro had run it.

My entire house was still under construction, so to speak. The men were huddled in my living room, surrounded by blank walls. Trevor had been my shadow every time I was at home. So far, he had finished the master bedroom and bathroom, my kitchen, dining room, and library.

I had to admit the work he'd done was spectacular. My bedroom had made me speechless the first time I had seen it. The soothing, green walls were accented by a slightly lighter shade on the ceiling. The ceiling had a crown jewel, knowing my heritage and pride in being Scottish, it had a Celtic knot that was actually a dragon if you looked close enough. It had been free painted by hand.

The bed was another piece of handcrafted artistry. It turned out Trevor didn't just do interior design and cook, he was a master woodworker. The bed had taken him almost a month. It had a rich, dark brown canopy and curtains. They were double sided with thick lining to keep out the light so I could sleep regardless of the time of day. Inside the canopied bed, it was always pitch black.

This was achieved by running the canopy cloth into a custom made slot on the headboard and footboard. Both had curved edges that slid around the sides of the bed about a foot and a half on each side. The curtains did the same thing, overlapping the canopy in both front and back and each other by more than seven inches.

On the inside of the bed, carved in the dark wood, you could see fairies, faces of Green Men, dragons, and pixies. He had even thought to make holsters for my guns and knives in the headboard. It was a bitch to make the bed, but making my bed only happened when I washed my sheets. Since this was something I was rarely home to do, Trevor ended up making my bed most of the time.

He had made the bookshelves in my library as well, but with a different theme. That was part of the reason it was taking so long, every theme required a different thought process. The library was themed with Medieval Russia. My bookcases had onion domes on them. The redeeming point was that they weren't kaleidoscopically painted like Saint Basil's Cathedral in Moscow.

The spare room he had tackled had a dark Gothic theme that reminded me of Notre Dame. I wasn't sure what the plans were for the living room. He just assured me that they were massive and I'd love them. I was hoping he was right since I had handed over almost a month's worth of pay for his design necessities.

Of course, I had made more in the last six months as a member of the Marshals than I had in the previous ten years combined. I had reassigned my trust fund to my nieces and nephews and was adding five percent of my monthly income to it. I was making well into six figures a year now, Nyleena kept reassuring me that I could splurge a little on the house.

"Well, are you ready?" Gabriel asked staring at the vacant room. Not only were the walls bare, but so was the floor and it lacked furniture. Needless to say, I spent a lot of time in my dining room, bedroom or library when I was home.

"No, I was told we were going to Alaska and I do not have a parka."

"You'll get used to it in a few days or we'll solve the case before that becomes necessary," Xavier smiled. I had learned he was a hopeless optimist.

Two

On the plane, I discovered the average temperature for Anchorage was 25 degrees in March. Yet, it was unseasonably warm with an average of 37 degrees this year. I was still pretty sure that I hadn't packed enough warm clothes and, if it came to it, I would have to do some dreaded shopping when we landed.

The plane touched down and we were met by our usual escorts. An FBI agent that I had never met and some local police that seemed to think we were intruding. However, most locals seemed to think we were intruding. I had come to expect it, even if I still didn't understand it.

There was snow on the ground. I instantly felt my feet get cold. This was psychological, not physical. I don't like the cold and my distaste for it seems to make it that much worse.

"I'm US Marshal Gabriel Henders and this is my SCT Unit--Lucas McMichaels, Xavier Reece, Michael Giovanni, and Aislinn Cain."

"I'm Special Agent Fred Arons and this is the head of the State Police, Commander Brian Neilson. Where do you want to go first?"

"How fresh is the crime scene?" Gabriel asked.

"Found her yesterday morning. The body is at the morgue. The scene has been roped off. Unfortunately, that doesn't seem to be deterring the press much." Commander Neilson said.

"I'll deal with them," Gabriel nodded decisively. "Take McMichaels and Cain to the crime scene. Reece can go to the morgue. Giovanni and I will go set up our command post."

Lucas and I were ushered into a waiting SUV. We drove about thirty minutes before we turned off the paved road and onto a well traveled asphalt path. Another ten minutes and the vehicle stopped.

"Here we are," one of the State Troopers informed us.

"This park, is it state or national?" Lucas asked.

"State." The trooper told him.

"Have they all been found in state parks?"

"Yes. We think he's been operating in the state parks to keep the feds out of it. We have our own system up here for that. However, we tried to contact you after the twenty-fourth woman was discovered and you all were busy."

"Sorry," Lucas managed to make it sound heartfelt. I wasn't sure it was genuine, but then Lucas was still full of mysteries and wonder, even after six months.

"The scene is about a mile or so down this path. You'll want to dress warmly, but not too warmly. Mostly cover your feet and legs. The cold will sink into your shoes pretty quickly."

I was way ahead of him. I had already started pulling on snow-boots with good treads that went all the way up to my knees. I grabbed an extra fleece and put it on. This gave me six layers of upper-body protection.

We got out of the SUV and the cold which had been starting to creep out of my bones rushed back into them. I didn't let it show that the cold was bothering me. I kept pace with the taller men, ignoring the protests from my knees and hips. My lifestyle was conducive to permanent joint discomfort.

The walk seemed to take ages. Barren trees covered in icicles and a crunchy snow covered landscape gave the impression of being in a winter wonderland. Hard to believe a dead body had been found here the day before, unless you looked at the ground.

The hard, crunchy snow was covered in footprints. Some of them were dirty, some clean, some buried under others, it looked like hundreds of people had come and gone down this path. My own snow-boots were leaving impressions as we continued forward, my footsteps falling in the impressions being left by Lucas's shoes. There were already enough prints without adding mine. So I carefully walked in Lucas's. His feet were almost twice the size of mine, making it easy.

Finally, the men stopped. I came up even with them and stared at the scene. There was a rope hanging from the tree with a hook on it. The rope looped over a branch and came down to where it was staked into the hardened ground.

There wasn't nearly as much blood on the ground as I had expected. A few drops here and a medium sized puddle there were all that showed. There was another area though. It was distinctly different from the other. It looked as if the snow had partial melted and refroze. "What is that?" I pointed to the altered snow.

"His signature," a trooper said to me. He walked over to it, I followed him.

"It doesn't look like much," I squinted to see if I could find any discernible features.

"We found skin here, laid out on the ground in the shape of a drawn back bow and arrow ready to be released. We removed the skin, but the salt melted the snow anyway."

"That is really gross," I knelt down to get a closer look.

"Yes it is, but it is how the press nicknamed him. Not sure who released that nugget of information, but someone leaked it and now the press knows that he signs his kills with it."

"What do you see?" Lucas knelt down next to me. We had developed a student/teacher relationship, but we seemed to take turns on which role we played.

"I see something that takes a lot of skill. Skinning a human is much harder than skinning a rabbit or fox or bear. The hanging implement is crude, nothing fancy there, but aside from the tree, nothing is improvised. He even brings his own stakes and hammer to drive them in with. What do you see?"

"I see a man disconnected from reality. To kill a person is one thing, to skin them is entirely different. He is obliterating their identity when he removes all their flesh. He is methodical, skilled, and completely lacking in empathy. He probably works with his hands for a living. I imagine there is also some military training, or martial arts, given his skill with a knife. People don't just become good with knives overnight. He may be a hunter who got bored with animal prey, but we aren't in a Joseph Conrad story," he shrugged at the last.

My mind instantly got the references, both of them. *The Most Dangerous Game* and *Heart of Darkness* were twisted works about twisted men who devalued human life to the point that it was about nothing more than showing superiority. I considered that. Was this a statement of superiority? Most likely, you didn't just skin a human because it sounded like fun. It required effort, dedication, and determination.

I stood up and continued to look around. There was a stained area in the snow; the blood had soaked in there, but how? Skinning, if done correctly, didn't bleed. And where were his footprints? Why weren't they marked off?

11

"Hey, where are the killer's footprints?" I shouted to the nearest uniformed officer.

"We didn't get here in time to save them. A TV crew found the body first. Instead of reporting the find, they reported the story, on the news. We learned about it that way. By then there had been two dozen people or more and we couldn't get elimination prints from all of them. They did a great job of trampling the crime scene."

"Why would a reporter not report it to the police before showing it on the news?" I frowned.

"Because she was some upstart local who thought it was her way to get national coverage." The officer informed me.

"Stupid woman," I sighed.

"Ambition and greed are amazing things," Lucas reminded me.

"They lower the intelligence of all involved," I responded.

"Yes indeed," he looked at the rope. "Get it down; preserve it the best way possible, we might be able to get skin, hair, or fibers off of it."

"Yeah, the reporter's," I muttered.

"Don't be a pessimist," Lucas whispered to me.

"Don't be such an optimist," I shot back. "It should be very hard to be an optimist when stupid people are trampling crime scenes and airing the grisly material on the news instead of reporting it to the police."

"Remind me not to leave you alone with her," Lucas gave me a quick grin.

"Probably a good plan," I turned a slow circle.

It was white. There were brown patches that belonged to trees, but that was the only break-up in the view. The rest was snow, snow, and more snow. It was all pristine and perfect. No animal tracks, no human tracks, aside from the path, nothing to indicate that anything had been touched outside of this small area.

On the flip side, it looked like everything had been touched on the inside. There were dozens of shoe prints around the stake in the ground. They circled the base of the tree. There was even an indication that at least two people had scampered up the tree or that the same person had gone up twice.

I moved in closer to the bloody snow. There was something else in it. It was yellowish and had caused a good deal of snow melt. It also smelled like Pinesol. I backed up and put a hand over my nose. Pinesol was like poison to people with migraines, the smell was strong, overpowering, and I hadn't met another person with migraines that could stand to be around it for very long. My stomach flopped, so I moved back another step.

The blood seemed to be frozen. Most likely it had been cold when it hit the ground. There seemed to be a large pool of it considering the victim was skinned. The hook from the rope was directly over the spot where the blood had frozen. If I had to guess, I'd say the Pinesol came before the blood. Lucas came up to me.

"See anything?" He asked.

"Blood and Pine-Sol; I am not sure why there is Pinesol, but that is what it smells like. Maybe he urinated on the ground here and used the Pinesol to cover it up?" I suggested.

"We'll have someone check it out," Lucas knelt down closer to the spot than I could get. He seemed to be inspecting it, memorizing its measurements. Of course, that was probably exactly what he was doing, he had a photographic memory.

"How far off the ground was she?" I asked.

"About ten feet or so," Commander Nielsen answered.

"Who went up the tree?"

"The coroner went up once. We don't know who the other was. We swabbed the tree."

"I can't think of a reason for our killer to climb the tree," Lucas said.

"Maybe the rope got hung," I offered.

"Maybe," he agreed doubtfully. "More likely, it was the reporter."

"She would have wished she had reacted differently if it was her hanging from that tree," I growled.

"Yes, she would have, but it wasn't her and human nature is what it is," Lucas tempered me.

"Because I need more proof that people suck," I gave him a small smile.

"That's better," he turned away from me again.

Someone was now carefully using a ladder to dislodge the rope from the tree. The hook was handed down and placed in an evidence bag. The rope was carefully being coiled up by a guy dressed in what appeared to be a HAZMAT suit. Someone else was prying the stake out of the ground. When it was up, it too got put into a bag and sealed.

"Let's go find Xavier," Lucas said to me. He looked over the scene one more time. I knew he was committing it to memory. He wouldn't forget a single detail. It was part of what he did.

I, on the other hand, wouldn't remember much of it. The blood stained snow, the weird melted spot where the skin had been laid out, the pristine condition of the snow all around the kill zone, those were what I would remember. After we finished the case, I would remember the bow and arrow in the melted snow. The rest would get lost as we started another case. I was not Lucas; I would not be haunted by it for eternity. Sometimes it made me wonder how he carried on, knowing that every

crime scene would be indelibly etched in his memory
forever.

Three

"Hello my lovelies, just in time," Xavier gave us a grin as we walked into the morgue. It smelled like Pinesol and my stomach gave a small flop. I grabbed a mask and put it on, trying not to gag on the smell.

"Did you find anything?" Lucas asked him.

"Loads," Xavier looked at me, "don't you dare break your streak. You have never yakked in the morgue, don't start now."

"It is not the morgue, it's the Pinesol," I informed him.

"Pinesol makes you yak?" Xavier gave me a skeptical look.

"Yes, it also triggers migraines. Why the hell is it so strong in here? Why not use bleach?"

"Because it is coming from the body," Xavier told me.

"That's just weird," I responded.

"Isn't it just?" Xavier gave me a look before grabbing something and handing it to me. It was a small brown bag. I wasn't big on dignity, but I wasn't going to toss my cookies in the thing. I held my breath instead.

"Why would you douse a body with Pinesol?" Lucas asked.

"I don't know, which is why it is so weird. There is nothing in Pinesol that would speed up decay and it isn't like this guy is looking to speed it up anyway. It won't work as a human preservative either," Xavier shrugged.

"Oh God," I gagged. I knew why it was covered in Pinesol. I left the room, motioning the others to follow me.

Outside, in the hallway, I took a deep breath. After a few more, I felt a little less like throwing up, but still not up to talking. I put my head between my knees and breathed.

"Are you alright?" Lucas asked.

Xavier fell to work, his fingers began lifting my eyelids, a flashlight appeared in his hands and blinded me for a moment. His fingers moved to my mouth and nose, opening both and looking in them. I pushed him away.

"Stop that," I finally told him.

"You look like you are going to pass out."

"If you had migraines and a nose as sensitive as mine, you'd look that way too," I said staring at Xavier and trying not to gag. The smell was still overwhelming. So much so, that it made me realize the purpose of the hideous floor cleaner. "The Pinesol is there to keep the wildlife at bay. There were no animal tracks within fifty feet of the body. It's barely spring in Alaska, where are the scavengers? The large birds looking for a snack? The wolves? The bears? Avoiding it like it has plague because it smells so badly."

"Bears eat car seats because of the formaldehyde," Lucas informed me.

"Yes, but it smells like a termite mound. I cannot imagine they would be attracted to Pine-Sol, and they certainly are not going to eat anything covered in it."

"I hadn't considered that. She may have a point," Xavier looked at me. "We need a zoologist."

"Pinesol smells worse than a dead body?" Lucas asked me.

"In large quantities, yes. Pinesol will give me a migraine and it certainly doesn't smell like food. I imagine it doesn't smell like food to the predators and scavengers around here either."

"Decomposing, half-frozen bodies smell like food?" Lucas continued.

"Not to me, but I'm sure it does to many animals. I think it smells like death, personally."

"Stop you two, I will take that under advisement. So, I also discovered that he torched the skin on the tops of the feet and on the hands, then peeled it off instead of taking it off with the knife. He did something similar around the lower genitalia and face as well, burning it off instead of trying to skin it. However, aside from that, the rest of the skin was removed with delicate precision. He rarely went too deep or moved the knife so that it exited the skin prematurely. The victim didn't lose much blood and there was evidence of searing, meaning he knew how to do it and kept the knife very hot. It reminds me of the Predator kills from the movie, only without all the dripping blood."

"Those were good movies," I commented dryly.

"They were and gave the wrong impression about how hard it is to skin a body. Of course, if you were Predator, it was easy, but for the rest of us . . . Well, it's an enormous task to undertake," Xavier looked at me. "Feeling better?"

"Some, but you smell like the damned Pinesol too."

"Shut up about the Pinesol, go get a HEPA-Mask. Now." Xavier looked at the counter pointedly. I grabbed the HEPA-Mask and shut up. "There were also no hesitation marks, no details overlooked, and I can't figure out the knife he used; but it is incredibly sharp, most likely carbon steel and designed for the job. I don't think it is something you can buy off the shelf at any local store. It was probably special order."

"Why do all our serial killers buy specialty items off the internet?" I asked.

"Because they can," Xavier responded. "Besides, why settle for something that's half the quality when you can spend a few more bucks online and get the good stuff? I wouldn't do that. I'd shop online. Besides, it is a lot harder to track down some anonymous knife purchase from the internet or gun show. But we could walk into a pawnshop or sporting goods store and figure out how many freaks and collectors have purchased specialty blades. Hell, ordering your knives was a chore. Even with the badges we still had to register to purchase them because they were customized and the guy wanted to keep all the spec information in case you had to have one replaced."

"Xavier, focus," Lucas said to him, eyes narrowed.

"Oh wow, he's high," I said, jumping from my chair. "Too much Pinesol."

"It would explain the rapid heartbeat and the feeling that I'm moving at a million miles a minute," Xavier answered. "Also it would account for the weird feeling of having my head detached from my shoulders and floating like a balloon. Maybe I should get a glass of water or something else not caffeinated. Maybe I should eat something with chocolate."

"Sit down," Lucas forced the slightly smaller man into a chair.

"Head between your legs, deep breaths," I told him. "Why chocolate?"

"Why not?" Xavier said, voice muffled, hands gesturing oddly between his legs as he talked.

As Xavier worked to get his senses back, I took a moment to survey my surroundings. I was getting used to morgues, this one wasn't much different. There weren't that many people around and the entire place smelled like disinfectant and Pinesol. There was only one other person. I hadn't been introduced to him yet, but he seemed important.

"Ok, I'm better," Xavier stood up slowly. "Dr. Ericson these are my colleagues--Dr. Aislinn Cain and Dr. Lucas McMichaels."

"I'm the medical examiner," Dr. Ericson shook my hand.

"Pleasure, sort of," I answered taking my hand away from him. "You did the first autopsies?"

"Yes."

"Did they all smell like Pinesol?" I asked.

"Yes, we weren't sure why, though it seems you managed to figure it out," there was a tone to his voice. I was also getting used to working with men like him. Most of the time, my presence was accepted, but once in a while I found a man that thought a woman shouldn't be working with this group of misfits. Most men didn't realize I was as damaged, if not more so, than my merry group of misfits.

"Only because I have migraines," I soothed his ego.

"When was your last check-up?" He asked, looking at me intently.

"A couple of months ago, but Xavier monitors them all the time," I assured him.

"And your last neurological screening was clean?"

"Yes, I just get tired when we go out on back to back calls, the eye glaze is a result of that, not of an oncoming migraine," I realized he understood what he was talking about. People who didn't have personal experience with migraines rarely understood.

"Are you sure?" He flashed a light in my eyes.

"Trust me; I have been dealing with them for as long as I could walk, I know my auras."

"I believe you; I'm just worried about your current state. You appear to be in the early stages of a migraine, which would significantly impact the investigation."

"Yes it would, I would remove myself for the duration of a migraine, because my judgment becomes flawed as does my thought process. However, that is not the case here. If I have a headache, it is exactly that, a headache, and is the result of the overwhelming smell of Pinesol in the other room. It is unlikely to be a migraine or any other medical condition."

"Your eyes are bloodshot and seem glazed, you have deep circles under them, meaning that you are not getting as much blood to your face as usual, these are all migraine indicators."

"They are also indicators of sleep deprivation," I reminded him.

"You're right. I'm sorry Dr. Cain. I am not only the medical examiner, I run a private practice and my daughter has migraines and a small benign brain tumor that causes them," he stepped back from me.

"Meaning migraines are personal for you," I gave him my best apologetic smile. "No need to apologize, I take my migraines very personally as well."

"Can you explain the blood at the scene?" I asked.

"I can," Xavier looked at me.

"Fine, you both can, if we can get the room aired out. I don't think you should go back in without a respirator."

"I think that is sound advice for all of us," Dr. Ericson walked out of the hallway, into another room. He came back with full facial masks complete with HEPA-Filters. "We also deal with diseased animals." He told me with a grin.

Masks in place, we walked back into the room. Dr. Ericson moved to one side, Xavier moved to the other. Dr. Ericson seemed fine with Xavier taking the lead.

"See here?" He pointed to the victim's neck. His voice sounded weird coming through the mask. "He is getting through most of the skin, but not all of it. After the victim hangs for a while, the blood stops flowing out of the head while the victim is alive. After the victim dies, the blood pressure continues to build in the head and face region. Eventually, since the killer has removed so much skin, the artery and vein that runs through the neck ruptures. The rupture breaks the layer or two of skin the killer is leaving. It isn't spray because it happens well after death, but it is a considerable pool simply because the blood is exiting the body. This seems to be increased, the pressure I mean, by the fact that it's so cold. The blood is clotting and starting to freeze, this causes the rupture to be larger than it would be in warmer temperatures."

"Wouldn't freezing have the opposite effect?" I asked, slightly confused.

"It would in the limbs," Dr. Ericson said, "but in the torso and the head the blood freezes slower because it stays warmer longer. Think of it as lividity. Normally, a hung body ruptures the vessels in the eyes, nose, and ears because that is the thinnest part. But here, because the body is missing so much skin, the rupture happens in the major vessels, creating a larger pool."

"Is the lack of skin an issue for keeping the body warm?" I asked.

"Yes, a serious issue. The feet are showing signs of freezing shortly after or in a few cases, before death," Dr. Ericson volunteered.

"How long does this take?" Lucas asked.

"Three or four hours," Xavier answered. "He is using a blowtorch on the hard parts and peeling the skin off, so the toes, fingers, and face all show signs of direct flame. But he is removing the scalp before he torches the face. From what I can tell, he starts at the feet. He skins the bottoms and torches the tops. This probably creates enough pain that he can untie the victim and begin skinning the ankles. After he is finished with the ankles, he reties their feet and strings them up. Once they are hung, he can work on the legs. What I don't understand is why he takes them down, unties them again, and takes the skin from the inner legs after he has finished everything else."

"Assault on their femininity?" Lucas looked at him. "You said earlier he takes the torch to their lower genitalia. Could it be that he skins the inner legs and then torches the genitalia?"

"Yes, that's possible," Xavier responded.

"Then maybe that's why he does the outer legs first, but leaves the inner legs for last," Lucas offered.

"Now for the odd part, Dr. Ericson, will you help me turn her?" Xavier asked and the two men rolled the victim over. Xavier pointed to the heel of the victim.

"He's leaving a patch," I said looking at it.

"That he is," Xavier answered.

"Why that patch?" Lucas asked.

I stared at the patch of skin; it was the wrinkled part on the back of the leg, where the calf muscle meets the tendons in the ankle. There was a flash of memory, the bow and arrow laid out in the snow.

"Achilles," I answered.

"Our brains don't work like yours," Lucas reminded me.

"There was a bow and arrow in the snow, made of human skin, and he's leaving the part where the Achilles Tendon connects to the calf muscle. Achilles was killed by an arrow shot into the heel; it was the only part of him not immortal."

"First, I think it odd that you made that connection," Xavier said, "second, you're right, that is the spot where Achilles would have been mortal, but why?"

"That sounds like a Lucas question," I said. We all turned to stare at the big man.

"I would have to think about it," Lucas answered. "I'm not often confronted with mythology and the mythological reasons for killing."

"I will tell you all about Achilles, the Battle of Troy, and the Elysium Fields when we get back to the motel and have some food in us," I told him.

"Thank you," Lucas looked at the ankle again. "What I can tell you is that this piece is purposely not removed."

"I might have a theory on that as well," I told them, "but I will wait until Lucas and I talk first."

"Then I think we can call it a night here. We are just waiting for the next victim," Xavier began removing his gloves.

Four

We ate dinner at a small diner. They had a decent menu with exotic fare such as bear burgers. I wasn't brave enough to eat a bear burger, so I settled for a Philly Steak with Cheese. Lucas was brave enough and ordered the exotic fare cooked medium and slathered with condiments.

After dinner, we went to the motel. There was an interior hallway, but it was only used by staff. All the rooms had double entrances and the exterior door that opened onto the parking lot showed the most use. The key card reader was tarnished, dented, and scratched. The knob had a slight jiggle to it. The paint was peeling from the frame.

Inside there were adjoining doors. Knowing how I felt about adjoining doors, Gabriel had been nice enough to put Lucas and Xavier in that room. Gabriel and Michael had the room on the other side of me. Being a girl, the only girl, gave me the advantage of almost always getting my own room. The rare occasions when I couldn't get my own room, I bunked with Lucas and Xavier, and Lucas made sure that Xavier stayed in line.

Not that Xavier needed to be kept in line. He was a flirt and a tease, nothing more. His rude and inappropriate comments were meant to be playful. He was only a danger to himself, when a woman mistook his playful nature and gave him a good tongue lashing or a hard slap for his comments.

Despite the fact that Lucas and I both understood Xavier was only teasing, Lucas seemed to have made it his mission in life to protect me from it. When Xavier stepped over some invisible vulgarity boundary, Lucas quickly put him back in his place. All he had to do was look at the smaller man and Xavier would be out with an apology; a second or two later, the tension would drain from the room. Xavier would go back to being Xavier, and the rest of us would go back to enjoying his company.

On the other hand, Xavier had developed a bit of a crush on my cousin Nyleena. He was very polite and gentlemanly around her, never a vulgar comment to be found. I had made it very clear to Xavier that if he and Nyleena ever hooked up, I would probably kill him. She had enough problems in her life with just me, she didn't need the complications of adding another serial killer chaser to it.

In reality, that meant that if Nyleena came to me and told me she had a thing for Xavier, I'd be planning their wedding. But for now, she didn't and since she didn't, I made it seem like I was the bad guy intent on stopping Xavier from having his prize.

My room was small with a single full size bed, a dresser that half the drawers didn't open on and a TV mounted with brackets sitting on top of it, to keep it from getting stolen. A nightstand with a drawer that did open contained a Bible. The other side of the bed had a nightstand with no drawer and a lamp. There was a small, mostly clean, bathroom. The shower curtain looked like it had been in existence since the 1940's and had dark spots near the bottom that were either built up dirt or mold, but they seemed to be on the side between the shower curtain and the tub, so I could shower in safety. If it really creeped me out, I could always use one of the other showers in our little three room block.

Finally, there was a table that looked like it had been built by IKEA during the Dark Ages. It was cheap and scarred; the top had been replaced by a slab of real wood that was sealed to keep things from seeping into it. No one had bothered to stain it. It appeared to be pine or some other type of evergreen. It also appeared to have come from a really old tree as the three foot circumference of the table top was made from a single slice of aged timber. Around the table were three chairs, which was weird, as there were normally only two.

Of course, we would still need another chair or two. I had strict rules about Xavier sitting on my motel beds after leaving the morgue. I actually had that rule for everyone. If you've been to the morgue, you were banned from sitting on the bed I intended to sleep in unless you had changed your clothes and showered. The morgues always had their own unique smell that was carried from place to place to infect other locations with the sickly smells of death and something darker.

I had been in my room a total of five minutes, when Lucas and Xavier came through the adjoining door. I smiled at them and made a mental note that the door was unlocked. If it had been someone else on the other side, I would have checked it immediately. Since it was Lucas and Xavier, I hadn't bothered. Of course, in the event that a serial killer busted down my door, if the adjoining door was unlocked, I could run there and the big bad scary men on the other side could run to my rescue. That thought made me smile even wider.

"Gabriel and Michael are coming in through the front," Lucas said as he walked over and unlocked the motel room door. Sure enough, Gabriel and Michael walked in, each with a chair in their hands. Xavier made a point to sit in one of the chairs at the table and gave me a grin while doing it.

"What's up?" I asked.

"Something about Achilles and the Hunter," Gabriel answered.

"Oh," I took my own seat. "Well, you all know the story of Achilles, dipped in the river to give him immortality except where his mother held him by the ankle?"

"Yes," most of them said or nodded.

"Well, he was killed in the Battle of Troy by being shot in that spot by a bow and arrow. I just think there is some connection between the killer leaving that spot with skin and the signing of his kills with a bow and arrow."

"But Achilles was male," Gabriel pointed out.

"That's true, but one tale says that Paris hid in the bushes and shot Achilles because Achilles was about to be privately married to Paris's sister which would have ended the Trojan War and forced Paris to give up Helen."

"I don't remember that story from my history classes," Lucas said.

"Well, it is just one of them," I answered. "There are generally three explanations for Achilles death. Paris shot him with an arrow guided by Apollo because the rage of Achilles could not be tempered and might defy the Fates. Paris shot him with an arrow as Achilles scaled the walls of Troy and was helped by the gods because it was not yet time for Troy to fall or that Paris shot him because he was marrying Paris' sister and bringing an end to the war. In each version, Paris is seen as a coward and denied being considered a victor over Achilles because each one has the gods helping Paris hit him where he was weak because Achilles was too strong to be reined in by Fate."

"Using that, I can go with him being Achilles, strong enough to defy his fate in his mundane life, or Paris, unable to stop killing because it is his fate. However, I'm still leaning towards a guy looking at life from the point of *The Most Dangerous Game*," he shrugged.

"But Conrad had his hunter use a gun," I countered.

"True, but he also had to use his wits, which is what our guy is doing. Besides, where does skinning fit into the story of Achilles and Paris?"

"They were Greeks and Trojans, so who knows. They did all sorts of things," I looked at him. "Skinning only sort of fits with the Conrad theory, I am sure the hunter skinned his game kills, but he also mounted the heads on his walls."

"True, but it would be a lot harder to get away with mounting a head on a wall outside of a book," Lucas said.

"That brings us to the next question, I think. What is he doing with the rest of the skin?" Gabriel interrupted.

"Good question," Xavier seemed to think for a minute. "I can think of a medical reason for leaving the skin on that part of body. It is where the rope goes, if the rope rubbed the area with only a layer or two of skin left, it's going to start bleeding profusely. You have a major artery and vein that run in that area."

"Well, that brings in an element of anatomy, he'd have to have a clue about the human body," Lucas stated.

"Yep," Xavier answered. "But it doesn't tell us where the rest of the skin went. And we should clarify here, he is taking the epidermis, meaning only the outer layer of skin. This averages only three millimeters thick and around the eyes it is thinner, around the feet and hands it is thicker. The dermis and hypodermis are being left, that's why they aren't bleeding much, but those layers are not thick enough to keep the veins and arteries from rupturing when the pressure gets to a certain point. This is serious precision and the knife would not only have to be of extremely high quality, but very thin and incredibly sharp. I'm not sure how well it could be done with a scalpel. I'd also like to point out how much the epidermis weighs on the average human. Most people have fifteen to twenty pounds of epidermis. That's a lot of skin to be carrying around."

"So, two opposing theories, and a man who walks around with fifteen to twenty pounds of skin that he then does something unknown with," Gabriel said.

"Not opposing theories," Lucas corrected, "just theories, Ace could be right about his feeling a need to buck the system or fate or whatever he believes controls his life. I could be right that he is hunting humans because he is tired of hunting other things, the thrill of the hunt gone until now. Or we could both be right. Or we could both be wrong. What he does with the skin could make a difference. Are they trophies? Is he disposing of it? Is it more about the act of taking the skin or is it about keeping the skin? If it's the act, he's disposing of it. If not, he's keeping it. But where do you keep that much skin?"

"Ok, so we know nothing about him except he can skin a person and not be bothered by it," Gabriel sighed.

"No, we know that it is a male, a female would not be able to skin another female like that," I told them. "Besides, women prefer less messy ways of killing. Yes, there are exceptions, but not like this. Exceptions are always quick and easy and messy, usually guns. Our last female serial was using a cult to kill for her because she didn't want to get her hands dirty with the gory work. Besides, I saw the hoist mechanism. There wasn't a pulley system, just a rope looped around a tree branch. I'm one hundred and thirty pounds, give or take, and in pretty good shape. However, to pull another woman my size off the ground without a pulley against the grain of tree bark is going to take it out of me. After I get her lifted, I'm going to need a break. And as a woman killing other women, I'm not very tall. I'm going to have to hoist

30

her and let her down and hoist her and let her down several times to get to all the areas. To get the precision needed, I'm going to need to keep almost everything at eye-level. This means if I start with her legs, I'm going to have to hoist her to five foot three inches off the ground and hope I can work with that. Then I'm going to have to pull her up more to get to her torso. After each time, my arms are going to be tired. I'm going to have to rest to keep my hands from shaking."

"I hadn't thought of that," Lucas looked me over.

"I did when I saw the rope on the tree. I realized then that it would take me forever to do something like that. A man like you, it probably wouldn't bother. A man like Xavier or Gabriel is going to get winded and Michael has less of a shot at it than I do," I told him.

"So whoever did it is either built like a wall or they took breaks," Gabriel said.

"Yes, it was a demonstration of both skill and strength," I said.

"Actually, it might have been a demonstration of prowess," Lucas said. "What if he climbed the tree and wrapped it around after he was done?"

"That seems like a waste of time," I told him.

"But it makes it easier to lift and release," Lucas answered.

"True," I frowned.

"But you're right, it would be a waste of time," Lucas said after a few more minutes. "And it might not be stable enough."

"We need to check the tree bark again on that limb," I said.

"They cut it down, it's at the lab," Xavier answered. "However, given either scenario, we are looking for someone who is physically fit and good with a blade. Military?"

"Or Predator," I smiled at him.

"Aliens aside," Gabriel said to me, "would a military guy have the precision to skin a human being?"

"I wouldn't," Lucas answered, "but Xavier might. Of course, he is also a doctor."

"So male, medical training, and military," Gabriel lit a cigarette. I was currently wearing a patch after Xavier decided that my smoking was bad for me. I had tried to convince him that not smoking was bad for everyone else. He had ignored me and for the last two weeks, I had been on the patch. However, I really wanted a cigarette.

"I don't know if you would need military training," I said, envying Gabriel.

"Why not?" Xavier asked.

"Why would he? Hunters don't always have military experience. Doctors don't always have military experience. I don't have any, but I can hold my own with any of you," I countered.

"No, Ace, we are all scared of you," Michael stated, "Lucas might put up a hell of a fight, but the rest of us would just go down with slit throats or lots of bullet wounds. You wouldn't need to hold your own because you are badder than the rest of us."

"I see the point," Lucas said. "Ace doesn't think the guy needs to have military training because she wouldn't need it. If she was willing to kill for the thrill, she could easily learn the tricks of the trade to skin a human being. She's probably right."

"She does know her personality disorders," Xavier admitted.

"Fine, we'll put a giant question mark next to military training. Anything else?" Gabriel asked.

"I imagine he is unimpressive," Lucas said. "He works his job and is good at it, but it will be something benign. I'd add he was a hunter, but that would include most of the male population in this area, so that would be worthless information. He has some medical knowledge, might be just an anatomy class or two in college while getting a degree in something else. Physically fit isn't necessarily going to help, because I'd guess he's also a psychopath and, therefore, better at physical feats than most. He wouldn't have to be my size for it not to exhaust him, just crazy enough."

"That is not a very helpful profile," Gabriel grinned.

"Well, give me a crystal ball and we will see what else we can dig up for you," I smirked at him.

"I think we'll leave Predator on the list of possible suspects for now, at least we have a physical description of him," Gabriel stood and left. Michael followed behind him.

Tedium

His cell phone rang as he left the morgue. His wife's shrill voice came over the line. She was upset because their daughter hadn't come home yet. He assured her that the girl was probably fine and that he'd check her normal hangouts before he hung up.

He didn't bother to mention that he already knew where the girl was; he had driven to her location while talking to the harpy he considered his wife. As he sat inside his Cadillac Escalade, he could see her through the large plate glass windows that spilled light into the darkened street. The SUV lights were off, but the engine was running. He lit a cigar. It was one of two places he could smoke; his wife hated the smell of cigar smoke. However, he had bought the Escalade himself, so she allowed him to smoke in it and in the backyard. As long as he picked up the stubs, of course, if he let any fall into the yard or left one on the patio, there was hell to pay.

As he smoked, he watched a group of teenage girls inside a pizzeria. The youngest was only fifteen. She was supposed to be home over an hour ago. Her mother was going to be livid. There would be shouting and screaming. After all, there was a serial killer on the loose.

This girl, though, wasn't his target. She wasn't his type. She was too young, too wild for his tastes. He preferred them to be prim, proper, full grown women. Besides, she was his daughter.

No one else in the group fit his purpose either, but their waitress, she was a different story. Her blond hair was pulled back in a very severe ponytail. Her face was hard set as she disapprovingly served the group of unsupervised girls. They were a little unruly in her opinion, and it showed on her face.

Then again, the fifteen year old currently shoving a slice of cheese pizza into her mouth, ensured that the waitress was safe, at least for the night. His wife had been insistent that he go find the girl and bring her home. If he didn't return with the girl, there would be hell to pay.

But he would give her a few more minutes to enjoy her pizza and her friends. He finished his cigar, put the stub in the ashtray, and got out. He adjusted his suit, smoothing out the invisible wrinkles.

He walked inside and made his way over to the girls. They were giggling and smiling. He was touched by their youth and innocence.

"Grace," he said to the fifteen year old.

"Hi, Daddy," she smiled up at him.

"You were supposed to be home by dark," he reminded her.

"Oh yeah," she blushed.

"Hi," one of the girls waved at him.

He smiled back, "Hi, Emily."

"Just one more slice?" Grace looked up at him with a smile and wide brown eyes.

"I suppose, slide over," Henry moved into the booth next to his daughter and grabbed a slice of pepperoni pizza.

The girls in the booth with them; Emily, Kara, and Brittany, were all seventeen. Grace was on the basketball team with them and despite being two years younger, the girls all clicked. But, as a result of the age difference, he and his wife insisted that most of the sleepovers happen at their house. Their daughter was still not able to drive and they weren't ready to let her start dating or participate in any other rites of passage.

This meant the girls were at ease with Henry too. Just a week ago, they had thrown a neighborhood block party that everyone had attended. Henry was still proud of the block party with bonfire and grilling in the snow, it had been a huge success.

Grace and Henry finished the pizza. Henry stood up and handed Grace her coat. He left money on the table for the three pizzas the girls had ordered as well as a huge tip. He would see the waitress again.

"Do you girls need an escort home?" Henry asked as Grace finished putting on her coat.

"No, my dad is coming soon," Emily told him. "It was the only way we could convince him to let us go out tonight."

"Maybe we should wait for him," Henry looked out the window as a SUV pulled into the almost vacant parking lot. He recognized the SUV, it belonged to the Sheriff, Emily's dad.

He walked out with Grace and the other girls. They waved good-bye as they piled into the SUV.

"Tucker," Henry said.

"Henry," Sheriff Rybolt responded.

"I was waiting to make sure the girls had an escort home."

"Glad you did, it was a bad one yesterday," Sheriff Rybolt looked at Grace. "We'll talk about it tomorrow though. Get some sleep."

"You try to do the same," Henry walked Grace to the SUV. It was still running, the inside was warm and welcoming as they slid into the heated seats.

"He did it again?" Grace asked.

"Yes, he did it again."

"Are you going to catch him?"

"I don't know, we've got some Marshals up here to help us," Henry thought about the female Marshal. She had struck him as odd. There was something different about her; he couldn't put his finger on it though.

"Took you long enough," Hilary, his wife, said as the two of them stomped snow off their shoes at the front door.

"She was having slices with friends, I went in and sat with all of them until Sheriff Rybolt showed up to pick up the other girls," Henry said, immediately defending Grace.

"Is that why you were out so late?" Hilary turned her eyes on Grace.

"Yes, Emily and Kara didn't want to leave until one of our parents came to get us," Grace took her book bag upstairs, away from her mother's piercing gaze.

"And you think that's an acceptable reason for her to be out late?" Hilary turned full force on Henry.

"Yes, Hilary, it's March, it gets dark early and I'd rather them have pizza at a busy pizzeria while waiting for parents than to have them be out on the streets, alone," Henry pulled off his coat.

"So their children are our problem?"

"There's a serial killer on the loose, I would hope that everyone is looking out for everyone else's children."

"Whatever, Henry," Hilary walked away, dismissing him with a wave of her hand.

Henry went to his study, glad the debate with his wife was over, at least for now. He was sure she'd bring it back up at breakfast, but for now it was quiet. They hadn't shared a bedroom since Grace had been born.

He pulled out all the case files from the drawer. Inside were all his autopsy photos. He had been meticulous about taking the photos. He wanted to make sure every nuance had been captured. The photos were good quality, they did his work justice.

Tomorrow held some promise. Tomorrow night he might be able to go out and find his prize. Or maybe he'd just grab the waitress at the diner. She had been just about perfect.

This thought brought him back to Dr. Cain. She was also just about perfect. She was very matter of fact. She was very proper. Her clothing had screamed loads about her. It had obviously been bought with meticulous care for color and shape. Even with the multiple fleeces on, she had been shapely. Yet, there was still something that nagged him about her. Something he couldn't put his finger on or identify. Something that was unique and screamed at him to be cautious around her.

He stopped thinking about her and went back to his photos. He did such good work on these women. He was a master in this domain.

There was a knock on the door of the study. His daughter, he thought as he stood up. Sure enough, Grace stood in her flannel pajamas outside the door. He closed the study behind him.

"Sorry I made Mom mad," she whispered.

"It's fine, honey, Mom is just freaked out because of the killer. But we had a group of US Marshals come in today to help with the search. We'll have him found out in no time," he assured her.

Grace gave him a hug and a kiss and went back upstairs. He went back to his study, locking the door behind him. His eyes fell on the photographs of the first three women. They were different. They weren't his.

Those three had belonged to his son, Henry Junior. He had come home from war a broken man. Too broken to even live on his own, he had moved back into his parents' house. His father had found the photos after Henry Junior had taken his own life.

A tear sprang to his eye. He wiped it away. His work made him feel close to his dead son·· the son that had taken a finely crafted blade to his own body, opening up over three dozen wounds. He had bled to death in less than three minutes. In the snow, in December, next to a freshly killed moose.

Henry still didn't understand the meaning behind the moose or the suicide. All he did understand was that his son had somehow turned into a killer when he arrived back in Alaska. A killer who seemed to hate women.

That was something Henry could understand. His wife was a monster. Always had been, always would be. He pushed the thought away, turned out the lights and left the study.

Hilary would be in bed by now. He climbed the stairs and when he reached his room, he hesitated for a moment. The fleeting glimpse of Dr. Aislinn Cain had distracted him again. Yes, she was his type, but she would be dangerous. The Marshals would double or triple their efforts if he went after her. He'd have to let her go.

He opened the door to his bedroom. The room was quiet. Hilary had the room next door and her snoring could be heard through the walls. But that was the only sound. He undressed as silently as possible and lay in bed for a long time, focusing on the waitress at the diner.

Five

Morning broke with no news of a new dead body. This meant our killer was two days off his mark. Something had changed his pattern. We were assembled at breakfast with our FBI liaison, Special Agent Arons, Commander Neilsen, and Sheriff Rybolt to figure out the "why" behind the time shift.

"Maybe he is being distracted," I finally offered after they had been throwing ideas back and forth for several minutes while my French Toast got cold and the waitress assured me for a fourth time that they did not in fact carry Karo Syrup.

"By what?" Special Agent Arons asked.

"By us," I suggested as I forked a mouthful of the unsyruped and rather plain French toast into my mouth. "We did finally arrive and you said it yourself, he has been killing in state parks, not federal ones."

"She has a point," Gabriel backed me up. "Not only did we arrive, but we kind of took over. As long as this stayed a local case, he was free to kill as he pleased; now that it's federal, we may be throwing up some roadblocks."

"Like what?" Sheriff Rybolt asked.

"I don't know, if I did, we'd be that much closer to catching him. However, our presence didn't go unnoticed by the news, so I'm sure it didn't go unnoticed by the killer. It wouldn't be the first time a killer changed his timetable just because we arrived," Gabriel told him.

I gave up on the French toast and moved to eating a piece of toast with strawberry-like jam on it. I was pretty sure it wasn't real strawberry or jam, but the packet had proclaimed it to be so. At the moment, I was more interested in my food than what any of them had to say. The killer had changed. There was a reason, but I didn't know what the reason was. They could theorize until they were blue in the face and it wouldn't help us.

As a matter of fact, I was pretty sure this meeting was all about who had the biggest set of balls. The Feds were here, worse, the Marshals "Death Squad," as I had heard one uniformed officer call us, were involved. The locals in this area were used to dealing with things a certain way. Everyone could tell that. They were also used to US Marshals, but they were used to the sort that banged down doors and served warrants and made arrests of known fugitives. That was certainly not us.

Even the FBI Liaison, Special Agent Fred Arons, was more local than we were. Sure, they had called for our help, but I think they had thought we would magically swoop in and catch their killer from the moment we arrived. The possibility of that happening was pretty much zero. It took time to catch a serial killer, no matter how crazy the hunters were.

"Ok, so if it isn't us, maybe it's something else," I interrupted again, finishing off the toast. "Lucas thinks he has a home life. Maybe something in that home life is creating a disturbance in the pattern."

"But it didn't happen until you arrived," Sheriff Rybolt reminded me.

"That's not true," I looked at him, remembering the case file. "There was a time period in December when it happened. It picked up again in January, after the holidays. Maybe he was visiting relatives in another town or state."

"Do most serial killers have family?" Special Agent Arons gave me a doubtful look.

"Almost everyone has family, this guy is probably married with children," Lucas answered for me. "This is a man who is highly functional, that means he has a job, a life, killing is an outlet for something, but aside from that, he is probably just like anyone else. He could be a neighbor, a church deacon, hell, just about anything. One thing we know for sure is that he is psychopathic, this means he is a highly functioning psychopath. He could be anyone and he is probably popular with his circle of friends and well respected."

"You get all that from the way he kills his victims?" Arons turned on Lucas.

"No, I get that from the methodical way he does it. I get that from the fact that he has killed forty-one women in Alaska of all places and not been caught yet. He's local, he's respected and he's dangerous."

"Why did you say Alaska like that?" Commander Neilson asked.

"Because this is Alaska," Lucas looked at him. "Tell me that each town, each city doesn't have its own way of working things. Tell me that each individual isn't adapted to deal with the way things work. This isn't Chicago or Kansas City or New York City, this is Anchorage. A serial killer here has to understand what he is working with. The city has three-hundred thousand people. It has its own FBI and US Marshal headquarters. And it serves as a jumping off point for most of the rest of the state. Yet, he isn't picking transients or people destined for areas north, he is picking locals. That says something about him."

"What does it say?" Arons pressed.

"It says he is comfortable here. If he wasn't born here, I would be surprised. If he is a transplant, it happened at an early age. He knows the parks as well as the city. And he knows that things get done a little different here than in the continental US," Lucas answered.

"It also says he knew you'd be resistant to call us in until it was absolutely necessary," Gabriel added. "There's a reason the FBI Agents and the US Marshals get traded out up here, it's so they don't go native."

"Are you implying that we don't do things the right way around here? Like we're breaking the law?" Sheriff Rybolt asked, eyes narrowed, lips pursed together, holding back his anger as best he could.

"Not at all," Lucas informed him. "What we are implying is that due to the harsh realities of your environment and your lack of cohesion with the rest of the states, you guys do things differently."

This seemed to diffuse the situation, at least for now. The men at the table all went back to sipping coffee and throwing out ideas. I gave up on the rest of my breakfast and waited on them. I didn't drink coffee, even in the frozen regions of Alaska. I contented myself with a second hot chocolate and ordered a soda to get my caffeine boost going.

"You eat terrible," Commander Neilson said.

"Thanks," I replied, looking at my plate.

"No bacon, no eggs, no sausage?" Neilson pressed.

"I have migraines, I don't eat pork for that reason, I limit my intake of beef for the same. I don't eat eggs just because I don't like the texture. That leaves breakfast foods a little barren. So, French Toast, regular toast, and biscuits it was. It would have been better to have Karo Syrup, but I understand this is an odd request everywhere. One day, I will remember to start carrying my own."

"What's wrong with maple?" Sheriff Rybolt asked.

"Migraines," I nodded once and pushed my plate away. It was easier to tell them it triggered migraines than explain that I hated maple syrup. That statement seemed to offend people as much as saying I hated baseball or cute little ducks.

A few minutes later, we loaded up into the SUV, heading for parts unknown. Gabriel got to drive because he had taken courses in evasive driving maneuvers. Since these courses were not standard for the rest of us, he drove while we sat and watched the world go past the windows.

With the engine running, Gabriel turned in his seat to look at Lucas and me, "Stop baiting the locals, both of you."

"How did I bait them? All I did was defend my eating habits," I protested.

"And suggest that we were the reason he changed his timetable," Gabriel reminded me.

"That was not baiting, that was pointing out the flaws of their logic."

"To you, maybe, to them, it was insulting that our appearance should be so special," Gabriel said.

"We are like US Marshal rock stars, our arrival is important," Xavier said with a smile, mimicking putting on sunglasses.

"A uniformed highway patrolman referred to us as the 'Marshals Death Squad,'" Lucas said.

"Huh, I wasn't sure you had heard him." I said.

"Oh yes, yes I did," Lucas gave me a look. The look was filled with anger and malice. It was one of his few scary looks. I was glad it wasn't directed at me. Lucas took each case somewhat personally. He did not like being referred to in a derogatory manner.

"Your personal feelings aside, we do not want to piss them off, we all have the same goal and we can't do that if there is fighting between us and them, so stop baiting them," Gabriel told us as he pulled into a parking lot.

It had been a very short drive, only three blocks. We were now staring at a large federal building that had a Marshals crest on the top of it. I didn't know if Alaska had a lot of crime, but they seemed to have a lot of Marshals.

We seemed to flash our badges to everyone in the building as we made our way to a conference room. It was so bad, that we didn't bother to put them up, instead holding them at the ready to be flipped open and shown off. Everyone else seemed to have a badge on a chain or cord. I was pretty sure I was going to ask for one.

"We'll be working out of here," Gabriel said as he led us into the conference room.

"Can we get those badges on chains so we can stop flashing ours?" I asked.

"No," Gabriel said as he turned a whiteboard around.

"Ok, can we get cords to hang our badges from?" I pressed.

"Ace, do you even care that we have a serial killer in Anchorage?" Gabriel turned on me.

"Yes, I do. I also care that my gun arm is going to get tired flashing my badge every time I enter or exit this building, which would be bad for all of us if a gun battle ensued. If you want to talk turkey on the killer without the pissing match that went on in the diner, that's fine, but I think that is going to be a hard order to fill since I see Agent Arons coming our way. Which means, I'd rather discuss the cords for badges," I answered.

"I'll get you a cord," Gabriel huffed.

"Thanks," I smiled at him as Arons walked into the room. He took a seat as far from me as he could and stared at the board.

"We think there is something different about these three," Gabriel pointed to photos on the board. They were gruesome and disturbing. Three faces without skin or hair. I frowned at them.

"Different how?" Arons asked.

"The killer doesn't have the same steady hand," Xavier got up and started putting up more pictures. "Occasionally he goes too deep or becomes too shallow, and a few times he comes out before the section of skin is cleanly removed. We don't know what happened between these three and the next thirty-eight, but our killer perfected his technique."

"That's when there was a four week delay, correct?" I asked.

"Yes," Gabriel answered.

"You don't perfect your technique without practice," Lucas said.

"I'm searching for similar kills in other places during that time, I'm of the mindset that Ace might be right, he might have been somewhere else for the holidays," Michael answered.

"Why not back me up when we were talking at the diner?" I asked him.

"Because the locals want it to be a monster," Arons answered. "No, they need it to be a monster, not a local. If you had pressed harder on your theories, they would have stone-walled you."

"So you are on our side?" I frowned at him.

"Well, I haven't gone native," Arons gave me a grin. "Dr. McMichaels is right; things get done differently around here. Even in a city as large as this. They are all sharing information among themselves, but not all of it is coming to me. That's why I requested your team. I knew that all the coroner reports, all the crime scene stuff, everything would start to flow into a workable area. I'm limited as an FBI agent here. The Marshals are limited because they are also federal agents, but your lot, well . . ."

He spread his hands wide and I understood perfectly. When we came in, we took over, literally. The US Marshals and the FBI began processing all evidence and then feeding it back to the locals, not the other way around. And we were not bound by the same codes of conduct as most federal agents. We had a special status that usurped the chain of command. If we wanted DNA, it would take three days, max, not six months or a year. The tools of the forensic world were at our disposal in minutes.

"Do you have any theories then?" Lucas asked Special Agent Arons.

"He's local and I think he's involved in law enforcement. He always seems to know what we are doing," he looked at me. "I think he is the one that leaked the signature to the press and I think he is inside the local investigation because we had evidence on victim number three that went missing."

"What kind of evidence?" I asked, leaning forward.

"A cigarette butt, we were going to DNA test it, but when I went to pick it up, it couldn't be located. The sheriff sent me to the city police, the city sent me to the coroner, the coroner sent me to the state police who said they had never seen it, but their techs did the crime scene analysis. There are about five of us that remembered it being at the scene, but no one remembers picking it up."

"That could be problematic," Gabriel looked at me.

"And you want me to stop baiting the locals?" I raised my eyebrow at him.

"Nope, go ahead and bait away," Gabriel said.

"Did I miss something?" Agent Arons asked.

"What do we know about the victims?" I asked.

"They are petite, dark haired, and from what we've found out from friends and family, meticulous in their appearance and dress," Arons asked.

"That almost describes me," I pulled off the Columbia branded fleece and revealed another Columbia branded fleece. "I do not actually give a shit what I dress in, left to my own devices it is jeans and t-shirts. But I'm a living doll for lack of a better term. I have a personal shopper who picks out my clothing, takes me to get my hair done, the works. He is meticulous in both dress and appearance, picking out clothes that are flattering in cut and color and of the latest fashion. He says I look like a bum when I pick out my own clothing. He has even color coordinated my dresser and closet."

"You think you can bait him out if he's involved in the investigation?" Arons asked.

"Ace has a way of getting under the skin of men and women who like to kill. If he's met her, he's already had his thoughts about her," Lucas said.

"And when she gets going, there is really no stopping her," Xavier smiled. "It wouldn't be the first time we've had a serial killer give himself away by coming after her. It happened a couple of months ago on a case as a matter of fact."

"Are you guys really as crazy as they say?" Arons asked, giving us a look.

"Probably more so," Gabriel answered. If he was going to say more, it was lost to the knocking on the door.

Six

Two hours later and all of us were back at the crime scene. Lucas and I had already seen it. However, someone had put a rope, a stake, and a hammer on the ground. I frowned at them.

"You are so not hanging me upside down," I told them.

"You're the right build," Xavier told me.

"Uh, and Doctor, what if it causes an aneurism to burst in my brain?" I pointed out.

"That's your concern? An aneurism? Really?" Xavier laughed.

"Serial killers I can see, aneurisms I cannot," I told him.

"We aren't hanging you," Gabriel told me. "Someone left these here while we were gone. During a shift change of the state police."

"That's disturbing," Xavier answered.

"You're telling me," I said. "But does that sound like something our killer would do?"

"Not really," Lucas said. "As a matter of fact, I'd say it was very out of character for him."

"So a fan?" I said.

"But whose?" Gabriel gave me a pointed look.

"Hey, I haven't heard from mine for a while, not since Christmas," I said.

"Yes, but it is hard to rule him out," Lucas said.

"True, this is theatrical enough for him," I admitted. "But it's terribly cold, would he follow me to Alaska?"

"I think he'd follow you anywhere, but this doesn't strike me as him," Lucas knelt down.

Xavier knelt with him, pulling on a pair of gloves, he picked up the rope. For several minutes we were all very quiet. Xavier moved every piece around, examined them one by one. Finally he dropped it all and stood up, pulling the gloves off.

"My guess, teenagers," he said.

"Why?" Gabriel asked.

"There's part of a joint under the pile and most of it smells like pot," Xavier answered. "If I had to bet, I'd say some stoned teenagers got the idea after watching the news last night and dumped these things afterwards."

"Drugs definitely do not sound like either our killer or Ace's fan," Lucas said staring at the rope.

"What do we do with it then?" I asked.

"We have it sent to the lab and processed," Gabriel said giving me a dumb look.

"Ok," I looked around.

The pristine snow was no longer pristine. A few animals had dared to venture into the area. I wasn't a master tracker nor could I identify the tracks, but that wasn't really the point. The point was that I had been right. With the Pinesol body safely tucked away at the morgue and the smell dissipating, the animals were coming back.

I pointed. Lucas caught the gesture and stared through the evergreens and the few struggling non-evergreens. His eyes found the tracks and locked onto them.

"Moose," he said after several minutes.

"Really?" I had seen a moose in the zoo, but never up close and personal outside a cage.

"Really," Lucas's eyes continued to stare into the abyss of the snowy wilderness.

"What's on your mind?" Gabriel asked him.

"I just hate when she's right," Lucas gave him a smirk.

"We all do, but that's bullshit, you have something on your mind," Gabriel was trying to see where he was looking.

"What if he watched?" Lucas slowly started turning in a circle. "What if he climbed one of these trees and watched through a scope?"

"You don't think we would have noticed?" Special Agent Arons asked.

"I don't know," Lucas was still looking thoughtful into something I couldn't see.

"Let me help you think through it," I said to him.

"How far do you think you could see out here?" He finally turned his striking, icy blue eyes to me.

"I don't know, I think snow-blindness would be a problem during the day," I answered.

"You've never been hunting," Lucas smiled at me.

"Can't say I have," I admitted, "but that does not change the thought process behind it. Sitting in a tree where you could see the investigation going on for hours on end, I would think that would be problematic. Back home, they hunt in blinds, I do not know if it's different up here, but they do not sit on a tree branch all day."

"That's true," Lucas looked back out into the woods.

"Besides, we would see his tracks somewhere," I told him.

"Not if we weren't looking for them," he pointed to the ground.

He was right, outside the path to this spot and within the spot itself, there weren't any other footprints. This meant that no one had bothered to secure an outside perimeter. This seemed like a major oversight. There weren't even footprints leading past this spot. We were in a natural clearing and outside the clearing was the rest of the world.

"We should search the area," Gabriel said.

"Damn," I looked at my feet. I was already ankle deep in the white powdery crap. I hated snow.

"Put ten feet between you and begin walking forward, we'll go one way until I say to stop," Gabriel shouted.

"Between us," Lucas said to me. I knew he meant between him and Xavier. I didn't think this would help with a sniper, but you never knew.

Xavier flanked me on one side. Lucas took the other side. Gabriel gave them a look, but said nothing. It had become somewhat obvious since I joined the group that Lucas was protective of me. That didn't mean he walked in front of me everywhere we went, quite the opposite. He helped me prove myself, making sure when I took point, I was calm and firing straight and fast.

We began walking. The snow proved deeper once we got off the path. It went above my snow boots, spilling into them. I could feel it squelch under my feet, soaking my socks.

There were other factors to contend with though. I didn't have the men's long legs; I was shorter by at least half a foot. The snow was nearly up to my knees in some spots. I struggled to move my legs.

The cold air didn't help. The wind was blowing and the forecasted high of thirty-one degrees hadn't hit yet. The cold air burned in my lungs. Together, they tired me faster. Two hundred yards in and I was already panting. My feet were cold and nothing I could do would warm them.

I'd had hypothermia before, only a mild case, but a mild case was still hypothermia. It hadn't felt like this. It had been instantaneous after jumping into Lake Michigan in late October.

"Stop," Xavier said. We'd made it maybe another hundred feet. He walked over to me.

"Go away," I huffed at him.

"Still have smoker's lungs," Xavier pulled off his gloves and felt my face.

"Then why isn't Gabriel panting?" I asked.

"Doesn't matter," Xavier pulled down my eyelids. I had no idea what that was going to show, but he frowned at me harder. "She's going to have to go back. The snow's too deep for her here."

"I'm fine, just needed to catch my breath," I pushed him away.

"Look, She-Ra, I'm sure you'd be fine if it was fifty degrees, but it isn't. You've got snow in your boots which means your feet are getting wet and you are cold. You've had hypothermia before, I am not risking you having it again," Xavier said.

"He's right," Gabriel said. "I know you don't want to hear it, but you should probably go back, get your shoes off, and turn the heat on."

"I'm fine," I repeated, my breath no longer escaping from me in ragged plumes that hovered over me.

"Come on, Cain," Lucas marched over to me.

"If I have the strength to get back to the vehicle, I have enough to continue forward," I pointed out. "Besides, I do not think it's a good idea for me to sit in the car alone when there is a serial killer out there, picking women like me."

"I would be more worried about you attacking him," Gabriel chuckled softly as he walked over to me.

"Let's just get on with it," I told them.

"The doctor thinks you should go back," Gabriel looked me over.

"I don't think we should risk her," Xavier repeated.

"Give me a minute," Gabriel walked away. He dug out his phone. Xavier went back to examining me. He put his hands on the back of my neck and adjusted my head.

"What do you hope to find out by doing that?" I asked.

"I am checking your muscle control along with your awareness," Xavier told me.

"I think you are making shit up," I told him.

"It gets all of us out of the cold," he smiled at me.

"Asshole," I smiled at him.

"Believe it or not, you are at an elevated risk in this weather with this sort of snow, considering you are a city girl," Xavier shrugged.

"Really?" I gave him a suspicious look.

"If you had been born here or conditioned here, then no, you'd be fine. You weren't and no matter how bad Missouri winters get, they aren't Alaska," Xavier told me.

"Ok, we'll go wait in the car, we have a search team on the way," Gabriel came back over.

"Come on, Ace," Lucas made a motion towards me.

"If you pick me up, I will shoot you," I told him.

He threw his head back and laughed. The sound was loud in the silence and seemed to make the snow crackle. He caught me with one hand on my coat.

"No you won't," he tossed me over his shoulder and we began moving out of the woods.

I was less than happy about being fireman carried out of the snowy woods. It was embarrassing enough to be the reason we turned back. This was just adding insult to injury. I watched his footprints as we moved.

"Wait!" I cried, hitting him gently on the back.

"What?" He asked.

"The women, how is he getting them in? We aren't finding any clothing out here. There are no shoes with the bodies, but freezing did not start in the limbs until after they were dead. So how did he get them out here?" I asked.

"You thought of that because he was carrying you?" Special Agent Arons tried to look at me. I righted myself, towering over Lucas as I did. His hands adjusted to hold me better.

"Well think about it," I looked at Xavier. "If he is carrying them out here then hoisting them up using that wrapped around the tree branch method, that's tiring. Lucas could do it to me all day long and never think twice about it, but most men are not Lucas and a woman being carried nude into the woods is going to be fighting."

"She has a point," Xavier walked over to me. "You think he carried them?"

"No, I think he made them walk out here and then stripped them down. He has to secure them while he either scurries up the tree to wrap the rope around the branch or he is doing something different than our original thought and is dropping them back," I paused. "I think I just confused myself."

"You got that because he was carrying you?" Special Agent Arons asked.

"I have weird thought processes," I told him.

"He's tied their feet and hands," Xavier said.

"So? If it was me, I would be attempting to crawl away. I know what comes next in the horror story and I imagine they do too. Yet, I didn't see any marks where our victim had tried to crawl away. Sure there were tons of footprints, but no knee prints, no rope marks, nothing to indicate that our victim tried to escape. Why not?"

"Too scared?" Lucas asked.

"Maybe," I admitted. "But, I am not so sure. I mean, you know there is a guy skinning women alive in your area. You have been brought to the woods and tied up. The dots get connected. Is anyone too terrified to try to escape at that point?"

"Hog tied?" Xavier suggested.

"I can wiggle while hog tied, probably better than with just my hands and feet bound," I told him.

"You know that how?" Special Agent Arons asked.

"I have been hog tied by a serial killer; I flopped onto my side and managed to get to a table where I knocked off a knife. I accidentally stabbed myself twice, but I got out of the ropes," I told him. That had happened in December. I hadn't been the target; I just happened to be at the right place at the wrong time and was kidnapped instead of Gabriel. I haven't driven the company car since. The windows are too darkly tinted for serial killers to accurately guess who is inside.

"But most women aren't you," Lucas pointed out.

"That's true, but I cannot imagine a woman going without a fight knowing that she is going to be skinned alive," I could only think of one death that was worse, and I had faced it already.

"Yes, but that's you," Lucas said more pointedly.

"You honestly think and want me to believe that faced with her fate, she just accepted it and let it happen?" I put my hands on his shoulders to look down at him.

"It wouldn't be the first time a victim has given up, Ace. Remember, you are never a victim," he said to me.

"That horrifies me in ways you cannot begin to imagine," I told him.

"I'm sure it does, but lack of evidence suggests she didn't struggle," he looked up at me. "If I put you down, do you think you can walk back on the path?"

"Yes, but go ahead and toss me over your shoulder again, I might think of something else useful along the way," I told him with a snicker.

Lucas didn't put me down, just adjusted my position again. This brought me more level with him, cradling instead of tossing me over his shoulder like a caveman. Xavier walked next to us. His face pinched in thought.

"If you are not thinking about sex, I will give you a quarter for your thoughts," I said to him.

"And if I am?" He continued to look at our feet.

"Then you owe me a quarter," I teased.

"Well, I'm not. I was thinking about the best way to drag someone into the woods. An average sized guy and an average sized girl," he said.

"If she had given up, it would be easy," I said.

"Yes, but they can't all have given up, some of them must have had the spunk and will to survive to fight back," Xavier responded.

"A gun," Lucas said.

"It's nighttime," I looked at Xavier. "I get where you're going. It's night, it's dark, it's been snowing like hell, and it's Alaska."

"This isn't the northern part of the state," Arons interjected. "Not everyone carries a gun."

"No, but Alaska has the highest gun ownership per capita of any state," I told him.

"Do you know everything?" Arons asked.

"No, if I did, I would win the lottery and buy an island where there were no serial killers," I told him.

"If you bought an island, it would be attacked by pirates who just happened to also be serial killers," Gabriel said.

"Ok, I'd buy . . . I don't know . . . I'd buy something. Anyway, so how do you get a woman who does not want to go into the woods in the dark, into the woods in the dark?"

"A gun," Lucas repeated.

"I'm not intimidated by a gun, especially if I am pretty sure something worse than death is going to happen first," I answered.

"You are not an average female," Lucas said.

"True, but there must be average females that will fight for their lives. I would run into the trees," I told him, "zig-zag my way around so that as he is firing shots, he does not have a good line of sight on me."

"You couldn't walk through the snow, Ace," Xavier looked up at me.

"Well hell," I couldn't argue that.

Seven

Two hours later, the search team had come up with nothing. Only our tracks and a few animal prints. My feet were wrapped in fleece and Xavier had them against his chest. Everyone else had gotten hot and climbed out of the SUV. Xavier was shirtless and the entire thing probably looked ridiculous. However, it turned out he was right. I was not built for cold weather. He was demanding a circulation test when we got back to Missouri. My feet had started turning colors by the time we reached the SUV. They were now warm and no longer weirdly shaded, but that didn't seem to stop Xavier from keeping them elevated and pressed, soles first, into his chest.

"Talk to me some more about getting the women in the woods," he said after he checked my toes again.

"I do not think I can help there. You are right, I could not run through this snow anymore than I could fly," I said.

"But you aren't a native," Xavier said.

"Does that matter?" I asked.

"Yes, a native, even a city girl, would be more acclimated to the climate. They would have more practical snow boots, for a start. Be him, how do you do it?"

"Honestly?" I frowned at him, uncomfortable lying down in the back of the SUV with my feet on his chest. "I tie them to me. It keeps them from getting away and it helps them keep their balance. I do not drag them that would be ineffective in such weather conditions. I keep pace with them. If they start to stumble, I can grab them. I do not want them face-planting in this stuff. The cold comes later."

"How?" Lucas opened the door and stuck his head in.

"What do you mean how?" I looked at him as he let some of the heat escape.

"What you said just now, you tie them to you? Do you tie their hands?" He looked at me. I could tell he knew the answer, he was testing me. He did this from time to time.

"No, that would result in jerky movements. I tie the rope at their waist and put them in front of me, especially if I have a gun. If I'm using a knife as my threatening weapon, I have to keep them pinned to my side. That seems impractical."

"What other weapons could you have?" Xavier asked.

"Beats me. We know he uses a knife, but what do you threaten a person with to get them to go with you? You use a gun, because in theory, it is scarier. They do not have to be close to kill you," I said.

"True, but there has to be other weapons that would be as effective," Xavier said.

"How about a crossbow?" Lucas asked.

"Uh," I gave him a look. As a medievalist, I found crossbows to be great for hunting, not so good at directing people.

"He marks his kills with a bow," Xavier agreed.

"Why not a harpoon then?" I asked.

"You think a crossbow is unlikely?" Lucas asked.

"I don't think it works, the arrow tip in my back sucks and it's scary, but he better have great reflexes because if I can run in this shit, I'm taking my chances with the crossbow. He has to reload and it is a lot harder to fire on the run."

"You've fired a crossbow?" Xavier asked.

"Hello, history degree," I reminded him.

"I don't know a lot of historians that have fired crossbows just because they have a history degree," Lucas frowned at me.

"Well, now you know one," I told him.

"Gun, knife, crossbow, what are we not thinking of?" Gabriel finally ducked into the car and joined the conversation.

"May I have my feet back now?" I asked.

"I suppose, but tonight I want them soaked in warm water and wear thick, dry socks to bed," he let go of my feet. I didn't have any dry shoes and he had already made it apparent that I wasn't getting back the snow boots or wet socks. I kept them wrapped in the fleece.

"What if we are thinking about it the wrong way?" I finally piped up as they all piled back into the SUV and the heat was turned down to allow for the living to breathe.

"You mean what if they went willingly into the woods with their killer?" Lucas pulled his bottom lip in and chewed on it for a second.

"That's what I mean," I said.

"That would imply that they knew and trusted him. It would also imply that he's single," Lucas said after a few minutes. Gabriel began backing the SUV up. Xavier and Arons were looking at me.

"Why does he have to be single? You're not," I told Lucas.

"Yes, but in that situation, it's different. You are not a sexual being and I am not interested in sex with you," Lucas said.

"That still does not mean he cannot be married. Married men cheat," I told him.

"So do married women," Gabriel added as we exited the park.

"See, married people cheat," I corrected myself.

"Picking up forty-one women in the space of a couple of months takes effort and charisma," Xavier said.

"Just because you couldn't manage," I teased, but he had a point.

"Maybe some were lured and others kidnapped," Lucas adjusted the theory.

"I know I am going to be odd man out here, but if you know there's a serial killer on the loose, why do you go into the woods for a bit of nookie? Also, it's really frucking cold out here during the daytime. Logically, I am thinking it isn't better at night, so that adds to the mystery. Why go out in the freezing temperatures for a bit of nookie?"

"Did you just say 'fruck'?" Arons asked.

"Ace only drops the F-bomb on rare occasions. When she does, look out, it means she's either had an epiphany or she is going to shoot someone," Gabriel told him.

"The promise of a warm sleeping bag and a campfire and a little forbidden passion. The cold makes it more intense," Xavier said.

"Spoken like a man who knows," I looked at him.

"Not everyone enjoys missionary, with the lights out and their nightgowns still on," Xavier replied dryly.

"I was not judging, just asking," I told him.

"From a medical standpoint, there is a reason for sex in the cold," Xavier went on. "It makes the capillaries in the genitalia contract. Like rubbing ice cubes on your sex partner."

"I will take your word for it, Doctor," I told him.

"I can get graphic if you want," Xavier said.

"Nope, I get the picture," I said. "I just do not understand it."

"And it is unlikely that you ever will," Gabriel spoke up from the front seat. "Ok, so he lures a few with the promise of sex. He abducts the others. He takes them into the woods and what?"

"He waits," Lucas said. "I think we should test Ace's theory about the hoisting being tiring."

"Waits for what?" I asked.

"If you're right, for his strength to return. Xavier said it would take a couple of hours to do this kind of work. However, if he's a slight man, it might take longer depending on how he is stringing them up."

"We need to go to the store, get her some shoes and socks," Xavier said. "Then we can conduct a few experiments."

"You are not stringing me up," I told them again as we turned into a sporting goods store. Xavier went in and came out with two large bags. He handed me one and I pulled out thick socks and weird snow boots. To my horror, he held onto the other one, refusing to let me even sneak a peek at what was inside. I was concerned that he had bought himself matching boots, or something worse. We continued on to the US Marshals building.

"They have a place we can use," Gabriel killed the engine. We all got out and followed him inside. I watched him swipe something off of someone's desk as we continued flashing our badges around the place.

We entered an elevator. Gabriel handed me a cord. I put my badge on it, smiling at him.

"I cannot believe you stole that," I told him.

"I wondered if you caught me," Gabriel smiled back. "They have a whole basket of them. They won't miss this one."

"You know an awful lot about this office," Lucas said to him.

"I was an FBI agent up here for a year. The US Marshals and the FBI work pretty closely in Alaska, more closely than anywhere else in the country."

"They have to," Arons jumped into the conversation. I was sure he felt like a fifth wheel. "Up here, if we want to catch a fugitive, we'd better call in the Marshals and not the locals, especially once you get out of Anchorage. The locals have been known to warn felons."

"Where is our geek?" I asked, realizing that Michael wasn't with us. He had been before we went into the frozen Alaskan wilderness.

"At the motel, sick as a dog," Xavier said.

"Anthrax, smallpox, polio?" I asked.

"You forgot to mention plague, but he actually caught pneumonia, a far more likely disease, especially in this cold climate," Xavier said. "Something in the air up here. He was fine last night, today he said he thought he was getting a cold, by the time we went to leave, he was running a fever. I put him on some antibiotics. He'll be good as gold in a couple of days."

"Today, he's not doing anything. Tomorrow, if he feels better, he'll work from the motel. I have a US Marshal catering to his whims and needs. I am also changing rooms," Gabriel said. The elevator dinged. We entered into a large open basement. I looked around.

"I have been in some creepy places with you before, but this may take the cake," I told them.

"This way," Gabriel pointed and started walking. We all followed.

We entered another cavernous room. There was a mock tree standing in it. I raised an eyebrow.

"We were already planning on doing this," Gabriel smirked.

"I am not being hoisted above a concrete floor by you lot," I reminded him. Sometimes I was pretty sure he heard me, but chose not to listen. I was also pretty sure they were about to tie me up and hoist me over a concrete floor.

"We're not going to put you through that, especially since I have concerns about the blood flow in your feet," Xavier shook his head at me. "We have special dummies for this sort of thing."

"That makes me feel better," I told him.

"Ace, go first," Gabriel said to me. There was another man in the room. He put a dummy on the floor.

I tied a rope around its ankles, put the hook from the rope through the tied area, and grabbed the other end. I got it about four feet off the floor, meaning its head and part of its torso were still on the ground before I had to take a break.

"Are your lungs all right?" Xavier walked over to me.

"Fine," I told him.

"Let me listen," he bent down and put his ear to my chest. "Deep breaths."

I took a few deep breaths. He stood up and frowned at me.

"What?" I asked.

"We do have cases of Alaska Sickness," Gabriel said. We all turned to look at him.

"I don't know what that is," Xavier said.

"That's because we don't either," Gabriel said. "We just know that some agents, when they first get up here, have trouble with shortness of breath, easily contract hypothermia and other illnesses. It seems to be a mix of the dry, cold air and getting the lower forty-eight out of your system."

"How do I treat that?" Xavier continued.

"You don't, she'll get over it in a week, maybe less. Until then, we just have to watch that she doesn't overdo it and kill herself by accident. I imagine that's why Michael got sick. Natives show a very high red blood cell count. I imagine you and Lucas already have high red blood cell counts for different reasons."

"And Ace being a woman already has a lower red blood cell count," Xavier said. He looked at me.

"Plus she just quit smoking and she hasn't been working out lately because her house is in chaos and she hates going to a gym. So the only time she gets her workout is when we are at the office and we haven't been there much lately," Lucas said.

I let the dummy fall to the floor. It thudded nicely. I looked at all of them.

"Are you implying I have let myself go?" I asked.

"No, we are implying that Trevor needs to tackle your exercise room next and while you are here, you are on restricted duty until you adjust to the climate," Xavier answered.

"Well that just sucks," I moved away from the body.

Lucas went next, he easily hoisted up the dummy even though the rope was double wrapped around the branch. He let it down and hoisted it again. To him, it was like lifting a feather. I watched him do it several times before he started showing any signs of fatigue.

"She'd be fighting," I said.

"What?" Gabriel answered.

"This test isn't accurate, she would be fighting, wriggling around, like a worm on a hook," I explained.

"Well, you vetoed using you as a hoist dummy," Gabriel said.

"I think it is disturbing that you used that analogy," Arons said.

"She's not like most women or men for that matter, in her mind, it is the best analogy," Lucas said.

"Do not make excuses for me," I said to him and turned the full weight of my attention on Arons. "You may find some of what I have said and will say offensive. I am fine with that. It happens. However, I know what I am doing and I am very good at it. So, suck it up buttercup, if you cannot handle the way I approach the world, you are welcome to walk your ass out an exit."

"And you just pissed her off," Gabriel said to him. "I've been in your shoes, take it from me, just let it go."

"At least she didn't 'f-bomb' you," Lucas said.

"Or cut off your ear, she has a thing about Van Gogh," Xavier added.

"I do not have a thing about Van Gogh, I do not understand his work," I defended myself.

"Hence why I thought you might emulate him. You understand things better when you practice it yourself, even if you use a stand-in for the painful bits," Xavier said.

"Whatever. As I was saying, if someone is pulling you off the ground after skinning your feet, not only are you going to be in a lot of pain, you are going to be pretty convinced that what comes next is worse. If she isn't passed out, she is going to be jerking and twisting. Lucas might be able to do it easily, even with that, but the rest of you, probably not," I said.

Xavier went next, pulling on the dummy. He got her fully off the ground. Her feet were over his head. His eyes were level with her knees. He stood and stared, holding the rope. You could see the wheels in his head turning.

"Damn, she's right. I can get her up, but now I'm going to have to secure her and it's going to take me a minute to recover to keep from shaking when I go to remove the epidermis," Xavier dropped the dummy. "And if she were jerking and twisting, that would add momentum and extra force and pressure to what I'm doing."

They all turned to look at me. I looked at the dummy.

"This just seems so . . .," I shrugged, unsure what to say.

"Because hoisting her up and down is a pain in the ass. He either has help or he isn't doing it this way," Xavier answered. "Because this way is exhausting."

"Exactly," I said.

"What are your thoughts, Ace?"

"I don't know, I just cannot imagine a world where this is the best solution for our serial. Unless this is absolutely part of the ritual, I do not foresee him doing it this way. I foresee him doing something to make it easier on himself so that when the time comes to skin the victim, he has the wherewithal to complete the task at hand."

"A winch," Lucas answered.

"That would be good, but we aren't finding a winch or evidence of a winch," Gabriel said.

"Then he's removing the evidence," Lucas looked at him. "Winches aren't cheap, not good portable winches, of course he doesn't leave it. That's what the rope and the stake and the hammer are for."

"You think he is using a winch, then using a rope to secure her after the work has been done?" Gabriel asked.

"It's better than this," Xavier answered.

"Do you have any idea how many people own winches in this city?" Arons asked.

"I'm sure it is just about everyone. The further north you go, the stranger the state becomes," I answered. "Eventually you get to a point where villages leave cars running all winter."

"How'd you know that?" Arons looked at me.

"I went to Siberia once, it was very cold," I told him. Cold was an understatement. I had been in Siberia in a "summer" month and had still froze my ass off. They told me about the danger of letting your car die in the winter.

"Why did you go to Siberia?" Arons asked, his eyes narrowed.

"Why does anyone go to Siberia?" I shrugged and walked over to the dummy. "If he's using a winch, we should find evidence of it."

"Not necessarily," Gabriel walked over to me. "If he's using coated cable and then rope, the rope burns on the tree would be more evident than the cable burns."

"Where does that leave us?" I asked.

"Getting lunch," Gabriel said.

Eight

We had less than twelve hours of daylight. By 7 o'clock that evening, the sun had set. I had taken a bath in very hot water, then a shower, because I'm like that. The second bag had contained men's pajamas, one size too big for me, that were crafted from the finest silk. The pajamas were also impractical; silk is not the warmest material on the planet. In his defense, he had purchased ladies' style long johns to go with them, but they were two sizes too small and wouldn't come up past my thighs. To fix this, Lucas had gone out a second time and purchased more practical pajamas. They were still men's pajamas, but they were dark red with black and grey striping and made out of heavy flannel with an insulated lining and had a matching robe that tied at my waist. I also had new snow boots that were made for Alaska and came up past my knees. I found them uncomfortable, but at least my toes wouldn't freeze off.

"Tell me about the first three," I said as we finished up dinner. We were assembled in the Marshals' conference room. Arons had been very quiet since I had gone off on him earlier. Gabriel and I had made a trip back to the motel-- me to get warm, him to check in on Michael or at least that was the excuse. The real reason was so that I could quietly and casually be reprimanded for going off on the Special Agent who was trying to be helpful.

I hadn't argued or pleaded my case. I had sat and let Gabriel tell me all the reasons I was in the wrong without saying a word. I considered it amazing personal growth because I really wanted to tell him where to shove Special Agent Arons. He rubbed me the wrong way, but that was probably just because I didn't know him or trust him or want to be around him in any way, shape, or form. I was like that with new people.

Now, we were back at the Marshals building. My badge was clipped to the pilfered cord and hung from my neck. Which was good since my pajamas didn't have a lot of pockets. They got me some interesting looks when we returned. I guessed suit and tie was standard dress for US Marshals in Alaska. I thought they should consider themselves lucky that I had bothered to put on a bra.

"Because they don't have the expertise and precision of the last thirty-eight victims, I have doubts it's the same killer," Xavier stood up and walked to the board. "See, with victim one, there are hesitation marks. The killer does not maintain equal pressure on the blade, making some of the patches too deep and others too shallow. He comes out early in a few places and has to start again. The legs are definitely not as cleanly skinned and he seems to have issues with the kneecaps, which isn't present on any of the victims after his break."

"I've been thinking about the break," Lucas jumped in. "This kind of training would take years, not weeks. I don't know what he was doing during that time, but you aren't going to gain that much proficiency skinning deer or moose in that time frame. I'm not sure you'd gain it skinning humans in succession."

"Why kill three, then stop only to be replaced by another killer?" Arons asked.

"Partners," Lucas answered. "If they were partners, one of them might have killed the other and taken over. The one that takes over has greater skill in this department, but without his partner, he has to find a new way to hoist the bodies. Maybe that's what the break was about."

"That might explain part of it," Xavier agreed, "but not all of it. Because while I see the work of two different men, I do not see a difference in the methods, just the skill level."

"But a partner might not change his methodology," I told him.

"True," Lucas said. He looked at the board. "His victims also change. Not much, just a little. The age goes up."

"That it does," Xavier said. "The first three were all in their early twenties. The rest have been in their late twenties or early thirties with an outlier that was almost forty. And their physical appearance changes a little as well. The younger women are all less 'natural', I can't think of a better way to put that. The people that were interviewed said they wore make-up, lots of jewelry, one even had implants. The rest of the victims are plain Janes-- no make-up, no excessive jewelry, and while their clothes are name brand, they aren't two-hundred dollar jeans or eighty-dollar shirts."

"I would consider the older women to be respectable. They dress nice, but not flashy. Their jewelry is small and tasteful. And judging by the photos of their make-up collection, I'd say they wear it on special occasions, but if they wear it every day, it is very light," Lucas clarified.

"Were any of them sexually assaulted?" I asked.

"Do you read the dossiers we give you or look at the pictures?" Gabriel asked me. The others had turned to look at me. I shrugged; I wasn't going to admit that I mostly looked at the pictures.

"We aren't sure," Xavier shook his head at me. "And if you thought about it for more than about three seconds, I'm sure you'd figure that one out on your own."

I did think about it. I thought about it for more than three seconds. I frowned at him.

"Whatever answer you wanted me to come up with failed to go to seed," I told him.

"Because of the nature of the body, specifically, the torched genitalia, we don't know if they are being sexually assaulted. There is no semen present in the uterus, but that doesn't mean anything other than there was no semen left in the uterus. If he does, he uses a condom," Xavier looked at me.

I looked back for a second before turning to look at Lucas. In hindsight, I could see that my question was indeed answerable by looking at the situation for a few moments. However, I was a master at getting hung up on small details and overlooking others completely. This meant that at times I was very good at this and at other times I wasn't.

"I would guess that he doesn't," Lucas said after I had stared at him for a minute. "It seems to be more about the suffering than it does sex."

"Sadist," I said quietly.

"I don't think so," Lucas said. "Sadism implies a sexual component. This is more about control."

"We are looking for a man that needs to be in control?" I gave him a look.

"I know, it's a broad generalization that fits most people, including you," Lucas answered.

I shrugged and yawned. He was right on both accounts. Although I didn't consider myself a control freak, there were instances where everyone else would disagree.

"Are we boring you?" Arons asked.

"This part usually does bore me to some extent. I do not like sitting on my hands waiting for him to take another victim. I like to go in, guns blazing, and rescue the damsel in distress," I answered curtly.

"What exactly do you do, Marshal Cain?" Arons looked at me.

"She provides valuable information in places where we can't," Gabriel said the words slowly, as if chewing on them before spitting them out. There was a tone to his voice that told me not to press that issue. Arons was oblivious to the discouraging tone.

"But what exactly? She's bored by the investigation, doesn't understand crime scene processing, doesn't seem to care about the victims. So, I'll ask again, what exactly is her role?" Arons pressed forward.

"Marshal Cain gives us all a sounding board. Most of us are intelligent but can't keep up with each other, we are all specialized. She is not. She can look at a problem with different eyes than us. And she has a unique perspective on serial killers," Lucas broke in, stopping Gabriel from using his sharp tongue again. "In a world where the serial killer is king and usually has an IQ that puts him over genius level, Ace levels the playing field."

"That doesn't answer the question," Arons huffed.

I stood up and walked to the white board. I pulled down all the pictures, placing the first three victims on top. I looked at Arons. The calm washed over me and I was unwilling to try to pull myself out of it. I wanted him to see just how angry I could be and just how different that anger was from anyone else's. When I got angry, it was like staring into an abyss, not a tantrum-fueled cartoon.

"When we figure out who he is, I am going to take point when we breech his lair. I am going to secure any innocents and hostages while keeping an eye out for our killer. Chances are good that if we get into a physical altercation, I am going to walk away with a few bumps and bruises, but he'll need a body bag. If he's smart, he'll surrender when I come through the door. Because that is what I do, I convince serial killers to surrender," I sat perfectly still after I finished speaking, staring at Arons.

"I love it when you're angry," Lucas stood up. "It always gives me ideas. We don't know how he is taking the ones that would normally resist, Ace suggested he uses some sort of device to keep them from struggling. Zip-cuffs wouldn't leave a mark."

"Zip-cuffs break," I answered.

"True, but most people don't know how to do it," Lucas replied.

"I like the idea," Gabriel said. "And if he is on the inside, he'd have access to all the zip-cuffs he'd want."

"Even if he isn't, he would still have access to zip-ties. They can be found anywhere," Arons finally started talking again.

"Very true," Gabriel looked at Xavier. "You seem hung up on something."

"It's the victims. I've been staring at these spots here for a few days now and I think I just figured out what they are from," Xavier started circling the marks he was talking about.

"All ears," I chimed.

"I think it's the hook end of a tanner's knife. And a tanner's knife would be sharp enough to do the work," Xavier answered.

"A tanner's knife?" Arons asked.

"A tanner's knife," Xavier repeated. "It's a very sharp blade used to separate dermis from the layers of fat under it when taking the hide from an animal. It usually has a weighted handle to keep the tanner from cutting too deep or not deep enough. Once in, it's stable as it cuts the flesh. It has a small curved tip used to puncture the skin without leaving much of a mark. In this case, I think they are mistakes made by the killer. They don't appear on any but the first three."

"Different knife?" Gabriel asked.

"I doubt it. Few things are made specifically for the task of removing flesh. A scalpel would work, but you wouldn't get the nice thick cuts that you would with a tanner's blade," Xavier looked at me.

"Don't look at me, dead animals creep me out. I know nothing about tanning," I shrugged.

"Dead people don't bother you, but dead animals do?" Lucas gave me a look. It spoke volumes. Mostly it said my lack of humanity and compassion had just shown through.

"I did not mean it quite like that," I adjusted my position. "I just meant that the process of butchering animals for food grosses me out. The same with tanning."

I stopped and sat down. I was just digging myself in deeper. I couldn't explain why animals bothered me more than people. It had something to do with the makeup of my psyche. Dead people bothered me, but I didn't eat people and for some reason, my mind made a distinction between the two. I would end up a vegetarian after a visit to a slaughterhouse. I was fine eating after a crime scene.

"Ace's mental state aside," Gabriel pressed forward. "There are probably dozens of tanneries in the area. So are we looking for a tanner?"

"The first three, I'd say yes," Xavier looked at the fourth victim. "After that, I'd say no."

"How many young men died in that four-week period?" Lucas asked.

"If I was in a team and murdered my partner, I would make sure he wasn't found," I said.

Everyone looked at me. I stared only at Lucas. He pinched his face up and frowned at me.

"You think he did something different with the body?" Lucas asked.

"I'm saying that if I was serial killer number two and I wanted complete control, I would kill serial killer number one and make sure that his body could not be found. I would chop him up and use him as bear bait or fish bait or something. I am sure there are tons of disposal methods around here," I met Lucas's gaze and held it firm.

"How would you dispose of the body?" Lucas sat down on the table, it gave a slight groan under his weight that he ignored.

"Me? I would use acid, but if I did not have access to such a thing . . .," I shrugged. "Bears would be hibernating. Most of the lakes would have been frozen over in December. There are carnivorous fish in Alaska and the food levels would be dropping along with the oxygen levels. I would go drill a hole, weight the parts, and drop them in. That would give me at least three months to make sure that the corpse was unidentifiable. I'd know the area, I'd know which lakes held things like white sturgeon. They'd make short work of it, good chance even the bones would be chewed on to some degree."

"It's late and there are extra patrols out. He hasn't grabbed a woman yet, nothing more we can do tonight. We'll go back to the hotel and get a good night's sleep and revisit everything in the morning," Gabriel stood up. "We'll be back here at eight, barring something happening during the night."

I followed everyone out to the SUV. The dashboard clock read that it was just after nine at night as we began the drive back to the hotel. It would be late in Missouri, but I had a feeling I needed a dose of humanity.

Once I was locked inside my room, I dug out my cell phone and dialed Nyleena's phone number. It rang six times before her sleepy voice came over the line.

"Are you alright?" She asked.

"Define alright?" I said back.

"Where are you?"

"Alaska, it's a bad one. I did a poor job of faking it tonight."

"The guys all know," she was starting to wake up.

"That may be, but there was another person in the room and he did not. Does not know? I'm not even sure how to word it."

"Are you feeling bad that you let it slip or that you couldn't connect?"

"Both perhaps."

"Talk to me Aislinn."

"I can't. I just needed a dose of humanity."

"My humanity?" I could hear the smile in her voice.

"I'm knee deep in dead bodies. My killer is probably out hunting at this very moment. I'm tucked safely away in my hotel room waiting for another woman to die and my only thought is, I wish he would hurry up. Another body means more clues."

"Yep, sounds like you need a dose of something. I know you want to capture him, but sometimes, waiting is all you can do. No matter how bad it is. Have you gone through the case files?"

"Yes, they were unhelpful. I think the locals are holding back from us. It would not be the first time."

"They called you in."

"Actually, no they did not. The FBI did because the agent in charge up here felt like he was also being kept out of the loop. He used a breech by a reporter to call us in. Can you believe some idiot reporter found the body before the locals?"

"That's not good."

"How was your day?"

"Knee deep in killers and trying to figure out what sort of deals could be made. I had one of your cases come across my desk today. He pled out for a life sentence in The Fortress, but he probably won't last long in there.

They are moving him to the secure ward, but sometimes things happen inside that place. I imagine he will have a nasty accident or something," I knew she was talking about a child killer that we had caught a few months ago. He had molested all the boys before slicing out their tongues and removing their eyes. She was right, he wouldn't last long in The Fortress. A needle in his arm would probably be a blessing compared to what the serial killers would do to him, even in the secure ward.

"Do anything not work related?"

"I went and had dinner with your mom. She's doing good. Worried about you. She said you hadn't called in a week."

"Yeah, I rushed from one case to another. I will call her when I have a few minutes."

"You won't wake her in the dead of night then?"

"It's only 9:40 here," I smiled at the phone.

"Have you felt the calm lately?"

"Yes, but not often."

"That's good."

"I suppose."

"It is, Aislinn, it means that just because you let your humanity slip, it doesn't mean you are out of control."

"Do I really value animals more than people?"

"No, you just have a different attachment to them. If you really valued animals more than people, you'd be tracking down poachers, not serial killers. Can you imagine yourself tracking down poachers? You'd be the scariest game warden around."

"I cannot imagine being a game warden."

"I can see you as a game warden. You'd be like Ranger Smith, talking to the animals and trying to ignore the humans. You'd drive a supercharged ATV with machine gun turrets to take out multiple poachers at one time. Possibly anti-aircraft missiles to take down hunting blinds that were illegally put up."

"Would I have to wear the tacky brown uniform?" I asked.

"Everyone has to wear the tacky brown uniform, but you could liven it up with dead lichen and the pinky bones of poachers."

"Thanks, Nyleena. I needed that."

"Aislinn, you may not always be on the same level as everyone else, but your dark moments are fleeting. You aren't Malachi or the killers you track down. You do value human life, even if you don't understand the human condition as it applies to the rest of us."

"Thanks, Nyleena. Go back to sleep."

"Will do, try to sleep, Aislinn," she hung up the phone.

The conversation had lasted less than ten minutes, but I was feeling somewhat better. Perhaps I couldn't relate, but I did believe life to be sacred. It was part of what motivated me to do this job day in and day out.

I pulled out the case files to see if I could glean anything new from them.

Prey

It was five minutes past ten pm when he looked at the desk clock. His wife and daughter were asleep, had been asleep for almost an hour now. The antihistamine he had slipped into his wife's glass of wine and his daughter's glass of tea had been very effective tonight. Sometimes it took longer to work than this, but by nine they had been hauling their asses up the stairs, too tired to watch the movie he had picked out for family night.

He had kissed Grace good night and told her to stop apologizing for missing the movie. The interaction with his wife had been more stilted. She had pulled her hair out of her bun and kicked off her shoes by the door. This had irritated him. Why couldn't she undress in her own space like other women? He had given her a quick peck on the forehead before shooing her upstairs. He despised the woman. He only stayed because of Grace, but Grace was getting older now. She'd be moving out of the house before long, going off to college to follow in the footsteps of her parents.

Within minutes of both ladies disappearing from view, he had heard gentle snoring coming down the stairs. It floated to him and made his heart beat faster. That deed was done; it was time to go hunting.

His first stop was the restaurant where he had enjoyed a slice of pizza with his daughter and her friends the night before. Henry watched for almost twenty minutes and never saw the waitress. It was obvious that she wasn't working tonight. This gave her a temporary reprieve. He would find her another night.

He wound down the road, blindly wandering the streets. He saw several police cars. Few took notice of him, they were used to his midnight wanderings. He'd been doing it long before the murders began, usually when he had a tough case on his slab.

Henry was lost in his own thoughts when he saw US Marshal Aislinn Cain. She was standing outside her hotel room. The door was propped open with a chair and she was arguing with Dr. Xavier Reece. Smoke swirled around her head from the lit cigarette she held. He watched with fascination as Dr. Reece took the cigarette and crushed it out. She lit another one in clear defiance of him. He threw his hands in the air and shook his head.

She was dressed in pajamas. Oddly male in style, they were pin striped red, black, and grey, including a matching robe and slippers. The robe was tightly cinched around her waist. The pants and sleeves showed creases from being ironed or pressed. Her hair was pulled back in a ponytail, not a single hair out of place. Henry wondered how much hairspray it required to get her hair like that.

He drove past without them noticing him. Watching her interact with Dr. Reece had infuriated him. How dare she talk down to someone as accomplished as him? However, Aislinn Cain couldn't be on his menu tonight. Maybe later, but not now. Now her death would be suspicious and he'd be at risk of getting caught. Someone might hear her.

There was someone else though. He had discovered her some time ago and had put her on the list for a later date. Her name was Ginny. She lived alone and taught fifth grade. But she was one of those teachers that students didn't like. He knew because she had taught Grace in fifth grade and Grace had hated her.

Carefully, he drove past her house. The street was dark. Everyone tucked safely into houses against the night and him. That last made him smile. If only they realized they could never be safe from him.

He parked in the driveway. Miss Ginny Jacobs didn't have many visitors, his car might be noticed, but it was unlikely. She was thirty-six, never married, no children. Henry crept around to the back of the house. He knew she hid a key back here in a potted plant. Reconnaissance was everything. He found the key and slipped in through the backdoor. As carefully as he could, he relocked the door.

Quietly he moved to the front door and unlocked it. He would go out that way. The hallway was filled with framed portraits of smiling people. If they knew his plans, it didn't show on their faces. They smiled with serene happiness eternally frozen on their faces. It made him mad to look at those faces. But he had a secret, the pictures would smile for eternity, but the people in them would not. Come tomorrow or the next day, they would huddle in groups and weep. They would curse and ask the important question: why her?

He could hear her in the bedroom. She also snored. Light and quiet, almost high pitched, as if it was coming out of her nose and not her mouth. Even in the darkness he could feel her, feel her life. The hole of bitterness in him opened wider, sucked him down even further into misery and despair.

Carefully, he switched on the small flashlight he had brought with him. He was careful not to turn it on her face, knowing the sudden stab of light would wake her. She lay nude in the bed, the sight transfixed him. It wasn't her nudity, but her beauty that caused him to pause. All his victims were beautiful while they slept. Their skin glowing under the beam of light, their hair let down for the night, they looked so innocent as they dreamed. It was these moments that made him catch his breath and just wait.

Finally, she moved, just rolling over, but enough to break his trance. Gently he placed the flashlight in his mouth and moved towards her. He was on her, his hands firmly placed over her mouth before she woke up. She kicked and fought against him. Her fingers dug into the fabric, trying to tear at his skin. She moved, trying to dig into his hands, but the leather gloves prevented it. The terror in her eyes filled him with joy. He loved that she was afraid of him. Slowly, she stopped fighting.

He let go. She was still breathing, not dead, but the lack of oxygen had caused her to pass out. Physically, he wasn't an imposing man. Yet, his build belied his strength. He looked around for a robe and found one in the small bathroom. He hated when they were nude. It was such a pain in his ass to have to dress them. He found socks in a drawer and forced them on her feet, anger starting to seethe in him again. Why did women sleep nude in Alaska? It seemed so impractical to him. And it meant that he would have to dress them to get them to the spot without them freezing to death. It was taking away from his time to enjoy them.

He roughly shoved her feet into slippers. She groaned. He had been prepared for this. Sometimes, they didn't stay out as long as he needed. He took a prefilled hypodermic neddled from his pocket and injected her with it. The sedative would need a few minutes to take effect. He waited until her breathing was steady again and her eyelids had stopped fluttering to continue.

Once her slippers were on, he searched around for a shirt. He found a dirty one in the hamper and with effort managed to get it on her. There were no sweats in the room. No lounge pants, no yoga pants, nothing to put on her lower half. He finally settled on a skirt he found in her closet and put it on her. Dressing the dead weight was tiring. He stopped after wrapping the robe around her and just sat on the bed getting his own breath back.

He hit the button on his watch, it was nearly midnight. If he didn't hurry, he wouldn't be able to finish in time.

Worse, he wasn't sure how long the sedative would last on her. He hadn't given her much. It should wear off in an hour, but that was another hour he was losing. He hated to rush. He might not do the job as cleanly as he wanted.

After regaining his breath, he grabbed hold of Miss Ginny Jacobs and tossed her over his shoulder in a fireman's carry. The photos still smiled at him as he passed. He slammed his fist into one that showed Ginny and two young children at a park, smiling. Breaking free of its hook, it crashed to the floor. In the dark, it gave the illusion of being thunderously loud. He looked out the windows.

It was a mistake to smash just the one photo. It would be noticed. Clumsily he tossed his prize onto the floor and began smashing the rest of the pictures in the house. To break one would be to show its importance. To break them all, would not reveal the secret.

The street was still dark. It seemed no one had moved since he had arrived. But it was late, his biggest dangers were teenagers up past their bed times and early morning workers on the way to their tedious jobs.

Yet no one was out. No lights shown in house windows. He opened the front door, locked it behind him, and slipped out onto the front porch with his prize. He tossed her into the backseat, ensuring that she was lying down.

He drove out of her neighborhood. A hint of satisfaction crossing over his face, he pulled into the hotel he had passed earlier. There were still lights on inside some of the rooms. He recognized that one of them probably belonged to Marshal Cain and the other Dr. Reece. If only they knew how close he was to them. They could walk out the door at this very minute and catch him in the act. Or look out their window and report a suspicious vehicle. The engine was still running. He turned and put handcuffs on Miss Ginny Jacobs. He shoved a rag into her mouth. Then he stared at the lighted rooms.

He'd done this before, sat outside FBI Special Agent in Charge Arons' home and waited for him to come out and notice the strange vehicle. He never had. But unlike the Marshals who appeared to be burning the midnight oil, Arons always seemed to be asleep.

The clock ticked past 12:30 to 12:31. He put the SUV in gear and pulled out. He had work to get done. There was a nice park not far from the hotel. He took the opportunity to use it. One more dig at the US Marshals. If he frustrated them enough, they would leave the case to the hopeless FBI Special Agent in Charge Arons and go to work another case. He'd have to pass on the infuriating Marshal Cain, no matter how much she pressed his buttons.

The park wasn't very big. It did hold enough trees to keep him from being seen from the roads. Even his car would be hidden.

Yes, this would get under their skin. His work found less than half a mile from their hotel. They would know that while they worked into the wee hours of the night, he had killed within walking distance of their hotel.

He pulled his prey from the car. She was starting to come to. Her head lolled side to side and she made small noises through the cloth. This was working out to be a good night after all.

Gently, he put down his tool bag. Inside was a blanket, he spread it out and placed her on it. Then he dug out a set of zip-ties and bound her feet. Next he took out a rubber mallet and a stake with an eye-hole. He pounded it into the frozen ground.

He went back to his bag and found the hook. He attached it to the rope and climbed the tree. He wrapped the rope over it, twice, and let the weight of the hook carry it to the ground. Holding tightly to the other end, he climbed back down and ran the rope through the eye-hole. He tied it off and went back to the bag. Inside was a miniature winch. He set the winch next to the blanket, untied the rope from the eye-hole and ran it to the winch. The winch whined for a moment and began to swallow the rope. Satisfied, he looked around.

It was time to create his masterpiece.

Nine

I wanted to yell at whoever was beating on my door. My eyes found the clock; it was just before eight in the morning. I'd gotten about three hours of sleep.

The entire night I had gone through each file carefully, looking at them individually, to see if there was anything we had missed. I hadn't come up with anything except sleep deprivation and a small headache.

"Go away!" I finally shouted. I knew it was Gabriel. We were due into the Marshals' Office at eight. However, I was pretty sure my brain wasn't going to function for another hour or so.

"They found a body!" Gabriel shouted back.

I got out of bed, stumbled to the door, and opened it. Gabriel let himself into the room. He carried a can of soda.

"You look like shit," he held the can out to me. "Get dressed, we have to go."

"Good morning to you too," I took the soda, put it on the table, grabbed my jeans off the floor, and slipped them on over my pajamas. I found a bra and a shirt, turned around, giving Gabriel my back, and put them on. My hair was still in a ponytail, but I took a few minutes to put any errant hairs back into place and tied it into a bun. I shed like a Saint Bernard in summer, so I always kept my hair up at crime scenes.

I grabbed my fleece and a coat and slipped into both of them. I was dressed in less than five minutes. Gabriel grabbed the soda off the desk, popped the top and handed it to me. I downed it as we walked to the SUV and threw the empty into a trashcan that was in the back of the vehicle. I belched loudly.

"How very ladylike. You look awful," Xavier said.

"I did not sleep much," I growled at him.

"Great, we're dealing with Cranky Cain today," Xavier gave me a grin and I couldn't help but smile back.

"We have Ginny Jacobs, age thirty-six, she teaches fifth grade at a local elementary," Gabriel interrupted us.

"How did we get an identity so fast?" I asked.

"Turns out, the locals have been holding back on us, he's been leaving the victim's identification cards at the scene," Gabriel smiled at me. "Today they decided to share that little piece of information when I asked the same question."

"Seems like a little piece of information they should have shared a while ago," Lucas said.

"It's worse when you get even more rural," Gabriel shrugged "and that applies everywhere, not just Alaska."

"I don't think it has anything to do with the locals," Lucas answered. "It's us. A call to us means very bad things are happening."

"That could be," Gabriel admitted as the car came to a stop. We had only driven a few blocks, but we were faced with a full wooded area. I stared at the snow, only a few footprints were visible and a dozen or so tire tracks.

"Is this one going to be trampled as well?" I asked.

"No, it was found by a park ranger. So far, the press hasn't gotten word because we've been using cell phones to communicate the find," Gabriel answered. "There are a few dozen locals and, of course, Agent Arons, other than that, the ranger that found the body. No lookie-loos and no reporters at this time."

"But you're expecting them," Xavier said.

"Yep, I imagine this little party will only last for an hour at the most. Word is going to spread fast about another one," Lucas said.

"Pretty much," Gabriel said, getting out of the car.

We all followed behind. I trudged through the snow with my new boots. They weren't exactly the right fit, just a hair too big. My feet slid around in them, making them almost treacherous on the snow. However, they were warm.

The walk lasted about ten minutes. The trail of footsteps ended at a clearing. The body was still in place. She hung about ten foot off the ground. Again there was a small pool of blood frozen in the snow. I looked around, still no animal tracks. A few more steps and I got my first whiff of Pinesol. In the fresh air, it wasn't strong enough to be overwhelming.

Xavier had already moved to the body. He was trying to get the crime scene techs to lower the victim down. Lucas was surveying the scene. His eyes swept back and forth over the ground. Gabriel stood next to him, his eyes doing the same thing. I knew what they were looking for, signs of our killer.

Lucas stooped down, examining something. Gabriel knelt with him. They were staring at something intently. I joined them. The snow had an indentation that someone had tried to cover up by piling more snow in it. However, it hadn't worked well, the additional snow had settled, bringing the indentation back into view.

"What is it?" I asked.

"Something heavy was here," Gabriel answered.

"Yes, I can see that, but what?" I continued.

"My guess, a mobile winch," Gabriel began moving the snow with gloved hands. Slowly he revealed a couple of holes in the ground.

"So he staked it to the ground?" I asked.

"You'd have to in order to keep it from moving when you hoisted the body," Gabriel informed me. "The only thing I can't figure is what sort of stakes you'd need to get them to hold the weight."

"That's what you cannot figure out?" I asked. "I am wondering why he does not just attach it to a tree. That would make more sense to me. He's picking good sized trees for his disturbing spectacles. Surely, a winch would attach to them."

"That would be obvious," Lucas said.

"And this isn't?" I stared at the holes. "Is anyone else bothered by finding it now. Could it be that the locals missed it every time, or is this another piece of information they have held back? If they did hold it back, what else are they hiding? How much more do they know that they are not telling us?"

"It is something to be considered, but not dwelled upon. This spot on the ground isn't nearly as obvious as the tree or somewhere else," Lucas answered.

"Then it's vanity? He wants us to think he can hoist them up and down while he does his work to throw us off?" I asked.

"Possibly," Lucas stood up. His gaze fell on Xavier and the body. I didn't turn around, I had a feeling I was going to be getting the up close and personal treatment soon enough. Gabriel always sent me in during at least one autopsy to give Xavier a new perspective.

"You don't sound very certain," Gabriel said.

"I'm not. I think it's just for convenience and expense. Mobile winches aren't cheap and it would certainly cut down the time needed to do this work. However, I'm not sure why he hides it. He knew we would find the evidence eventually, so what does he gain by taking the time to cover it up?" Lucas was still staring. I followed his gaze. It wasn't at Xavier or the body, it was aimed at the tree branch that the rope was wrapped around.

"What is it?" I asked.

"Why go through all the trouble of simplifying the process, only to overcomplicate it at the same time?" Lucas answered.

"Meaning?" I pressed.

"Why not attach it to the tree where the angle would be better and the tree would be more secure than the ground? The ground isn't very giving at this time of year, or in December, it seems like extra work to secure the winch to the ground. And look at the distance. There is at least twenty feet between the body and where we found the winch secured. So he would need to stand here to hoist her up or down, move back to the victim, work for a while, then walk all the way back here to the winch and readjust her position," Lucas turned his blue eyes on me. His eyebrows were drawn in, frown lines created deep creases in his forehead and around his mouth. His lips were pulled tight, set in a hard frown that drained them of color. "So securing it to the ground has nothing to do with convenience. Why do it?"

"To keep it clean," I offered.

"The moment he starts working on the body, every time he goes back to the winch, he is contaminating it further. The victim's skin cells are going to be all over him. Just because she isn't bleeding, doesn't mean he isn't being covered in traces of her, especially in this situation. I can't imagine he doesn't realize that. He's been very smart about everything. He is going to know that he is getting her DNA all over him and everything he touches. Her skin cells alone should be creating an evidence trail," Lucas turned back to the tree. "Besides, there should be evidence of it. There should be a path of him walking back and forth from the winch. There should be trampled snow and melt marks. None of that seems to exist."

"Why does someone skin another person alive?" I asked.

"That is the part that makes even less sense," Lucas's voice sounded far away, as if he were somewhere else. His eyes had glazed, his face relaxed. It wasn't like the calm that I felt, it was his thoughts. Lucas could get locked in his own head, almost literally. When he did, he got this look and countenance that was hard to decipher. "One person, I could see. But we are working with the theory that it is two. It is hard enough to find two killers who want to kill in the same manner and hook up. Something this bizarre, something so painstakingly difficult as this, I can't even begin to fathom how they found each other. In no scenario can I see them finding each other. The fact that they did is mind-boggling."

"Internet?" Gabriel asked.

"Do you know how few serial killers have ever skinned their victims?" Lucas snapped out of it and looked at him. "I can count them on both hands. Parts, yes, but the entire victim? No. It is probably the rarest form of murder. Even cannibalism is more common than this. And the two are usually linked, you skin your victims so that you can eat them. Not this. This is something different."

"It's art," I said.

"That's what it seems like to me," Lucas agreed.

"That is not art," Arons joined us.

"Yes it is," Lucas looked at him. "Art is subjective. You may like Renoir or Monet, but the person next to you will not. And many artists from painters to sculptors to writers have found beauty in death."

"Art," Arons shook his head. "Well, you may consider it art, but I don't."

"As he said, art is subjective," I shrugged and turned away from the scene. "The bow and arrow melting the snow can be taken as art. The precision with which it has to be laid out along with the time necessary to have the salt from the skin melt the snow, there is beauty in all of it. You just have to change your perspective. He practically tip-toed over to the area to lay it out and then got down on his hands and knees to carefully put each piece down."

They continued to talk, but I tuned them out. I was once again faced with a pristine winter scene. Evergreens covered in snow. The ground covered in the white devilish stuff with a thick, crisp crust on the top of it. It would crunch when you walked on it. I closed my eyes. How many people had trampled the path before our killer had used it? How many boots had crunched in the snow? There was no way for me to know these things.

Most people would consider the body in the tree a desecration of both the body and the pristine winter. I did not. Crime scenes were a hallowed area for me. Until the area became a crime scene, it was just a picture to put on a postcard. This was reverse of what most people thought. I knew that, but couldn't change my logic.

"What are your thoughts?" Lucas whispered to me.

"Was the area tracked up when we arrived?" I whispered back.

"Yes, it's a well used public area," Lucas gave me a look.

"Then the point is moot," I opened my eyes.

"What was it?" Lucas pressed.

"I was thinking that if he had picked an area that had been untouched since the snow had fallen, it might have been significance; desecrating nature, despoiling the virgin beauty of the snow."

"Sadly, that is not the case. Although, I like the way you think," Lucas gave me a wink. We both turned back to look at Xavier. The body was now coming down from the tree. He was barking orders to those doing the lowering. Dr. Ericson, the normal medical examiner, was standing with him.

"What do you think of him?" I asked, nodding towards Dr. Ericson.

"Married to his job and he's let it take its toll on him and his marriage. I know he runs a regular practice along with it, so he avoids being home as much as possible. He volunteers to work the evening and night shifts with the coroner's office. On his nights off, he probably bowls or does some other team sport with other men. He is slightly phobic of women, which makes me wonder if his marriage crumbled first or if work crumbled his marriage."

"Why do you think he is phobic of women?"

"He doesn't talk to them unless he absolutely has to. As he made his way into the crime scene, he merely nodded at the females, but called the men by name. I would consider him misogynistic, but your confrontation with him would prove otherwise. He wasn't upset that you were a woman in charge of yourself, it frightened him."

"And Arons?"

"Special Agent Arons is in Alaska trying to salvage his career. Whatever he did, it was not enough to fire him, but it was enough to send him away. They sent him here. He is bright and capable as an agent, but it's all about treading water at this point. He was hoping this case would be his return to the light. It isn't working out that way, but if we solve it he'll be able to point out that he helped and put the feather in his cap. It might get him transferred out of Alaska and back into a more hospitable climate."

"He's a jerk," I pointed out.

"He is a jerk, that is probably why he was transferred. He probably didn't get along with a female superior. He is a bureau man through and through, but he isn't much on females in the job. I'd say he is a misogynistic jerk; however, not to the point of doing this."

"I was not thinking of him as a suspect, just wanted confirmation that he is a jerk," I gave Lucas a brief smile. The body was down. Xavier was still talking to Dr. Ericson. Gabriel had wandered away to talk to someone else. Arons had followed at his heels.

"And Ericson?" Lucas asked, before I could walk away.

"Ericson was very blasé about Xavier taking over his case. I don't do well around strangers, especially strange strangers. Most coroners throw a fit when Xavier walks in."

"Most coroners want the feather in the cap."

"Ericson doesn't?"

"What would notoriety do for him? Ericson is a man who has accepted his place in life and doesn't believe it can be changed just because he solved a case. I'm sure Xavier will continue to include him, but Ericson won't care who gets credited with the solve at the end. He'll just be happy to move on to the next case."

"That's almost pathetic," I said.

"He has become a broken man. Once, he was probably great, but we are looking at a shell. He plods forward because he doesn't know what else to do. Most people would find him pitiful."

"You think I should adjust my opinion?"

"Not in the least, why fake an emotion when it is just the two of us?"

"Thank you," I looked at Xavier. He nodded at me. I hesitated.

"I heard your argument with him last night and he came in and told me about it. It's fine," Lucas reassured me.

"He was pretty pissed."

"He was pissed because you didn't take the patch off first. You'll get nicotine poisoning doing that," Lucas told me.

"We all stray once in a while," I commented.

"Next time you stray, make sure to take off the patch first."

With that, I left Lucas and the safety of the woods. I would be present at the autopsy. They may not emotionally bother me, but I still find them gross, making them my least favorite part of this job.

Ten

There were three of us in the autopsy room.
Xavier, Dr. Ericson, and myself, we were all wearing
respirators and vinyl suits to help with the overwhelming
smell of Pinesol. I sat on a stool, just a few feet from the
medical doctors. They were busy examining things. I
was busy trying not to examine anything. I knew the
moment would come when Xavier called my name and I
would have to get up and go look at something horrifying,
but I'd delay that moment as long as possible. In the
meantime, I just listened to Xavier talk into his recorder.

He was busy describing the body. There were only
a few ways to say that the victim didn't have any skin
left, but Xavier managed to turn this into a ten minute
sentence. He might not be meticulous in appearance, but
almost nothing missed his attention when he was with a
body.

Dr. Ericson was closer to the body. Almost at
Xavier's elbow to be honest, but, like me, he was silent.
He was more interested in watching what Xavier was
doing than I was. My face was starting to sweat beneath
the mask.

"Eureka!" Xavier said. It sounded muffled and
strange through the respirators. If there hadn't been
another person in the room with us, I would have made a
sarcastic comment.

"What?" I asked instead, standing up and walking
to the body.

Xavier looked at me. He was wearing goggles that made him look like a goldfish and, with the respirator, the picture he made was completely comical.

"Look at this," Xavier was pulling apart two pieces on the arm of our victim. I saw nothing.

"Ok," I said. He let go of the arm and then did it again.

"Don't you see it?" He asked."No, but I do not have bug eyes either," I pointed out to him. Dr. Ericson gave me a look. Most coroners have to have a sense of humor. In our line of work, it isn't just a necessity, it's a life preserver. Without it, we would all go insane and most likely be locked up or practicing vigilantes.

Dr. Ericson seemed to be the exception. He was frowning at me.

"Sorry," I said to him quietly.

"I understand," Dr. Ericson dismissed it. "Most of my colleagues develop it as well."

"There is a tiny puncture mark on her arm," Xavier interrupted.

"And that means?" I asked.

"That means I think we know how they are subdued," Xavier told me. "Nothing seems to be showing up on the toxicology screens, so I don't know what he's using."

"It seems unlikely that in the few hours they are in his care that a sedative would leave the system," I said.

"True," Xavier took off the goggles. "Maybe she got a shot for something else."

"Shingles, flu, pneumonia," Dr. Ericson offered.

"She's a teacher," I added. "It could be anything, even a tetanus shot."

"Damn, so much for the eureka," Xavier sighed. "This body doesn't seem any more remarkable than the others."

"Not remarkable? It has no skin," Dr. Ericson pointed out.

"That's not what I meant. I meant that the body doesn't seem to give up any more clues than the others," Xavier corrected his wording.

"Let's get outside, get some fresh air," I suggested.

"You just want a cigarette," Xavier looked at me.

"Come on," I yanked on his arm and dragged him out into the hall. There we stripped off the vinyl protective suits and the respirators. Sweat showed on the foreheads of the two men. I was sure my forehead would look the same. I shoved the vinyl suit into a closet and then wiped my brow.

"I could use a smoke," Dr. Ericson said, heading outdoors.

"Come on," I grabbed Xavier again and we followed Dr. Ericson out.

Dr. Ericson had already lit up a cigar and was puffing on it when we got outdoors. I stared at the burning tip and had my own cravings flare up. Xavier handed me a cigarette. I handed it back to him.

"So, the hole in the arm is useless," I said. "Is there anything that you might have missed? Anything different in the way the knife was used or the actual knife used?"

"Doesn't seem to be. I'll know more after I cut her open," Xavier sighed.

"We've been at it for an hour and learned nothing," Dr. Ericson commented. "That's what we've been up against all along."

"Yes, but you have never had Xavier looking at the bodies," I smiled at Xavier.

"I don't think there is much to find, despite your faith in me," Xavier was not smiling. "Come on, let's get back to work, especially since you seem sensitive to the cold."

The reminder of my "fragility" was not necessary. Like most people, I did not like to admit to weaknesses. I liked it even less that there was an interloper around to hear the comment. Dr. Ericson, regardless of his profession or his association to the case, was not one of us.

I cherished that "us." It was almost hallowed in my mind. A part of me felt slightly betrayed by Xavier's slip of the tongue. I had built cohesion with my Marshal unit and that was not something I did easily or often.

Xavier must have noticed. When we were in the hall, he gave me a look. It would have said nothing to the outside observer. To me, it was an apology.

We suited back up and entered the autopsy room. The respirator was already uncomfortable. I imagined lines were deeply set in my face from the plastic digging in to the flesh. The bridge of my nose would sustain the most damage. It would take hours for that line to disappear.

"Ok, let's talk about this," my own voice sounded strange to me through the respirator. "There is nothing different except the possible injection site?"

"Not that I see at this time," Xavier shook his head and picked up the leg. "Come here."

"Really?" I asked, moving around to him.

"Really. See this here," he pointed to a thin membrane that was covering the muscles on the calves.

"Yes."

"This is the body's last layer of defense. On the two bodies I've examined, I have found tiny nicks in it. Or like this spot," he pointed somewhere else on the leg, "too much skin was left. Oddly, these distinctions were not made on the other bodies and no close-ups were done. I don't think they mean that much. I imagine Dr. Ericson believed the same, hence the reason they weren't given any focus."

"Sure," I said it slowly.

"It shows the level of skill involved Ace. It is nearly impossible. I can't think of a single person that could do this. It doesn't matter how good any of us are with a blade, we couldn't do this," Xavier put the leg down.

"None of us?" I asked, doubting him. I had seen his skill with a knife. I had seen him remove tattoos from bodies with a scalpel.

"Not even me. The closest I can get with that thought is Alejandro."

I hadn't been to see my former supervisor. He'd been in a wheelchair since his encounter with arsenic on my first case. He'd been my boss for less than two weeks and that time had been rough. There was no need to spend time with him now. He was living with his sister and I understood his drinking was worse. This meant he was probably living on alcohol calories.

"You think Alejandro could do it?"

"Honestly, no. Not even on his most lucid, coordinated days, but he'd be the closest."

"On a scale of one to ten, with ten being the best you have ever seen, how would you rate this work?"

"Fifty, easily," Xavier said without hesitation.

"That seems high," I said.

"Someday, try to take only the skin off of something and then come back to me," Xavier answered.

"I will take your word on it."

"That's why these little nicks and slips aren't that important. I would expect more of them. This really is almost pristine."

"So they are important, but only because there are so few of them," I said.

"If you want to look at it that way, then sure, but in all reality, they aren't going to tell us much other than what we already know. The person doing this has serious skills."

"Butcher, doctor, tanner?" I rattled off a list of persons who would work with skin.

"Sure, or something completely unrelated who just happens to be very good at skinning things as well."

"I have no suggestions based on that information."

"I didn't expect you to, Ace." Xavier shook his head again. "I know there are clues here, I just can't seem to find them."

"Why don't you give it a rest? I got a message from Gabriel, I have to go to her house. Why don't you come along and see how she lived? Maybe it will help you identify something with her death," I suggested.

"I don't think so. There's still more to do here," he waved me away.

In the hallway, a woman was talking with Dr. Ericson. She wore a no-nonsense business pants suit, black with very fine white pinstripes. Her hair was pulled back in a fashionable braided style. It also seemed to be expertly colored. I imagined when she wasn't in work clothes, she was still perfectly fashionable.

"Marshal Cain?" The woman looked at me.

"Yes," I answered.

"Special Agent Fiona Gentry, I'm here to escort you to the victim's home."

"Great, catch you later Dr. Ericson," I motioned my escort forward.

Dr. Ericson waved, but said nothing. Special Agent Gentry led the way to her waiting car. The engine was still running in the parking lot. We climbed in and the heat was on full blast. I sat quietly, waiting for my body to adjust from the outside. It didn't seem to matter that I had been outside for less than a minute, I could already feel the bone-chilling cold seeping into me.

We didn't talk much on the way to the house. I was guessing she had the same impression as most FBI agents. The Serial Crimes Tracking Unit had a tendency to think about comfort first and business-looking attire last. Today, I was in a black T-Shirt that glowed in the dark, had flames on the front and a stylized-R for Rammstein. I was also in jeans that were fading and my black snow boots. The final touches were two fleece hoodies and a light coat.

In stark contrast, she had a very nice grey dress coat that hung below her knees and tied at the waist with a wide belt and fastened with large buttons. She also had on dress shoes that would cause my feet to freeze. I wondered if she had raided Scully's *X-Files* wardrobe for the coat and the suit.

Anchorage is a beautiful city, when it wasn't full of serial killers flaying their victims alive. The streets were well maintained. The areas we traveled through had manicured yards with evergreen shrubs and bushes. The houses were not the cookie-cutter ranch-style that I associated with artificial suburbs.

I was sure there was a seedy side, all cities have them. However, we hadn't gone through any of them. They were well hidden behind the parks and pines.

In this neighborhood, the police cars looked even more out of place. There were six of them, plus two unmarked SUVs that had flashing lights. Neighbors huddled at windows or stood brazenly on the street, uninterested in hiding their gruesome, voyeuristic behavior.

The house was a pretty two story painted a light shade of gray with darker gray shutters. Part of the front had a brick facade with a large window set high off the ground, curtains drawn, showing the platoon of officers on the inside. I noticed Gabriel walk past it as we parked.

A brisk walk and I found myself climbing the front steps. A large sheltered porch covered the entryway. There was a rug that said: Keep The House Clean, Please Wipe Your Feet. I ignored it. There would be no keeping the house clean. It would be covered in fingerprint dust and grime from dozens of shoes. The rug wouldn't be able to handle all the dirt from our snow encrusted feet. Our very presence proved that someone had already soiled the inside.

"Cain," Lucas stuck his head out the door and motioned me forward. I walked past the rug and into the house, stamping my feet on a sheet of plastic. From where I stood, there wasn't much to see. A foyer with hardwood floors and bright pink walls greeted me.

I followed Lucas out of the foyer and into a living room. The first thing I noticed was the fireplace. It was the dominating feature, dark bricks around the exterior and a grate full of ashes. The second thing I noticed was that all the framed photos were smashed.

The glass littered the floor, reflecting the light, causing the carpet to dance with prisms. The pictures were unrecognizable. Some had been scratched by the breaking glass, others were just obscured by the plethora of cracks. There were ten photos total on the mantelpiece, each of them smashed near the center. It looked as though someone had gone through and slammed their fist into each of them.

"There's more," Lucas said, turning from the living room and moving towards the stairs.

Glass was sprinkled on the stairs. Most of the photos had fallen, bringing down their nails with them. The few that remained fastened to the wall were like the ones in the living room, cracked to the point of obscurity.

At the top of the stairs, the trail of glass continued. The walls of the upstairs hallway had been lined with framed family photos that were now lying on the floor.

Most of the frames had broken, spilling the glass and the photos into desecrated heaps of trash.

I slipped on a pair of gloves and reached for one of the pictures. It showed our victim, smiling and happy, with a group of children. The children were all smiling. I turned it to Lucas.

"She was a fifth grade teacher for sixteen years," he told me.

"That's a lot of suspects," I answered, my eyes returning to the photo. All those smiling children seemed grotesque in the glass littered hallway. I put it down.

"Someone was very angry," Lucas said as I stood.

"Yes, they were. Why didn't she get up and investigate someone smashing all her photos? It would have been very noisy," I continued to stare at the glass.

"That is the question for the ages," Lucas frowned.

"Maybe Xavier is right," I said.

"Right about what?"

"He found a puncture mark on the victim's arm. Since she was a schoolteacher, it could be nothing, a flu shot, tetanus vaccine, so I dismissed it. But what if it was a sedative?"

"Something that works fast and vacates the system just as quick?" Lucas shook his head.

"I do not know much about sedatives, but anything is possible."

"While he is waiting for it to take full effect, he goes through and smashes all the pictures, then grabs her and walks out of the house?"

"Sounds like a good theory."

"He hasn't smashed pictures in the other places."

"You are the one that is always talking about escalation," I smiled at him. "Maybe this is an escalation of behavior. Or perhaps he has and we just do not know about it."

"Something else for the locals to keep back?" Lucas raised an eyebrow.

Eleven

Several hours later, we were back in the conference room at the US Marshals office. The conference room was many things, but comfortable wasn't among them. The walls were a drab beige color with grey industrial carpeting. Up to this point, I had always considered grey to be one of my favorite colors, but a few days in Alaska had changed that. When things weren't white, they were grey. I wasn't sure if it was to hide the cinder residue that seemed to permeate the streets or just because color hadn't happened in Alaska.

The conference table was a rectangular monstrosity of plastic and metal. There were ten office chairs done in fake black leather. There were four whiteboards on the back wall and one on each of the side walls. The final wall was covered with panes of glass that looked into the Marshals office.

The windows had blinds that were closed. White in color and in need of a good dusting, it was obvious that they weren't down very often. Oppressive fluorescent lighting was stuck in the ceiling at regular intervals.

The whiteboards were covered in photos and handwritten notes in different colors. Gabriel, being cute, had given me a pink marker for my notes. So far, there weren't many. I got up, went to the boards, and found the picture of our newest victim. Over her head, in my messy handwriting, I put the word "sedated" with an arrow pointing at her grisly remains.

Both Agent Gentry and Agent Arons were now in the room. They had integrated themselves into our part of the investigation. I agreed with Lucas, they were both looking for a way out of Alaska and this was their ticket. I also agreed with Lucas that bringing us in to solve it wasn't going to get them the promotion to warmer climates they desired.

I stared at some of the other stuff written on the boards. Lucas, Gabriel, and Xavier had all put their stamps on them. Their handwriting streaked colorful stains across the whiteboards, providing not just information, but a colorful piece of artwork in the white and grey room. We didn't really require different colors to distinguish us. We all had unique handwriting styles.

Xavier's was like mine, something just above a scribble that took a while to get used to reading. Lucas's was more stable, cautious, his letters articulated. Gabriel's was surprising, loopy and almost feminine in nature. My eyes fell on the repetition of the word "drugged". Each had written it on the boards in a different place.

My eyes found another word, "loner", above another victim. I thought about it. Our teacher was a "loner" as well. Outside of work and family, she didn't associate with many people. I wrote it above her picture and took a step back. My eyes fell on variations of words. The synonym for "loner" was used several times. So was "severe".

"Lucas," I said, pointing at the boards.

"What?" He looked up from a file.

"All these women seem to be social misfits," I said.

"I know," he stated. "They were all very meticulous as well."

"So, I'm not pointing out a pattern we had not realized existed," I made it a statement.

"Nope, we know. We can't find any links though other than those."

"Well, our teacher seems to have been personal. You don't smash photos at one person's house and not another's if it isn't personal."

"I agree," Lucas said. "But she was a teacher for sixteen years."

"As I said earlier, that's a lot of suspects. If you go by the national average, that means at least half of her students have divorced parents. And single women in societies such as these are more likely to get remarried quickly. So, if she averages thirty students per year, that's four-hundred and eighty parents. Mark off two-hundred and forty because they are women, which leaves two-hundred and forty. Of course, then you have to add another eighty, give or take a few dozen because of divorce and remarriage. So, three hundred men who might have known this woman just because their child was in her class. Then there are a dozen or so coworkers that are male, and I do not know how large her family is, but it seems good sized, so another dozen plus that are related by birth or marriage."

"What are you getting at?" Agent Arons asked.

"Exactly that, this one seemed personal, our killer knows her. Up to this point, all the others might have been complete strangers that he snatched at random because they fit some perverse fantasy. This one was not random, he had her planned. So the first question is: why wait this long? And the second: why now?"

"Those seem counter-productive questions," Agent Gentry said.

"Not at all," Lucas jumped in. "He's waited this long to take her as a prize, so why did he pick this moment? Was she all that was available because of the stepped up patrols? Or some other unknown factor that fell into place? Most killers start with people they know or end with people they know. So either he grabbed her now because he didn't figure he'd get to her later, since

110

we are here or he grabbed her because something else changed."

"You make it sound like she was always a target," Gentry said.

"She was," Lucas answered. "Most of his victims are going to be opportunistic, they are in the wrong place, wrong time. A few of them though, they are going to be planned. This one was among the planned. If we can pick out the ones he always intended to kill from the random jumble of victims, it will get us closer to his identity."

"Not all serial killers grab victims they know," Arons pressed.

"That's true of most serial killers. I would say that is not true of this serial killer. This serial killer is doing both. He is grabbing victims of opportunity as well as eliminating some women that he isn't very fond of. The level of anger at this victim's house proves that. He was probably angry at the pictures of happy people at the homes of the other victims' houses, but he was pissed that there were pictures of happy people at the house of this particular woman. So he smashed the pictures, figuratively, he was obliterating her happiness. I imagine there are signs at some of the crime scenes as well. However, since we haven't found all the crime scenes..." Lucas spread his arms wide.

"Damn you are good," I told him, a small smile forming at the corners of my mouth. "You could be a profiler."

"Profiling is dodgy business," Lucas said to me. "I don't profile."

"We all profile, it is in our genetic makeup. For example, when we see a man driving a Hummer, we instantly think he is compensating for something. Probably a small penis or short-man syndrome. When we

111

see a buxom blond in the same car, we think trophy wife to a man in his hundreds or stripper," I told him.

"That is bias, not profiling," Lucas corrected.

"Fine, when we see a man driving a Hummer who has all gold teeth, we label him a drug dealer," I grinned.

"You got me there," Lucas said. "However, I try very hard not to profile."

"Or have a sense of humor about it," I turned back to the whiteboards. Lucas had history with profiling and profilers, he hated the profession and considered them about as useful as psychics. Instead, he looked at situations and ran the information through his psychology background to generate emotional information.

We had all had our run-ins with bad guys and evil people. Lucas's happened in the military. One of his comrades in arms had gone on a killing spree. The profiler involved had pretty much described Lucas to the letter. Lucas had been in the middle of a court marshal when the killer struck again, effectively exonerating him. He hadn't liked FBI profilers since then and had gotten his psychology degree primarily to thumb his nose at them. The real killer had been nothing like Lucas in looks or personality. However, because the victims had been carried for nearly half a mile, the profiler had decided it had to be someone of extreme physical girth. In reality, the killer had been less than six feet tall and weighed as much as I did, making him very small. But true psychopaths are stronger than your average person; I knew one that was stronger than the average bear.

"Ace?" Gabriel asked.

"Sorry, I just had a thought. We were talking earlier about the physical requirements of someone hanging a woman and skinning them. While I know we found the winch marks, we also know that his last victim was unconscious to some degree when they left the house.

So, maybe we are looking at it wrong. We were thinking it had to be someone of well defined build and muscles. But a psychopath is not limited by the normal constraints of a person, so would it really take someone of physical strength to do this? I am guessing the guy could be my size and manage," I answered.

"Do you think he is that far gone?" Gentry asked.

"Uh, he skins his victims while they are alive, that requires a certain amount of detachment. So, yeah, I think he's stepped off the 'personality disorder' train and jumped onto the 'fully functional psychopath train,'" I told her.

"He has always been functional," Lucas answered.

"True, but I do not see anti-social personality disorder induced psychopathy creating that much detachment. That seems more like a borderline type of detachment," I answered. I had learned much from Lucas about the world of psychology in the last six months. Most of it was self-relevant, but you couldn't explain me without using others as contrast.

"I have trained you well," Lucas smiled. "I agree that it has all the hallmarks of being someone with borderline personality disorder. His level of detachment is astounding."

I uncapped the pink marker and in all capital letters I wrote "PSYCHOPATH - BPD" at the top of the nearest whiteboard. We all stared at it for a while, silently thinking our own thoughts about the declaration. It was one thing to have the thought in the back of your mind, it was another to see the word expressed in front of you. We had dealt with true psychopaths before; they always proved to be the most challenging.

A pall fell over the room after we had digested the word. The grim reality was simple; he would kill over and over again. Each time would bring him pleasure. Each time would leave us just as clueless. This was not a man to make mistakes often. The few he had made hadn't gotten us any closer to finding him.

Of course, we had an incredible success rate. It was in our genes to catch him. He couldn't be smarter than all of us. He couldn't be stronger than all of us. Somewhere, there would be a slip and we would put the puzzle together. His reign of terror would end. It was the getting there that bothered us. How many more bodies would he have to his credit when we got there?

"Aislinn?" It was unusual for anyone on the team to call me by my full first name. Since Xavier had nicknamed me "Ace" when I first started, it had stuck. Even Nyleena used it more and more. To hear it slip through their lips now, brought them my full attention.

"What?"

"You seem distant, even for you," Xavier said.

"I was just thinking dark thoughts," I admitted to him. "He's made it personal, possibly for the first time, probably not. And we do not have a way to decipher the personal ones."

"Why wouldn't he just stick to smashing photos?" Arons asked.

"Because I would not. He did not want this woman happy. We cannot guarantee that it's the same with all of them. If it was, then it would not be personal," I said.

"Somewhere in that twisted sentence, I see where you're going," Lucas said. "You think he hates all the personal ones for different reasons."

"Exactly," I said. "Why didn't he want this one to be happy?"

"I don't know," Lucas admitted.

"I didn't figure you did, I do not imagine any of us can guess the reason, unless the woman somehow slighted his own happiness. However, if denying happiness was his goal in this instance, what about the others? What did he want to obliterate in the lives of the others?"

"That seems like a lot of motives," Gabriel said.

"I don't think it is the motive," Lucas said. "I think killing for the sake of killing is the motive, I think the other is just extra stuff."

"A bonus," I quickly chirped.

"That's one way to put it," Lucas said. "If the other is just a bonus, then he targets those women for that reason. He kills them because he is going to kill someone, might as well be them."

"Because of the lack of evidence in each case, we are having trouble connecting them," Xavier said.

"This guy is a nightmare," Gabriel kicked his chair back and folded his arms behind his head. He stared at the whiteboards.   "We can't even take an educated guess which killings would help us figure him out."

"An educated guess rules out the first one, it was probably important to his partner, not him," Lucas answered.

"But figuring out the partner could help identify him," Gabriel said.

"Probably, but three kills isn't enough to go on. We know he wasn't as skilled, liked his victims younger and probably did the first one alone," Lucas answered.

"I hate dead ends," I sighed.

"We all do, Ace," Xavier responded.

Twelve

I awoke with the knowledge that I was not alone. My hand searched under the pillow and found my boot knife. My guns were on the nightstand, but it was too far away. In one smooth fluid motion, I pulled the boot knife from under the pillow. The light flipped on.

"Seven seconds," Gabriel said to me.

"What the hell?" I groaned at him.

"It took seven seconds for you to wake up after I got into the room. Are you on something?" He asked.

"Xavier gave me something to help me sleep. Obviously, if I woke up in seven seconds, it isn't working," I told him. He flashed a smile.

"Come on, Sleepy, we have somewhere to be," Gabriel handed me a Mt. Dew. I had come to the conclusion that Gabriel's job was less about leading the team and more about keeping the team from killing FBI agents. I knew when he woke Xavier and Lucas he did so with cups of coffee in hand. He was not only our liaison but our handler. I didn't envy his job. I would have hated waking up this lot.

"Where?" The clock on the nightstand read 4:17 a.m.

"Patrol car pulled over someone suspicious. They were carrying a knife, a winch, and a bag full of bloody clothing."

I took the Mt. Dew as I climbed from bed. I drew my hair up into a bun without a brush. It was permanently misshapen into that style so it went easily.

I pulled on the rest of my clothes, redid my bun, and followed Gabriel into the parking lot.

The SUV was already running. Lucas and Xavier's shadows could be seen inside it. I pulled open the door.

"Sleeping pills must be slowing your reflexes. It took almost four minutes for you to get up and moving," Xavier said to me.

"I don't think Ace should be taking sleeping pills," Lucas said adding emphasis to my name.

"Would you rather her have a sleep-deprivation induced psychotic break?" Xavier countered.

"This is the first time I have taken one while working," I told everyone.

"Why did you take one tonight?" Gabriel asked.

"Something about the photographs being broken. It bothered me. He did not just obliterate her happiness by smashing the pictures, he got rid of her memories," I told him.

"And that bothers you?" Lucas asked.

"Wouldn't it you?" I countered.

"You think it was about the memories or the happiness?" Gabriel asked.

"I don't know, that sounds like a question for Lucas. I just got to thinking, I do not have many photos, but the ones I do have are important to me. They are about more than just smiles and faces frozen in time, they are about specific memories. Especially that photo of her with her class. That was a special photo because it was not a class photo, it was set outdoors. They were doing something, a field trip or an Easter egg hunt. It was a memory that she wanted to look at every day."

"I will think on that," Lucas said.

"So we think our killer pulled a Bundy?" I asked.

"Anything is possible," Gabriel shrugged. Even in the darkened interior I could see it. The tone of his voice told me that he wasn't buying it.

"Not our boy," I whispered.

"Probably not, but we may have caught a different serial killer or just some schmuck who can't figure out that driving around with a bag full of bloody clothing and a knife is a really bad idea," Gabriel replied.

"Ten to one, he's a poacher," Xavier said.

"People," I shook my head in the dark.

The city was deathly quiet. Our car was the only one I saw on the road. In a city this large, there should have been traffic, even at this hour. The fact that there wasn't proved something about the fear level of the city. I had only seen it once before, in Colorado Springs, once the sun went down, the town closed up. Their killer had been pretty stealthy, sneaking up on his victims and slitting their throats as they walked down the street. His mistake had been an ATM camera. Once we found the picture, it had only been a matter of time.

We arrived at the police station a few minutes later. Gabriel and Lucas went into the interrogation room. Xavier and I sat in a different room.

Despite what people see on TV, interrogation rooms do not have large windows that allow you to see everything going on. Instead, we were shoved into a room with two other people, one of them Agent Arons, and a small TV. The camera for the TV was inside the interrogation room, a room that was overcrowded with just three people. Lucas was wide enough for two or three normal people.

The suspect sitting in the chair opposite the Marshals looked like many things, including a Viking warrior or a Russian muscle man. He was well muscled with a beer gut. His clothes looked slept in or worse. I imagined he didn't smell very well. He hadn't shaved in ages or by the looks of it, washed the beard that had grown in. I would have guessed him homeless and a car thief before our meticulous skinner.

Deciding this guy was guilty of poor taste and maybe a few other things, but not our serial killer, I turned to our surroundings. Something told me this had once been a janitor's closet. It was five foot wide by seven foot long. The walls were a strange muted yellow color. The TV sat on a skinny folding table. Our seats were metal folding chairs that were missing their rubber coated feet. They made horrendous noises when they were scooted across the linoleum tile floor.

A uniformed officer came in with four cups of coffee. The coffee looked strong and smelled stronger. Growing up in a house with a serious coffee drinker meant I loved the smell despite hating the taste. It also meant that I could tell the strength of the coffee based on the smell. It wasn't quite *Snow Dogs* thick, but it was getting close.

"Sugar? Cream?" The officer asked me. I shook my head and put the coffee on the table. Some would consider me a germ-o-phobe. I wasn't, but the thought of drinking coffee from a coffee mug that had been in a police station for an unknown number of years, bothered me. All those lips and hands of strangers made me not want to touch the cup. It wasn't about the germs, it was about the strangers. I had the worst case of "stranger danger" on the planet.

On the monitor, Gabriel and Lucas stood up. We followed their lead and met them in the hallway. Gabriel was shaking his head. Lucas was trying not to smile.

"You might check him against other open murder cases, I'd bet he killed someone, but he isn't our serial killer," Gabriel said.

"He had a bag full of bloody clothes!" Arons protested.

"But no skins and he's not coordinated enough," Gabriel answered. "This guy couldn't kidnap and then skin our women. He's a barely functional alcoholic. He's already starting to detox. He's dirty, smelly, and his mental state is a mess, but he isn't our killer."

"However, I wouldn't rule him out as a killer in general," Lucas jumped in. "He probably killed a guy or girl that pissed him off and is trying to figure out what to do about it. That's probably why he ran the light. Not only is he detoxing but he seems to be in a state of mild shock. I associate that with people who have done something out of character. In this case, he said something about trouble at home. You might check his girlfriend or wife or any of their lovers if they exist."

"He lives alone," Arons answered.

"That doesn't mean he does not have a girlfriend," I pointed out.

"Or a mother," Lucas said.

"How very Norman Bates," the unidentified detective said.

"In the movie, Bates just preserved his mother, she died of natural causes," Lucas said dismissively.

Agent Arons visibly paled, "This guy is an amateur taxidermist."

"Oh, how creepy," I said, shooting a glance at Lucas.

"Which part?" Lucas asked.

"Both. How does one become an amateur taxidermist and why would you stuff your mother?" I answered.

"We don't know that it was his mother," Xavier reminded me.

"True," I answered, "but stuffing anyone is pretty creepy."

"I'll give you that," Xavier looked at Arons. "Do you want us to go with you to check on the rest of his associates?"

"No, we'll organize it. You concentrate on our killer," Arons and the detective left.

We loaded up and headed back to the hotel.

I hate being trapped in a car. There is nowhere to run when people start asking you questions. I had found the same applied to showering. Lucas had a tendency to corner me in the shower if he wanted to know something that I didn't want to talk about.

"Now, back to your drug use," Gabriel said as the car pulled out of the parking lot.

"They are not drugs," I said. "They are sleeping pills. I normally only take them when we are not on a case. The neighborhood we live in is secure enough that I should be able to get a good night's sleep. My brain does not let me. Between my past and the history I am building as a Marshal, I am having more nightmares. The pills keep the nightmares away. I do not dream at all when I am on them, or if I do they never wake me and never let me remember them. It isn't a problem. I took one tonight because I was having trouble erasing the image of the photos being smashed from my brain."

"I need you completely functional, Aislinn," Gabriel said from the front seat.

"And I am, Gabriel. Seriously, I am fully functional. However, I have not slept much since we arrived and was starting to feel the effects. I thought I would get one night of sedated sleep and be back on the job tomorrow as my usual self. I never expected to have you walk into my room to tell me that they had caught a guy with bloody clothing in his car. I expected at seven or eight tomorrow morning you would burst in and tell me we had another victim in a tree. Since I average four hours of sleep on the pills, it wouldn't have been a big deal."

"How much sleep do you get off of them?" Gabriel pressed.

"When we are on a case? About two and they aren't very restful. When we aren't on a case, about four. Of course, my body reacts differently to the pills when we aren't on a case and I can usually get six if I am home and in my bed."

"Ace requires less sleep than most. She is at her best when she has between four and five hours of real sleep. That's all the pills do," Xavier defended me.

"And you're sure that she is fine on them?" Gabriel continued.

"Her? Yes. Anyone else would be comatose. Aislinn doesn't have any groggy side effects or feelings of slowness that is normally associated with these types of medications," Xavier responded.

"What is she on?" Gabriel asked.

"Quazepam. It's a benzodiazepine used to treat insomnia with very few side effects. Aislinn has no side effects and I write the script for thirty tablets but she only fills it every couple of months. She isn't abusing it or misusing it," Xavier assured our team leader. A weird look came over his face.

"What?" Gabriel asked.

"I had a thought," Xavier turned to look at me. "You tried other benzos, didn't you?"

"Several. I have been on and off them for years," I answered.

"Ever try triazolam?"

"Yeah, it was terrible. It did not improve my sleep, something about the half-life. It would make me sleepy, but by the time I fell asleep, it only kept me asleep about ten minutes. While in college, I was on and off diazepam and clonazepam. It worked much better."

"Don't care about the others. Did they say why you had such problems with it?" Xavier asked.

"Yeah, I metabolized it too fast due to a stress induced high metabolism. The half-life is normally something like two hours, but for me, it was more like thirty minutes. As a result, I would fall asleep, but I would be awake within a few minutes."

"If I injected you with triazolam, how long before you woke up?"

"Twenty minutes, maybe less."

"That's it," Xavier looked at Gabriel. "There's my fast acting, quick to leave the system sedative."

"Speak English," Gabriel told him.

"Well, I'd been racking my brain since we got the case about what sort of sedative it would take to keep them from fighting, but have them awake for the skinning. I was leaning towards full anesthetics, but while Ace would only sleep for twenty minutes or so, most would sleep for hours before it started wearing off. But triazolam, since it is such a fast-acting benzodiazepine, it wouldn't take long for the drug to wear off and wake you up."

"But I have failed drug tests because of benzos," I told him. "Hell, I failed the Marshals drug test and had to get a note from my doctor in Washington that I did have a prescription for the Valium they found."

"True, and triazolam would stay in the body since they die within twelve hours of injection," Xavier hung his head. "I'll go back to thinking on it."

"Glad my medication use could almost help," I told him forcing myself to sound cheery.

"Yeah, well, it was a great thought. I hadn't considered some of the weaker benzos because they aren't used much in the US. Some are even banned," Xavier told us all.

Indecision

He knew he had screwed up by smashing the pictures at the teacher's place. Marshal McMichaels would have figured out that it was personal. He just hadn't been able to help himself. To see his child smiling out at him from her photo had enraged him.

His Grace, smiling, staring out at him, with her fifth grade teacher behind her, also smiling was too much. Grace had hated her. She had been mean and cruel. Grace had been sent to the office one day because she was sneezing in class and the bitch found it disruptive. But the bitch was the cause, Grace was allergic to cats, she always sneezed around them. And that bitch teacher had owned three of them at the time.

One by one, they had all disappeared from the teacher's house during Grace's time in her class. By the end of the year, Grace was back to being a healthy child.

She had even had the nerve to call him and his wife in to talk about Grace's problem. Her suggestion had been homeschooling the girl if her allergies were that bad. But Grace's only allergy was cats and she could handle them to some degree. She just couldn't handle all the dander the teacher carried on her clothes.

Henry picked up a cigar and a photo album. He took both outdoors. The women in his house were sound asleep. He had ensured it. His original plan had been to go hunting, but that hadn't worked out for him. He'd had a flat tire. It was the second time he'd been delayed this month. He wasn't happy about it. He had a schedule to keep.

Instead, he would content himself with the album. There were two hundred pages in it. Each page could hold four, four inch by five inch photos. However, that wasn't what was in the photo album.

Each photo holder carried a three inch by four inch swatch of skin. Under it, in meticulously neat handwriting was the name of the person the skin belonged to and the date they had died. He'd found it in his son's things.

The first three swatches had his son's illegible scrawl under them. It reminded him of Marshal Reece. His handwriting was nearly illegible on his autopsy notes.

His best estimate was another two weeks before they finally caught up to him. Marshal Reece had been muttering the entire time he had done the autopsy. Now the results of toxicology were going to go straight to the Marshal. And Marshal Reece, despite his unkempt appearance was a man who didn't miss much.

Henry had been unable to stop the basic tox screens that identified the sedative he was using to subdue unruly victims. However, he had been able to make them disappear. It wasn't hard. But Reece would see everything, find the clues. It would take a while to put it all together, but they would.

He had three women on his list. The whore upstairs, snoring her head off, was among them. Maybe a fourth, if they figured out it was him and he could manage it, he'd get Marshal Cain before they arrested him. She hit all the wrong buttons. Her dismissive wave today had been irritating. She thought she was so smart and so superior to him. He'd show her.

The waitress was still on his list. If his fucking tire hadn't been flat, she probably would have been on the menu tonight. The Marshals seemed to bring bad luck with them.

Tomorrow night would be her turn. After she was found, he'd go after the uppity bitch at the police department--the one that wrinkled her nose and walked away every time he came to talk about a case with her.

Then there was his secretary at the doctor's office. She had the audacity to think he was hitting on her, flirting with her. She'd been with more men than anyone on the planet. He had treated her for several sexually transmitted diseases and yet the bitch still thought that he wanted her.

In response to these imagined sexual advances, she had taken him aside and quite firmly told him that she would never be with a man as small as him. His slight size told her that he would have a small dick. And she just couldn't handle that.

She was just like the rest of them, convinced of her own superiority. He had almost fired her, but she threatened him with a lawsuit about sexual harassment if he did. That was the last thing he needed. This was the best solution.

And of course, the nag upstairs had been harping at him for years. He never did anything right according to her. He also knew that Grace was not his biological daughter. It didn't take a genius to figure it out; Grace had genetic features that couldn't have existed if she had been his daughter. Hilary still didn't know he knew. She still thought she had cuckolded him. She was wrong.

Grace would be his only regret when it was all over. He had written a new will, one that stated Grace was to go live with his brother and their family. His brother had been concerned when he got the call, but it had been shortly after the death of their son, so his brother had dismissed it. Henry remembered that conversation vividly.

His brother had kept reassuring him that nothing would happen to Henry or his wife. Henry had been insistent that bad things happened all the time. They could have a car accident or something equally tragic and Grace wouldn't have anywhere to go.

So, his brother had relented and Henry had set about to do his son's memory proud. The twisted world in which he had grown up had turned him into a killer. Henry could relate to that. He found himself capable of it when he had dispatched those damned cats. He hadn't turned it on people though until four years ago. He had killed a homeless woman, stabbing her six times.

She had been the first to stoke his rage. It had been October. The winter had descended early with huge snowfalls. He had been walking from the doctor's office to the coroner's office when he saw her. He offered her a dollar.

The homeless woman had made a snide comment about how he could do better than a dollar. She deserved more than that. It would barely buy a cup of coffee and she needed the warmth and the food in this cold.

He had agreed, lured her to his car with the promise of a hot meal and a place to stay. They had arrived at the cabin only twenty minutes later. He had walked her inside and stabbed her. The release had been euphoric.

All his stress and worries had melted away in those few minutes. He had held her and watched the life drain from her. For the first time he had felt free. He had done it a few times since, always with the homeless and never the same way. There were computer programs to detect that kind of stuff. There was never a pattern.

Until now. His son had given him a pattern and a purpose. The release each time was just as euphoric. He had control over these stupid women that had beaten him down to a shell of a man.

In high school, Henry had been the man going places. He'd been voted "Most Likely to Succeed." And he had. He had just started his practice when he met his wife. She had come in with a kitchen knife injury. Chopping onions or something, the knife had slipped. He had thought she was about the most beautiful woman he had ever laid eyes on.

Six months later, she was pregnant and they were married. Their lives had been hell since the wedding rings slipped onto their fingers. She had done nothing but berate him since then. But he would get his own back. He was determined to find the man that might still reside in the shell.

He wanted to see her skin gone, wanted to listen to her cries and screams as he removed her evil covering. However, killing her was a huge risk now that he had screwed up and smashed all those pictures. If his wife died at the hands of the skinner, someone might take notice of his little girl smiling from the picture.

The first swatch caught his attention. It belonged to a girl named Amanda Turner. She had been pregnant when his son went overseas. She gave the child up for adoption and told his son she never wanted to see him again during a Skype conversation.

His son had been devastated. When he got back, he went to talk to Amanda. Henry wasn't sure what happened after that. His son had spiraled into a darker and darker mood until finally, the police had knocked on their door. It had taken over a week to find her body. They ruled him out as a suspect. A week and a half after that day, another girl had been found. Then another. Then his son had butchered himself, slicing into his flesh over thirty times before slitting his own throat and bleeding to death in the cold, white snow.

Three days after Christmas, Henry had agreed to go through his son's room. That's when he found the album he was now holding, with the names and swatches of skin inside.

He stubbed out his cigar and returned to his den. The radio he kept in there was chattering. The secure line was talking about a patrol officer pulling over a driver for running a light. They had found bloody clothes in his trunk. They suspected he was the serial killer.

Now would be a good time, Henry thought. While the Marshals and FBI wasted their time, he could go out and find himself a woman to fulfill his needs. But he still had a flat tire and it needed to be there in the morning. If it wasn't, his wife would nag him about going out so late and was he having an affair. She kept all the finances, she would notice him paying for the tire.

She had caused him social impotence with her strict checkbook balancing and money management. She even did the finances at his office. She knew exactly how much he got paid and it went into their joint account every week.

The same was not true of hers. Her money went into a private account. He didn't know what she did with hers. He guessed part of it went towards hotel rooms with her lover, Grace's real father. He didn't know why she just wouldn't give him the divorce. He had asked once, she had responded over her dead body. Henry thought that was ironic.

His mind still jumbled and screaming at him, he gave up on the night. Sliding the album into a hidden drawer in his large desk, he put his second greatest treasure away. Finally, he turned out the light and went to bed.

Thirteen

Another day staring at whiteboards, I thought as we trudged into the Marshals office a little after ten in the morning. We had slept in because of our early morning call. So far, patrol units hadn't found a body. Another delay in his pattern.

Agent Arons and Agent Gentry both sat in the room, watching us. I didn't know if they were waiting for us to pull a rabbit out of our hat or what, but I was pretty sure they weren't going to get it. Another Marshal stuck his head in the door.

"Uh, Marshal Henders," he said.

Gabriel was technically not a Marshal. I gave him a smile. He was supposed to be a suit and tie man with black shoes polished to a high shine. Working with us made him an Extra Special Agent, but most people just identified him as a US Marshal.

Gabriel stood and left the room. We all stared at the door like our grip on reality had just walked out of it. In some ways, this was true. Of the five of us, Gabriel was the least nuts.

Michael Giovanni walked into the room looking like warmed over death. He sat down and flipped open his laptop. Then he sneezed.

"Should you be out of bed?" I asked. "Your complexion matches the carpet in this room, like a turkey that has been baked in a pizza oven for six days by an incompetent fry cook."

"At least I am color coordinated. Just don't expect me to do miracles," Michael answered.

"I always expect miracles out of you," I told him. "That's why you are the computer guru and I am just the gunman."

"Gunwoman," Michael corrected. "And I think we should go with computer emperor, since I'm here with pneumonia."

"Are you still contagious?" I moved away from him.

"No, he hasn't been contagious since yesterday. We all know about your issues with germs," Xavier told me.

"Do you have a legally binding document that says that?" I asked.

"You have my expert opinion as a doctor," Xavier answered.

"Oh great, we are all going to die from pneumonia or plague," I said.

"Is this relevant?" Arons asked.

"Does it matter?" Lucas looked at him. "Are you in a hurry to return to the land of death? If so, perhaps you should seek a therapist."

Arons sat there for a moment, looking at Lucas. Lucas stared back, face set in stone, not cracking a smile. Finally, Arons sighed and looked away. Lucas had won the staring contest. I tried not to giggle.

"I've been keeping up with things and everything is tenuous at best," Michael brought us back into the land of death. Then he stopped. Agent Gentry offered him a mask. Michael waved it away and winked at me.

"Who is this?" Michael asked, then coughed. Agent Gentry gave up offering and tossed the mask at him.

"Special Agent in Charge Fred Arons and Special Agent Fiona Gentry," Lucas informed him.

"Feds," Michael said it with a grumble.

"We are feds too," I reminded him.

"We're different kinds of feds," Michael said. "Where's Gabriel?"

"Doing Gabriel things," I said.

"Do I wait?" Michael asked.

"Do you have world-altering news?" I asked.

"Not really," Michael sighed. "I do have the geographic profile built. It's a mess."

He hooked some stuff up to his computer and we were suddenly staring at a map of Anchorage on one of the whiteboards. In the corner was a "key." Red dots were kill sites, blue dots where the victims lived, and green dots where they worked. The dots were speckled all over the place.

"If we try to find a center and draw a circle, it is nearly impossible. If we draw a square, it works better, but you have to use the FBI office as the center. If we draw an oval, the center changes to the hospital. So, I drew a free form. There is no way to encompass all the dots and when you start leaving out a dot here because it's an outlier, you have to leave out this one and that one and . . .," he shrugged. "There is no way to create any geometric shape to include the majority of the dots unless you just circle the entire city of Anchorage."

"What if you eliminate all but the first three," Lucas asked. Michael typed some stuff into his computer. There were two dots in the north, two dots in the south, one in the dead center, and one way off the marked areas. It was red. I stared at that red dot.

"Which one is that?" I finally asked.

"Victim two. The first three were not covered in Pinesol. Something caught hold of it. The guess was a pack of wolves based on teeth marks, but we don't know how far from the original spot they moved it. The police never found the tree with the rope. They theorized that the rope had broken and the wolves had carried her off," Michael answered.

"How gruesome," I continued to stare at the dot. "Maybe it didn't break, maybe he dropped her to be found by wolves or other predators and carried off."

"You think victim two could have been known to our killer?" Lucas asked.

"It's possible. She seems to have gotten the most punishment," I shrugged.

"Who is victim two?" Xavier jumped into the conversation.

"A woman by the name of Gina Leeks. She was reported missing over a week before some hikers found her," Michael answered. "The police did the usual stuff, but they didn't find anything in her background or any of the interviews with her associates. They marked it as a dead end."

"Maybe Lucas should spend some time talking to her family," I suggested.

"That's the dead end part, there isn't any. Well there is, but she didn't associate with them. She hadn't talked to her parents in over eight years. She ran away from home when she was sixteen. They live in California, didn't even know she was in Anchorage. She had a couple of friends and a roommate, but they all came back squeaky clean. You might have more friends than her, Ace," Michael added.

"That's sad, humans should have more connections than that," I said off-handedly.

"One day, I'm going to put a shock collar on you and every time you distance yourself from us frail and pathetic humans, I'm going to give you a good strong jolt," Lucas smiled at me.

"Just do not scramble my brains too badly, we might need them," I grinned back.

"Well," Gabriel made a grand entrance with a stack of stuff in his hands. "Our guy from this morning is

Norman Bates. It sort of looks like his whole family might have some of Bates' insanity."

"What's up chief?" Xavier asked him.

"The blood was the suspect's father. But the father died of natural causes. When the police raided a storage unit, they found grandma, grandpa, great aunts, and uncles. It looks like they have been doing it for generations. It's a learned behavior."

"How did that go unnoticed?" Xavier held his mouth open.

"That would be a question for someone else. What are we looking at?"

"The geographical profile. It's a disaster," Michael answered. "And Lucas is considering fitting Ace with a shock collar."

"That might not be a bad idea," Gabriel smiled. "So, geographical profile. It looks like an amoeba."

"That it does, look like an amoeba, I mean. I am not real keen on the shock collar," I answered. "However, Michael, remove the first three victims."

Six dots disappeared from the screen. I turned sideways to look at it. There were still a ton of dots.

"Remove all workplaces that have daytime only hours or where our victim worked in the daytime," I said.

Dozens of dots disappeared. The screen looked clearer, but it was still spread out. Too spread out to really get a good idea of what we were looking.

"Wait, put those back on," I said. With a clacking of keys, the dots reappeared. I grabbed my pink marker and drew a circle on the whiteboard.

"What's in the center of that?" Gabriel asked.

"The FBI Headquarters," Michael answered.

"Did they build it in the exact center of town?" I asked looking at the two visiting agents.

"I don't know," Gentry answered.

"What about restaurants, diners, coffee shops?" I asked.

"The FBI is located there, of course there are amenities. There are at least two dozen restaurants, a half dozen diners, and about fifty places that sell coffee, including a Starbucks in the FBI building," Michael answered.

"Why stick a Starbucks in an FBI building?" I asked.

"Have you seen how much coffee Feds drink?" Gabriel asked.

"You've got me there," I looked at the circle. "So this is useless. Based on it, our killer is most likely an FBI agent picking out victims while he has lunch and gets coffee."

"You think this is an agent?" Arons scoffed at me.

"No, I think it is a coincidence of enormous magnitude. I think our killer wants us to think it's an FBI agent," I said.

"Or his fixation might be an FBI agent, so he frequents where she frequents and picks out victims while he is there," Lucas offered.

"Oh, that would be good," I told him. "How many female FBI agents do you have here?"

"At least fifty," Gentry said to me.

"Well, that does not help," I looked at Lucas.

"She would have to be a woman in power," Lucas reminded me.

"All our directors are men and the Special Agent in Charge changes based on seniority and who is leading the investigation," Arons answered.

"Maybe he's just some nut who likes to hang around places that the FBI hangs around," I said.

"That would make him nutty," Arons quipped.

"Not really," Lucas countered. "It would give him a fixation or fetish. Maybe he wants to be an agent and can't for whatever reason."

"He'd probably fit in with our lot, if he wasn't a serial killer," Gabriel sat down. "Are we in agreement that this geographical profile is pretty unhelpful?"

"Yes, but it's because we do not have the data. Not all the victims were kidnapped from their home. Some were abducted leaving work, some we don't know where they were before they went missing," I said.

"The computer is limited by the information we give it," Michael agreed.

"Ok, so change the information," Gabriel said.

"To what?" Michael asked.

"Remove all the dots except the places where the bodies were found and the known sites of abduction," I said.

The keys clicked and clacked as Michael began furiously typing. The dots slowly began melting away. I noticed the problem as the other dots left my field of vision.

"Ok, so most of the outliers are the kill sites," I said.

"Most, but not all," Lucas answered.

"Most is better than what we were looking at," I told him.

"Agreed," Lucas gave me a look.

"But the known abduction sites fall into a pattern," I continued. "Unfortunately, it isn't a circle, but a shape is a shape."

"That's my neighborhood," Agent Gentry said pointing at one of the dots.

"And mine," Agent Arons pointed to another one.

"Check the other dots with known FBI agents," I told Michael.

More clacking. The dots began changing colors. Michael updated the key at the bottom to show how many were near homes of FBI agents.

"I think someone is stalking the FBI," I said.

"We'll need a list of how many staff the bureau employs here," Gabriel told Arons. Arons looked a little green.

"Since they haven't struck the FBI directly, it is just a power play. A show if you will," Lucas assured them.

"Why taunt the FBI?" I asked.

"Why not? Around here, the Marshals and the FBI are the enemy," Gabriel answered.

"Ok, we'll go with that," I answered unsatisfied. For a killer that targeted women, the FBI agents in the area seemed out of place. Besides, how did our killer have so much time to stalk FBI agents as well as his victims? It was another jigsaw piece that didn't fit and seemed to belong to an entirely different puzzle.

I went back to staring at the map and the whiteboard. Nothing made sense with any of it. The geographical profile was all over the place. The whiteboards were filled with information, none of it useful. I sighed without realizing it.

"What?" Gabriel asked.

"I do not know, I just feel like we are chasing our own tails," I answered. "The geographical profile is useless. The information on the whiteboards aren't getting us anywhere and now, he's broken pattern again."

"You think the pattern breaks are the most important?" Arons asked.

"Overall? No. But today? Yes. I mean twice in a week? He's been at it for months and only broken the pattern once. And it was a long break. So either he was away for the holidays or he was in the hospital or something," I said.

"Why not jail?" Gentry answered.

"Because this guy is not the jail type. The worst he's probably had is a speeding ticket," Lucas answered. "You don't get where this guy is with a criminal record."

"Thought you didn't like profiling?" Arons asked.

"I don't, it isn't profiling. I don't know much about him, but his victims are all women who do not trust easily and, yet, they go with him. So he has to be clean-cut and somewhat attractive. You don't get that with a serious criminal record," Lucas said. "Think Dennis Rader."

"It took over twenty years to catch him," Gentry said. "And then it was because of his vanity."

"True, but vanity is an interesting thing," Lucas said. "Our killer is vain as well. He just isn't ready to send us a floppy disk with all his information on it."

"Speaking of vanity, is it possible that's why he's taunting the FBI?" I asked.

"Yes, quite likely. The women in the FBI are his type. They are usually no nonsense when on the job. There isn't a lot of room for personality in the FBI," Lucas answered. "Unlike the Marshals. There is more wiggle room for personality and expression of such. Using the two females in this room, we can see the difference in the way they dress, carry themselves, everything. Part of it is just because of Ace being herself, but the FBI wouldn't allow her jeans and T-Shirt. They would approve of the bun though."

"That's why I am not an FBI Agent," I reminded him.

"There are a lot of reasons you aren't an FBI agent, Ace," Xavier gave a snicker.

"Or you," I smiled at him. "How is vanity going to help us catch him?"

"I'd say all are sparked by the need to dominate a woman, but a few are also vanity kills. Women that personally slighted him, we find them, we find him," Lucas said.

"We have talked about that and other than the teacher, we have no idea which ones are vanity kills," I said.

"No, but if you and I go through all the crime scene photos . . .," Lucas was interrupted.

"That might have to wait," Gabriel said. "They want us to talk to Norman."

"Who's Norman?" I asked.

"How did you forget the creepy guy who is stuffing his dead relatives that quickly?" Arons asked.

"He is a nonentity for me. He isn't a serial killer. I do not have to chase him down. I do not need to wrestle victims from his clutches. Why remember?" I asked.

"You're strange, Marshal Cain. I mean this in the best possible way, I think alligators are more socially oriented than you," Arons said.

"They are," I agreed. "You guys do that, I will stay here and stare at the whiteboards to see if I can find anything."

Fourteen

Seven hours later, I was stiff; my head hurt from my vending machine lunch and my eyes were tired. The whiteboards were now covered in pink notes. I had even had portable whiteboards brought in.

Michael and I had taken all the photos and arranged them in chronological order. He had made a few notes in bright green. Together we had found something. It was a minor something, but it was still better than where we had been when everyone left us.

"What do you think, dinner and then the hotel?" Michael asked as he stretched.

"I thought hackers were supposed to be able to sit for long periods of time?" I teased him.

"They are. I'm losing my touch. Being a Marshal is making me soft," he yawned and stretched again. "And I am getting over pneumonia."

"Ok, real food and then we go back to the hotel and await our fearless leaders," I agreed. Agent Gentry had been left with us. Most of the time, it didn't bother me to have a handler. Sometimes, it felt like I was on a short leash with armed guards just in case I went crazy and started killing people. This was one of those leash moments.

She ferried us to a restaurant that was close by and proclaimed that it's special of the day was something weird with lobster. I was sure the lobster was fine, but there was no way in hell I would order it from here.

We took a table near the back. The restaurant was decorated in 1950's decor. There was a faux car front that worked as the counter. The floors were black and white checkered linoleum that had seen better days. The walls were white with black pin-striping. However, the white had yellowed with age and grease. It had been a while since someone had taken the time to clean them.

The tables were all done in a car theme. The booths looked like the bench seats out of Buicks. The tables were formica and metal. Both showed wear and tear.

A waitress looking about as old as I felt most days, handed us menus and sloppily poured us glasses of water. She stood there, hand on her hip, waiting for us to order. I glared at the menu.

The choices were limited. Most of it was seafood. My brain instantly turned to mercury poisoning. I didn't really believe eating a piece of fish or shellfish would instantly cause me to fall to the ground with convulsions and begin hyper-salivating, but why take that chance? The cook could be a nutcase with an easy method of administering extra doses of mercury into the seafood.

This was not the kind of place that served low-calorie items other than diet sodas. Most of the items were fried or served with fried foods. Even the salads were heaped with ham or fried chicken or seafood. The dessert portion touted triple chocolate cake and pies of different varieties, all served with ice cream and, if you wanted, fudge or caramel sauce.

"Ace?" Michael said my name.

"Sorry, I was thinking about mercury poisoning," my eyes unglazed, I looked at the menu again. They had chicken salad. Chicken and tuna salad were some of the fastest ways to get food poisoning. I frowned.

"Just order something that isn't likely to be toxic," Michael chided after a minute more.

"What cuts of meat are on the Philly?" I asked our waitress.

"Brisket," she answered. I marked it off the list of possible food options. "Ok, well just give me a roast beef sandwich."

"Do you want fries, waffle fries, seasoned fries, or a baked potato?"

"Um, do you have onion rings?" I countered.

"For a buck more, I can give you onion rings," she walked off.

"What was that about?" Gentry asked.

"Ace is very careful about the food she puts in her body," Michael snickered.

"I have migraines and a track record with serial killers, paranoia and concern are just standard operating procedure at this point," I commented dryly.

Dr. Ericson walked into the diner. Gentry waved to him. He joined us at our table.

"We just ordered," Gentry told him.

Dr. Ericson waved his arm and brought the waitress back to our table. He ordered the special and water. She frowned at me as she walked away.

"Marshal Cain, you have a headache," Dr. Ericson said.

"I know," I told him. "Too many hours in a room with florescent lighting. Hence the dinner break."

"Ok, back to the 'it took ten minutes for her to order food' thing," Gentry pressed.

"It isn't that exciting," I told her.

"Marshal Cain has migraines, food can trigger them," Dr. Ericson said in my defense. "As a result, I imagine it is very hard for her to eat out."

"How is the cut throat world of doctoring?" I asked him.

"Boring. How's the case coming along?" He countered.

"Slowly. But we did find a guy who pulled a Norman Bates on us. The police found dozens of taxidermied corpses in a storage unit. Xavier is doing something with the bodies; Lucas and Gabriel are talking to the guy," I answered.

"No doubt that headache isn't helping your thought processes either," Dr. Ericson pulled out a script pad. "Take this."

He scribbled something illegible on the pad and then handed it to me. I read the words and raised my eyebrows.

"Well, I'm guessing you have migraine medicine with you," Dr. Ericson said.

"I do, I am waiting on food to take it," I admitted.

"Take this if it doesn't work. I know those lights can be a real bitch. Tomorrow try to bring in lamps and work under those," Dr. Ericson answered.

As I was folding it up, Michael took it from me and handed it to Gentry, "Know any all night pharmacies?"

"Yeah, I'll drop it off and pick it up for you," she sighed as she said it.

"Thank you," Dr. Ericson and I said in unison.

"So what brings you out tonight, Doc?" Gentry asked.

"Nothing much, my daughter is at a volleyball game. My wife is at work, so I thought I'd stop in for a bite to eat. The lobster here is always good and I had a craving for it," Dr. Ericson said.

Our food was brought to us and we finished the meal with light conversation. Michael tossed out a credit card and paid for everyone. We had per diems, but we rarely adhered to them. Add the fact that we discussed the case for about three seconds and suddenly, it had become a business dinner on the US Marshals.

If anyone ever questioned our expenses, they did it to Gabriel. And whatever Gabriel said, kept them from coming to us with more questions. He probably included phrases like "whack jobs" and "nutcases."

We said good-bye to Dr. Ericson. He still wasn't growing on me, but it would be more surprising if he did. Gentry started the car and we headed to a pharmacy.

We all unloaded and went inside. The store was brightly lit, making my eyes hurt even more. I handed the prescription to the pharmacist who made a face. Gentry pulled out her badge and showed it to him. Then she dug around my coat pockets, found my badge, and laid it up on the counter. The prescription was filled in record time.

As we made our way to the exit, Michael was standing in a check-out line. He had gobs of stuff that the poor night teller was scanning. I smiled.

"Good grief, is he going to eat all that?" Gentry asked.

"The others will help him," I assured her.

"What about you?"

"I don't really snack much," I shrugged. "Every now and then, I will steal a bite of something they are snacking on, but I am just not a snacker."

"I'd fail my next physical if I snacked on all that."

"We do not have physicals. If you're slow, you're dead," I shrugged again.

"What's your story?"

"Me? I have Anti-Social Personality Disorder from being kidnapped by a serial killer when I was eight. I also have an anxiety disorder and migraines."

"You were kidnapped by a serial killer? How'd you get away?"

"I killed him," I told her.

"At eight?" She looked astonished.

"Yep, that's why I'm here. Then it happened again at sixteen, nineteen, twenty-two," I paused, "actually twice at twenty-two and at twenty-six. Not all of them were serial killers, some were just rapists, but a bad guy is a bad guy regardless."

Agent Gentry stared at me for a moment. Her mouth worked, but no sounds came out of it. I gave her another second to recover. When it failed, I looked at her.

"Sometimes, shit happens, particularly to me," I told her.

The blank look cleared, I'd shaken her from astonishment. She cleared her throat and pointed at Michael, "And him?"

"Michael was a hacker, stealing identities off the internet. He stole the wrong one. It turned out to be a serial killer who came looking for him. During the struggle, he put several million volts through the serial killer. He's a brilliant engineer. The FBI arrested him for hacking and identity theft. The Marshals recruited him for this team."

"Has everyone in the Serial Crimes Tracking Unit encountered a serial killer in civilian life?"

"No, Xavier encountered a mass murderer. Gabriel only does it as a profession, never as a civilian. Most of us are just mentally broken for different reasons. Mine makes me think like a serial killer. Michael is a genius, might be smarter than me even, but he's never fit in. He was bullied in school and became a recluse. Until the serial killer broke down his front door, he had not seen another person in almost six months. Lucas went to trial as a spree killer that turned out to be someone different from his unit, but his story goes a lot further back than that. Xavier, well, that's a story for another day," I told her.

"Why?" She asked.

"Because it is a painful one," I answered.

"Aren't they all painful?"

"Some more so than others. Xavier's is just, well, he does not like to talk about it," I shrugged again.

"Girl bonding?" Michael asked as he pulled his bags from the conveyor belt.

"Me?" I raised an eyebrow at him.

"Fine, sociopathic bonding?" He smiled and handed me a bag.

"Something like that," I agreed, taking it and looking inside. He had remembered. I smiled wondering when I'd enjoy the sweet treat inside the bag.

Back at the hotel, Agent Gentry followed me into my room. I gave her a look, but she ignored it and sat down at the small table.

"Are you planning a girl's night?" I frowned at her.

"No, but I took the liberty of looking at the warnings on your box. If you take that, I'm staying right here until Dr. Reece shows back up," she stood as if remembering something and walked over to the adjoining door. She opened it and then returned to her seat.

"I'm not entirely sure I'm taking it," I told her.

"How long will your migraine medicine take to work?"

"It should have already started."

"Well, hacking boy, pun intended, isn't going to be much good to you, I believe he's already asleep. I can't leave knowing there is the possibility that you are taking death serum without someone around, so I'm here. No worries, I understand no TVs, no lights, no excessive noise."

"You know someone with migraines?"

"My father had cluster migraines. They got so bad that when he was in his forties, he ate a shotgun."

"I am sorry to hear that," I told her.

"He waited to see me graduate from Quantico. I remember what life was like for him. While I miss him every day, I kind of understand why he did it. They never could control the migraines. Then again, I don't think he was ever on a special diet. He ate whatever he wanted. I didn't even know food could trigger migraines."

"Mine are controlled pretty well. Besides, I will probably be slaughtered by a serial killer before they get that bad."

I pulled the vial and the needle from the bag. Agent Gentry took hold of the paperwork. She looked at it and then me.

"You've done this before?" She asked.

"DHE is not unknown to me."

"One of the known side effects is death, Marshal," Gentry looked concerned.

"Your own experience tells you that is also a side effect of migraines," I told her.

"You have a point."

I inserted the needle into the vial and sucked up the liquid. It was perfectly clear. It was also going to make me sleepy and possibly sick. I slid out of my jeans, pulled up a patch of thigh fat, and rubbed it with an alcohol pad. As it dried, Agent Gentry moved closer.

"What?" I asked.

"Can you inject yourself?"

"Yep, not a problem," I gave her a weak smile, grabbed the syringe, and jabbed it into my leg.

The medicine burned as it filled the fatty tissues. The liquid dribbled out just a little and ran down my leg. I'd been too quick with the plunger; the death serum filled the tissue in my leg too fast to contain it all.

I wiped the dribbles away. I didn't bleed; I never really bled from injections. Agent Gentry sat back in her chair.

"You are a brave woman," she said.

"Some would consider it stupidity," I responded.

"What happens now?"

"Now I go to bed and hope I wake up," I said.

I stood up and was overcome with vertigo. For a moment, I thought I'd crash to the floor. Somehow, I stayed on my feet. I jerked at my clothes and collapsed onto the bed. My heartbeat increased with the effort, so did the throbbing in my head. Minutes earlier it had just been a dull ache. Now it was a drum line beating a steady cadence of intolerable pain in my brain.

My blood throbbed in my ears, seemingly audible. My heart rate kicked up another notch, increasing the speed and pain of the rhythm of the pulsing in my skull. Rational thought left me. All I could think of was removing my skull to release the pressure that seemed to be building.

Agent Gentry did seem to have the experience she spoke of. As I closed my eyes, willing myself to die, she went to work. I felt my hoodies unzipped and my body jerked and rolled as she stripped them off of me. She spoke, but her words were unintelligible to me, sounding foreign and coarse. In response to my non-action, the younger woman sat me up and yanked off my shirt.

Finally, I felt another tug, followed by an explosive noise that sent me reeling. I stumbled for the bathroom. My knees shook, my body churned. Somehow I knelt down. Agent Gentry put a washcloth on my neck. It was cool and brought some relief. My hair was twisted back up and into place.

When I felt the wave pass, I lay down on the cold bathroom floor. The lights flicked on above me, sending shockwaves of pain deep into my skull. Gentry covered me with a towel, got a pillow from the bed, and placed it under my head. She wet the washcloth again and replaced it on my neck. The lights went out and her footsteps retreated.

I cursed my own body and weaknesses. I was no good to anyone in this condition and to be helped by a stranger was embarrassing. She had seen the weakness rear its ugly head and cripple me in seconds.

My aura hadn't come. Instead, the headache I had been creating slowly all day had triggered the migraine.

The DHE slipped into my blood stream. It wasn't an instant cure, not even close, but it was bringing relief. I felt slow, but the crushing pressure was releasing in my brain. Sleep was descending over me. Coupled with the blessedly cold floor, I had no choice but to allow myself to sleep.

Fifteen

A really smart serial killer would wait until I had injected myself with DHE before trying to kill me. Then again, I was smarter than that. I never injected it when I was alone. They'd have to kill Malachi or Nyleena first.

At some point, Lucas picked me up and carried me from the bathroom to the bed. I woke up enough to realize it was happening, but not enough to care.

Morning did not bring an annoyingly happy and shiny Gabriel into my room. It brought a very concerned Xavier with a bag full of tools and Lucas with a Mt. Dew. Xavier was taking my blood pressure. All the lights were still out, Lucas was holding a flashlight for him.

"I'm fine," I told them for the millionth time.

"That's twice already this year that you have injected yourself with DHE," Xavier said without looking up from the pressurizing cuff.

"It happens," I answered.

"Yes, but it shouldn't happen. Agent Gentry said you had no warning," Xavier continued.

"Bad lighting and vending machine food, Xavier. You know how I am under those conditions," I pleaded my case.

"You should have ordered in lunch, not eaten from a vending machine. And you should have turned the lights off for a while. You know these things, Ace, why the fuck can't you follow them?"

I couldn't really argue with him on that. I did know these things. The lights in the Marshals' office were terrible for me, and a bag of chips and a thing of trail mix did not equal lunch.

"I will do better today," I told him.

"Because you aren't leaving this room, I imagine you will do better today," Xavier nodded to Lucas. Lucas turned the flashlight off and began flipping on lights. "It's almost noon. We're going to make sure you have lunch, a real lunch, then bring in some case files for you to look through."

"What?" I let myself sound as enraged as I felt, nearly yelling the question at him.

"If you hadn't taken DHE last night, we'd let you come into the office, but you did. We can't risk you having a rebound migraine with DHE in your system. I am staying with you. Gabriel and Michael are already at the Marshals office, and Michael has set up a video session so we can hear what they are doing."

"This is bullshit," I flopped back into the pillows.

"No, Ace, this was your decision. Agent Gentry says you tried to send her away last night. Luckily, she wouldn't budge. We didn't get back until well after one in the morning, you would have been here alone for over four hours with that poison coursing through your veins. Michael was zonked out. He wouldn't have been any good had you reacted poorly to the medicine. So we are taking all precautions. We need you at 100% and not worrying about rebound migraines or the fact that the drug is still in your system. You could still have a bad reaction to it," Xavier pulled away from me.

"Then what are we doing today?" I frowned at him.

"We are going through associates," Xavier handed me a stack of print outs. "This is a list of anyone that has been connected to more than three of the victims."

"Great," I grumbled.

"You could be doing nothing," Lucas told me.

"That's true, bring it on," I tried to feign some enthusiasm.

"So what I did was build a different geographical profile. Since we didn't learn much from the original profile, I had the idea to track their debit or credit card usage. I mapped out each purchase for the six months prior to their deaths," Michael said through the computer.

I frowned at the computer screen. I wasn't sure when it had been installed and connected. The migraine had caused a loss of time for me. Everything had been set-up and linked while I had slept in the bed not seven feet from it.

"And that does what for us?" I asked.

"Think about it," Michael looked confused. "Humans are creatures of habit. We stop at the same gas stations, get coffee from the same coffee shops, etc. Everything we do is part of a routine. Even the most varied individuals still create patterns. If I were to analyze your debit and credit card usages . . ."

"Yeah, I get it," I said interrupting him to stop him from pointing out how boring my life really was.

"So, we'll add the victims' purchases one person at a time," Michael said. On a second computer, a map appeared. Green dots began to appear. Then a second set of green dots. Where they crossed, the dots turned darker. Slowly, the city of Anchorage began to turn green.

"We cannot check all those employees," I said before we had gotten very far.

"That's the beauty of it, we don't have to," Gabriel came into view. He pointed at a dark green dot that was almost black, "This is a coffee shop. Fifteen of our victims visited this coffee shop. That makes it statistically significant. Whereas this dot is much lighter, only three of our victims visited this fast food restaurant in the six months prior to their deaths. Therefore, it is not statistically significant."

"Still seems like a lot of people," I pointed out.

"It is, but we can start to whittle down employees pretty quickly," Michael pushed some buttons on his side. Something popped up in place of the map. It had a list of names on it.

"These are all the employees of the coffee shop," Gabriel said. "We can automatically remove all the female employees."

All but five of the names disappeared. Lucas printed out several sheets. Xavier went to work on yet another computer. I was beginning to wonder how many laptops we had between the five of us. I knew we all carried one, but I was beginning to think that the others might carry two or in Michael's case, more.

Xavier hit the print button and a second, unseen printer came to life. I glared at them. For the first time, I realized the amount of furniture in my room had swelled. While I'd been sleeping, another table had been dragged in and my bed had been moved, probably with me in it.

"Should I be around all these electromagnetic fields?" I asked.

"Are you EMF sensitive?" Xavier grabbed something from the printer I couldn't see.

"I do not know," I told him.

"I think it's fine," he handed me a stack of papers. "Read these and tell me what you think."

The papers turned out to be background reports on each of the five names from the coffee shop. The first person proved why I wasn't on the internet much. Xavier, or more likely Michael, had scoured the internet and brought up crap that should have been private. He was an avid hunter and an anarchist according to his online profile. He couldn't seem to hold down a job, switching from one menial task to another every couple of months. He spent far too much time gaming. I had information about his avatars from World of Warcraft and Halo. They were violent. I pushed it aside.

"Not him?" Lucas asked.

"Not organized enough," I said. "Besides, according to his World of Warcraft stats, he spends too much time online to take the time to kill anyone that isn't in the video game. Do I want to know how we got his WoW information?"

"Probably not," Michael answered.

"Ok," I moved to the next file.

He was an assistant manager. Married with one child, age three. No online gaming, but he had several online profiles, including a dating profile. I raised my eyebrow at that, but moved on through the file. I wasn't the marriage police and they could have an alternate lifestyle. His career was steady but average. Nothing seemed to stick out about him. I added it to a different pile, close to Lucas. Lucas looked at it.

"That would be the 'maybe' pile," I told him. Lucas picked it up and thumbed through the paperwork as I moved onto the next file.

By the time dinner arrived, my eyes hurt. We had four piles. One was my 'may be our serial killer pile', one was my 'should be investigated for other crimes' pile, one was 'ok', and the final one was 'might be a different serial killer' pile. Lucas was currently thumbing through the final pile.

I had sorted through an unknown number of lives. I had also remembered why I wasn't a people person. People were just unfathomable to me. I couldn't believe the stuff we had dug up on the males we had taken the time to investigate. It wasn't hard to imagine everyone having secrets, that I got, I had my own, but putting them

154

out there to be discovered by someone looking was a whole different story.

"You get the vegetarian meal tonight," Xavier handed me a container. I opened it and discovered pasta with white sauce, mushrooms, black olives, and onions. At least they had an understanding of what I liked.

There were seventeen people in our "might be our serial killer" pile. The others were much thicker. I stared at the files as I ate my pasta.

"What's wrong?" Xavier asked.

"There is a 50/50 chance that someone in that stack is going to go out tonight and skin a human being alive while we sleep. That means tomorrow, we will be back in the Pinesol saturated autopsy room with Dr. Ericson wondering what we should have done to speed up the process," I told him.

"Sometimes, your affinity for humanity is almost encouraging," Xavier smiled at me.

"I am not an alien," I defended myself.

"You might as well be. You are as different from most people as ET was from Drew Barrymore," Xavier bit into a large meatball.

"Well," I shrugged. "I just think all life should be considered sacred. Serial killers break that rule, which pisses me off."

"Uh huh," Lucas looked up at me. "There's only seventeen. They'll be knocking on doors tonight. Most of these people will spend the night in an interview room dealing with Gabriel or myself."

"Michael is going to have a live feed for us to watch the interviews," Xavier told me.

"I cannot even go to the police station?" I asked.

"Nope," Xavier chewed noisily. "You screwed the pooch when you decided to inject DHE a mere two hours after injecting sumatriptan. I'm not real happy with Dr.

Ericson for giving you a prescription for the stuff without consulting me. But, I'll deal with him at another time."

"He has a medical license," I pointed out.

"So do I," Xavier said defensively.

"Yes, but it only applies to us. It is a special case medical license. You couldn't write a prescription for Nyleena and not get in trouble," I reminded him.

The government seemed to have this theory that it was fine for Xavier to medicate us. It saved on doctor visits for simple things as well as allowing him to prescribe and monitor any medication we might need while working. They were not convinced that he wouldn't become an "Angel of Death" if he could prescribe to anyone else.

"You just like to needle me," he smiled. Xavier was pretty damaged too. We got along great.

"Agent Gentry asked me what your story was," I suddenly remembered.

"Did you tell her?" Xavier asked.

"Nope, I figure it isn't any of her business," I answered.

"Thanks," Xavier seemed to sigh in relief.

"I did tell her Michael's and she sort of knew Lucas'," I added.

"Profilers suck," Lucas said automatically. He handed a file to me.

I took it and looked at it. The details flooded back to me. Single male in his thirties works in lingerie at a department store. I thought that detail odd at the time, it still struck me as odd.

"What?" I asked.

"He's probably not our guy," Lucas said.

"He's a bit different," I responded.

"Yeah, like Trevor different," Lucas said with emphasis. "Wanting a human Barbie doll is odd, but it doesn't make you a serial killer."

"I am aware of that," I was currently Trevor's human Barbie doll. "But the other stuff in the file is why I flagged it. He does not seem to like women much, he got a degree in cooking, and he had a terrible relationship with his mother and four sisters."

"So?" Lucas asked.

"So it raises red flags," I stated.

"He could be Trevor's brother then," Lucas said.

"That he could be, but I still think he's worth checking out. Just because Trevor isn't a serial killer, doesn't mean that this guy cannot be," I said.

Lucas took the file back. I was right and he knew it. Lucas was usually the one that got personally involved in every case. From experience, I knew he slept soundly and well, but the how was still a mystery.

Xavier took vitals for the hundredth time that day. Lucas grabbed the files and walked out the door. Satisfied that I wasn't going to keel over, Xavier slumped in his chair.

"I don't think he's in those files," Xavier finally said.

"Me either, but we might get lucky," I leaned back against the headboard.

"Yeah, we might find a different serial killer," Xavier said. His voice held an edge to it. The wheels of his brain were churning. You could tell just from the way he spoke.

"Or another Norman Bates," I said.

"What are your thoughts on this case, complete thoughts."

"I think it's a cop. What better way to find victims?" I responded.

"There would be tickets."

"Not necessarily. When I was in high school, my friend had this car with some sort of weird short in the taillights. She got pulled over dozens of times for it. She always showed them the mechanic's receipt saying he had worked on it. They would let her go. No warning, no tickets, nothing. Occasionally, they would thump the car to see if the light would come on, but there was never any evidence that she had been pulled over, except the cop reporting in that he was making a traffic stop," I shrugged.

"Then he uses the police computers to find the victim's address," Xavier said.

"Not necessarily. Even if you just have a taillight out, they want identification. Someone with a good memory could remember it and write it down when they got into their squad car," I said.

"That is a terrifying thought," Xavier said.

Sixteen

With the new serial killer and mass murder laws in place, the police served warrants on our seventeen suspects. They could be detained for forty-eight hours without being charged. During that time, they would be interviewed and while they were in their cells, their behavior monitored.

Xavier and I were sitting at the desk in my motel room. Michael had patched us into the feeds coming from the police station. Lucas and Gabriel were currently interviewing the third suspect on the list.

Suspects one and two had been about as useful as a nun in a swearing contest. Three wasn't turning up anything useful either. Xavier and I listened to the audio and watched the interview in silence. Xavier was munching popcorn. It smelled really good, but I also knew that chewing popcorn while listening to the audio was nearly impossible. The chewing and crunching noises inside my head would be louder than the speakers on the computer.

"I think finding Bigfoot would be easier," Gabriel said as suspect three left the interview room.

"Agreed," I said into the little microphone on the table. It fed into earpieces that Gabriel and Lucas were wearing.

"What is that noise?" Lucas asked.

"Xavier chewing popcorn," I answered.

"What did you think of that one?" Gabriel asked.

"He should remove his online dating profile before his wife finds out," I answered.

"We're taking a quick break and will then start on number four. Why doesn't Xavier finish his popcorn, it's distracting as hell, and you get twenty minutes of sleep?" Gabriel told us.

"A whole twenty minutes?" I smiled.

"Well, maybe fifteen by the time you get out of that chair and into bed," Gabriel took out his ear piece and put it on the table.

"I can give you something," Xavier mumbled through the popcorn.

"Thanks, but I think I will just go wash up," I told him, brushing chewed popcorn bits off my jeans.

The harsh lights in the bathroom did nothing to improve my looks. I looked rough. My eyes were blood shot and had dark circles under them. My cheeks looked sallow and sunken in. The visit to the stylist some weeks earlier was wearing off, exposing grey patches of hair. The shorter pieces of hair were jutting out at all angles from my scalp, making me look unkempt and possibly deranged.

When we got back, Trevor would probably insist on making me an emergency appointment to get my hair done. If he found out about the migraine, he'd also insist on a day of homeopathy. He'd put cucumbers over my eyes, make me soak in a bathtub, and he'd hire someone to come in and give me a massage. All the things you'd do to rejuvenate your living doll. Of course, a massage sounded like an excellent idea and I could stomach the other crap to get it.

I ran hot water in the sink and used one of the scratchy washcloths to wash my face. I pulled the hair down from the bun. It was getting long, well past my shoulders. Fake curls flowed around my face from where the hair had been twisted and put up. There was a visible line where the curls started.

Using the washcloth, I wet the hair and started pulling it back.

"Leave it down for a while. You aren't at a crime scene," Xavier said, tossing his popcorn bag into the trash.

"But I could be," I told him.

"So, run a brush through it now, and if we get called you can spin it up then," Xavier shrugged and left the bathroom doorway.

I considered it and left it down. I picked up the brush and roughly yanked through the tangled curls. It took a few minutes, but I finally got my hair brushed.

Xavier was stretching when I exited the bathroom. He smiled at me and I heard something pop as he moved his arms.

"Better?" I asked.

"Much."

"Are they back yet?"

"No, but they will be soon. Sit down."

I sat down and Xavier took my blood pressure and heart rate. I ignored him while he did it. The routine was familiar. I rarely got migraines while we were working, but I got them often when we were off. Xavier said it was because my mind was too busy putting together the puzzle pieces to hurt when we were hunting down serial killers or mass murderers.

"They're back," I said as Xavier counted my heartbeats.

"They can wait another minute," he said starting over.

"Are you with us?" Lucas asked.

"Need a minute, Xavier thought he needed to check my vitals again," I answered.

"She'll live," Gabriel said.

"Maybe," Xavier sat down. "Ready."

Time passed slowly as they went through one suspect after another. My eyelids felt heavy and my body was cramping from sitting in the chair for so long when they stopped. Gabriel and Lucas both stood up. They stretched. I mimicked their behavior. We'd made it through seven more suspects. None seemed to fit the bill.

"It's morning," Xavier said.

"We know," Lucas yawned. "I think we are going to catch a nap before we interview anyone else."

"Sleep would be good," Gabriel rubbed his face. "How many of us think we are barking up the wrong tree?"

"Me," I said.

"Me," Xavier answered.

"Me," Michael's voice came through the speakers.

"Suggestions?" Gabriel asked.

"Not really," I lied.

"Ok, we are coming back to the motel for a while," Lucas disconnected.

Xavier shut the laptop lids. He glanced at me, a frown appearing on his lips.

"If I thought you looked bad earlier, life has proven you can look even worse. You have about as much color as a zombie," he said to me.

"Sleep deprivation."

"No, this is different, I've seen you sleep deprived and this isn't it. Are you having a rebound?"

"No," I told him.

"Hangover from the migraine meds?"

"That is possible," I yawned.

Xavier booted the laptop back up. He did something with the keys and Nyleena appeared on the screen.

"Does she look as bad as I think?" Xavier asked the flickering figure on the screen.

"Yes," Nyleena answered. "I'm guessing she has a migraine."

"Had," I corrected.

"She eating properly?" Nyleena asked.

"She is now," Xavier answered.

"Then she needs some sleep. How long has she been up?"

"Twenty-three hours," Xavier answered.

"Give her something to get some sleep. She'll look better when she wakes up. I have to be in court in three minutes," Nyleena hung up.

"I think we can avoid drugs, I think I will sleep without them," I slipped out of my jeans and into my pjs.

"I'll stay here for a while longer," Xavier shut the lid on the laptop. I curled up into bed and slept.

I didn't dream. I didn't sleep long enough to get to that point. I felt better when Gabriel came through my motel room door. He looked awful.

"Come on," he handed me something that wasn't a Mt. Dew. I stared at it blankly.

"It's a Coke, Xavier said to cut your caffeine intake today," Gabriel explained.

"You always bring me a Mt. Dew," I whined as I crawled from the bed.

"Yes, but the doctor said no Mt. Dew today and I have to listen to him or stick you in this room all day today again," Gabriel said.

The sun was up. I saw it as Gabriel exited the room. The clock told me I had slept about two and a half hours. It had been good sleep though. I felt refreshed and ready to face the horrors of the day. And since Gabriel looked terrible, I was guessing it was going to be horrific.

We pulled into a parking area of another state park. It had snowed sometime during the night. The tracks leading into the forest were partially obscured by the new snow. I counted, too many footprints.

Gabriel locked the doors and whipped around in his seat to face me. His lips were curled up, eyebrows pinched forward. I knew the look, I wasn't going to like something.

"You are not allowed to kill anyone you see here, do you understand?" He asked.

"Yes," I answered.

"I want your word, Aislinn, that you will not kill, shoot, or stab anyone at the crime scene," Gabriel continued

"I promise not to shoot, stab, or kill anyone at the crime scene," I told him, raising an eyebrow.

"You have to let her out," Xavier said.

"She's no good to us locked in the car," Lucas added.

"And she did promise," Michael was trying not to smile.

"Fuck," Gabriel unlocked the doors.

The scene in the car put my guard up. I cautiously got out of the SUV and walked behind Gabriel into the forest. The first thing I saw was the clearing. Why did so many forests have clearings perfect for killing? I wondered.

My eyes found the reporter. She was smiling as she talked to the police. Her cameraman was not smiling. He looked green. He was trying very hard not to look at the body in the tree.

I reached for my gun and then remembered the conversation in the car. This is why he had grilled me into the promise. Gabriel had known I'd like nothing better than to bash her skull in with the butt of my gun. I couldn't do that.

I walked up to her. Gabriel and Lucas were at my side. She smiled at me and motioned her cameraman to start paying attention.

"You're Aislinn Cain," she practically squealed at me. "I feel so honored to be working with you on this case."

I punched her in the face. Blood smeared her cheek and oozed from her nose and upper lip. Tears filled her eyes and she gave me a stupid look.

"Did you broadcast this?" I asked.

She muttered something unintelligible.

"Did you broadcast this scene?" I asked again.

"No, just filmed it," the cameraman finally answered.

"Give me the goddamn tape, right now," I told him.

He began to fiddle with his camera. The reporter now had a tissue and was holding it on her face. She stopped him.

"So help me God, if you do not give me that fucking tape right this second, not only will I have you arrested for hindering a Serial Crimes investigation and watch you rot in jail, but I will break your face open so badly that a plastic surgeon will not be able to put it back together again," I said. The calm washed over me. I was outraged that she would dare to film such a thing without calling in the police. This was twice she had done it. Her respect for human life was so low I put her in the same category as our serial killer.

The cameraman must have noticed the change in me. He swatted her hand away and magically produced the tape. He handed it to Gabriel. Gabriel tucked it into an evidence bag.

"I want to press charges," the reporter suddenly began screaming.

"Funny, me too," I said and walked away from her. No one touched me. No one tried to put handcuffs on me.

Most of the police stared at me in a mix of horror and admiration.

"What the hell was that?" Gabriel reached me, grabbed my arm, and spun me around to face him. He instantly dropped my arm.

"That was me delivering on my word. I did not stab, shoot, or kill her."

"Next time I'm going to ban all grievous bodily harm," Gabriel growled.

"That's fine, I am sure I can find something else. Maybe I will glare at them and clack my teeth together," I answered.

"She wants to press charges. You'll be arrested, Ace."

"Then I will be arrested, Gabriel. At least you got the tape before the victim's family could see it," I told him.

"We were going to get the tape regardless."

"No, you were not. She was going to invoke her rights as a journalist. You would have arrested her. She still would not have given you any information. We'd dance around for weeks to see what she filmed without seeing it on the national news at six."

"Damn, I hate when you are cold and logical at the same time," Gabriel's face went slack. He turned his eyes towards the victim. "That's Agent Gentry."

"She would have put up a fight," I told him. There was a part of me that didn't believe the vivacious FBI Agent with sensible shoes and impeccable dress could be the body hanging from the tree. The other part said that it was and that she had put up a hell of a fight. There was no way she would have just let him lead her into the woods and kill her. She had squared off with me and won when I had been weakened. Not for the first time, I thanked the calm that occasionally swallowed me.

Without it, I probably wouldn't have been able to do my job.

"Marshal Aislinn Cain?" The sheriff's voice came from behind me. I turned to him.

"What?" I asked.

"I'm going to have to arrest you," the sheriff told me, warily.

"That's fine," I turned back to Gabriel. "There may not be anything useful on the tape, but I am guessing she did not get here by accident nor did she arrive very long after his exit."

"Marshal Cain?" The sheriff said my name again.

"Do you want to use your handcuffs or mine?" I asked.

"Handcuffs won't be necessary," he said. I was betting it was more because he didn't want to touch me at that moment. He motioned me forward, away from the body and the clearing in the woods. Gabriel would use the information I had gotten him to his advantage.

"Figure out why there isn't a bow and arrow," I shouted to Gabriel as the sheriff led me down the path.

Interrupted

He watched with unease as Marshal Cain was escorted off the crime scene. He couldn't believe she was being arrested. She had done the world a favor hitting that bitch reporter in the face.

The reporter had caught him in the act, so to speak. She wouldn't have evidence of his face on her tape, but she would have his build. She'd have his movements. He didn't know how much of the ritual she had caught on film.

Her cameraman had thrown up. That had been the first sign they were there. He'd just finished. He had dashed down the path the other direction. They may have found his clearing this time, but they hadn't found the parking lot he had used.

Henry had been driving home when the call came over the radio that another body and the nosy reporter had been found. He had turned around and returned to the scene via the directions given to him by the dispatch. He had also been told that the Marshals were on the way.

He had gotten lucky. After driving away from the scene, he had taken a moment to stop in an alleyway. He'd removed his murder garb and replaced it with street clothes as the first crackle of static hit the radio.

Now, they had the tape because Marshal Cain had scared the pants off of the cameraman. Six other officers had tried to convince him to turn it over. Only Marshal Cain had managed to get it.

"What do you think?" Dr. Reece asked him, breaking his thoughts.

"Looks like the others," Henry answered.

"Since my second set of eyes has officially been arrested, would you like to join me in the autopsy?" Dr. Reece asked.

"Of course," Henry looked at him. "Arrested for hitting the reporter?"

"Cain internalizes some situations pretty personally. Filming a crime scene for personal gain is one of them."

"She doesn't like reporters," Henry said.

"Pretty much. She's been hounded by them in the past."

"She get much TV time?"

"A few times, never good encounters. Cain's brother is a prisoner in the Fortress."

"Her brother is a serial killer?" This shocked Henry, maybe that's why she seemed so determined. Even after encouraging her to take the DHE she had seemed determined to carry on like nothing had happened.

"No, mass murderer," Dr. Reece said. "By the way, I don't mind you giving her migraine medication, but please make sure you ask her for a list of her meds when you do. She won't lie to you about it, but she'll omit when she has a migraine. She went straight back to the motel and self injected the DHE."

"Is she heavily medicated?" Henry raised an eyebrow at Xavier.

"Not in the least, quite the opposite, she takes fewer drugs than she should. However, Gentry said she self injected sumatriptan at the diner, a mere two hours before filling her blood stream with DHE. My guess, she didn't mention the sumatriptan or the time frame to you."

"No, she didn't. She said she had taken migraine medication earlier and it had helped, she'd only use the DHE if it was necessary," Henry recalled their conversation. It had been shortly after that he had decided to take Agent Gentry to the woods.

"That's the problem, she'll take anything you give her when she has a migraine. You could offer her heroin and she'd shoot up with it if you said it would help."

"I didn't realize."

"No one does. She has an incredibly high pain threshold. She seems functional when she has a migraine, but as her doctor, and her friend, I've discovered that this isn't the case. She feigns being healthy quite convincingly. Then she gets alone and suddenly she raids everything in her medicine cabinet to get rid of them."

"How high is her pain tolerance?"

"Things that would make you and I pass out, might make her flinch," Dr. Reece turned to look at him. "If Cain was strung from that tree, even as the killer was burning her feet, she'd be plotting how to kill him. And she'd probably succeed."

"That's impossible," Henry knew from experience that no one ever stayed conscious for very long once the propane torch started.

"She isn't like us." Dr. Reece walked off.

Henry tried not to smile. He had thought Agent Gentry would be different. Her training and survival skills were at their apex. She'd been in combat. She had been posted in Alaska after shooting a cuffed suspect in self-defense. However, she had been right to do so. Something in her gut had told her that the frisking hadn't been good enough. She had probably saved half a dozen lives by shooting him. After he gurgled and bled out on the sidewalk outside the FBI headquarters, they had found a small bomb on him. Set to be triggered when they sent him through the metal detectors.

But Fate was a fickle mistress and instead of being hailed as a hero, she'd been shipped to Alaska, shipped to Alaska to answer to inferior FBI agents like Arons.

Still, she hadn't been strong enough to put up a fight against him. Once the drugs had worn off, she'd swung from the tree trying to free herself for only a few minutes. He had turned on the torch, and she had turned into a sobbing mess. She'd even pissed herself.

Despite Dr. Reece's assumptions that Marshal Cain would be different, he knew better. She'd cry and whimper and pass in and out of consciousness. She'd probably piss herself and he'd laugh, like he always did, when it ran down her body.

He'd had to change the injection site on Agent Gentry. He was still dumbfounded that Dr. Reece had found the site on the teacher. So, he'd injected Agent Gentry in the mouth. Then he'd burned off her lips. He was still searching for a way to get the toxicology report before Dr. Reece.

Shrill yelling jarred him from his thoughts. It was the stupid reporter. She was swearing loudly and demanding the return of her tape. The cameraman was not yelling. If anything, he looked like he wanted to run away, leave the psycho bitch behind, and maybe find a new job in a new city. Henry felt sorry for the cameraman stuck with her. The louder she got, the smaller he seemed to become.

"What a pain in the ass," a uniformed officer said to him.

"To be sure," Henry answered. He turned away from the scene and walked towards the body.

"What is this?" Dr. Reece was pointing at the ground. Henry's eyes followed the finger and found cigar ash. He'd made another mistake. His admiration of Dr. Reece grew a little. No one else had noticed the darkened area of snow.

171

"It appears to be ash," Marshal McMichaels answered moving in closer. He squatted down and examined the fresh snow.

"Our killer is a smoker?" Marshal Henders frowned at it. "We haven't found it at any other sites."

"Because we were looking for it?" Dr. Reece said. It struck Henry as odd that the man occasionally seemed to lose the ability to speak properly. It was a strange idiosyncrasy that no one seemed to notice. He wondered how much time they all spent together. Would killing Marshal Cain cause them significant grief? Would it be the lynchpin that would send them back to wherever they came from? Could it be used?

"Maybe it was one of the first responders," Henry offered.

"That would be stupid of them," Marshal McMichaels frowned. When he spoke again, his voice boomed through the assorted personnel on scene, "Was anyone smoking when they arrived?"

His ice blue eyes leveled on the reporter and her cameraman. The cameraman shrank. The reporter held it for a couple of seconds before turning to look away.

Lots of people began shaking their heads. Marshal McMichaels scanned the crowd, daring someone to step forward. No one did.

"I think we can safely add 'smoker' to our killer's list," Marshal Henders said.

"Seems like a lot of ash," Marshal McMichaels said.

"This would be a Cain moment, take some photos before they bag it," Marshal Henders stood up.

"She won't get out of jail until at least tomorrow," Dr. Reece said.

"True, but she can still see the pictures," Marshal Henders walked off.

This was a problem. He hadn't considered that she might not get out of jail today. He had hoped to swoop down on her tonight as she slept. He would have to change things. His mind churned for a moment. If he could send them skittering away with their tails between their legs, he'd have more time. But if he couldn't, he'd better speed up his plan a little.

Tonight, his bitch wife would have to become a victim.

Seventeen

The cot was about the most uncomfortable thing I had ever laid on. It didn't matter though, now that I was out of the game, I could sleep, at least for a while. I wasn't exactly as good at the occupation as Xavier, but then I didn't think many people were.

My dreams were fitful. I dreamed of Agent Gentry. Her skinless body staring at me. I hadn't been the last to see her alive, but I had been close. Had she been in the room when we were making notes on the suspects? I couldn't remember. I rolled over again and sleep sucked me down one more time.

Agent Gentry wasn't there this time. It was Nyleena. My life support had been skinned alive and stood before me. Her eyes held accusations. That woke me up again. I sat up, my shoeless feet brushing the concrete floor. I felt the chill seep into them. The eyes, Nyleena's beautiful stormy colored eyes had been staring at me. The others hadn't had eyes. They had fallen out or been plucked out.

"Rise and shine," Gabriel's voice came to me, echoing down the long hallway.

"Have Xavier check on the eyes," I shouted out to him.

"Ok, why?"

"Were they cut out? Torn out? I don't remember him making notes about the eyes."

"They fell out once the eyelids were removed."

"I get that, but what happened after they fell out? Eyes will heat and explode in the sockets, but they still leave a trace. So what happened to the eyes?"

"I'll ask. In the meantime, look at this," he slid a picture through the bars.

"It's cigar ash," I told him.

"You think?" He frowned.

"Pretty sure. Cigarettes make a mess, but the ash is lighter in both texture and color. Cigar ash tends to be thicker, chunkier. This looks like cigar ash that has been spread out somehow."

"Spread out?"

"Check shoes," I said testily.

"You think someone stepped on it?"

"You are a smoker, have you never smoked a cigar?"

"Nope, never even thought about it. They smell."

"Well then," I shrugged. "Cigar ash falls in clumps and tends to stay that way. So either it was stepped on or something interfered with it on the ground. We did not find ash at any of the other scenes."

"We know. We don't know why there is some at this scene."

"Are we sure it belongs to our scene? What if it was deposited there the day before?"

"Would it still be there?"

"I do not know. I don't know what happens to cigar ash in snow."

"I don't see why not, you know everything else," Gabriel grinned at me.

"Don't be ridiculous," I frowned at him.

"What's wrong?"

"I dreamed it was Nyleena," I told him.

"Oh," Gabriel seemed to think for a few minutes. His face aged as I watched. "I guess it's a good thing she is in Missouri."

"I suppose," I shrugged. "So, check the eyes and talk to Dr. Ericson. He smokes cigars, the good ones by the smell of them."

"Eyes, Ericson, cigars, got it," Gabriel seemed to pull a chair out of thin air. "The reporter is willing to drop charges if you give an interview and an on-air apology."

"I will rot here, but thanks," I chirped.

"It might not be a bad idea to do the interview," Gabriel pressed.

"I am not letting that thoughtless, self-absorbed, barbaric bitch interview me."

"That's a lot of adjectives to describe one person."

"I could throw in a few more if you want."

"Nope, I'm good. So that's a no on the apology and interview?"

"Yep."

"Your bond will be set later today, we think it will be low considering the circumstances, and eventually it will go away altogether."

"Talk to Xavier about a theory I had yesterday," I told Gabriel, remembering the talk about our killer being a cop.

"Why don't you just tell me?" He asked.

"You will see, when do I get my phone call?"

"Do you want one?" Gabriel gave me a weird look.

"I do," I told him.

"I'll see what I can do."

He left. I couldn't see a clock. I wasn't sure how much time had passed, but I was sure it was at least half a day. To get someone's attention, I began singing loudly. Since I can't carry a tune, it was pretty effective. I was nine lines into *Closer* by Nine Inch Nails when an officer came in. He frowned at me.

"Food? Time? Cigarette? Phone call?" I asked.

"Here," he slipped a cigarette between his lips. There was a big "NO SMOKING" sign posted across from us on the wall. He lit it for me and handed it through the bars. He took the chair Gabriel had vacated and I realized I was talking to the sheriff. I didn't know his name.

"Won't allowing a prisoner to smoke in a non-smoking building ruin your chances for reelection?" I asked as I took a drag. My patch had fallen off hours ago.

"We've been chasing a serial killer for four months and failed to catch him, I think my chances of re-election are nonexistent regardless," he lit a cigarette for himself. "You have guts and principles. You also seem to be very smart and very stupid at the same time."

"I am what you would call a loose-cannon or a wild card," I admitted.

"So I see. Threatening the cameraman into giving us the tape was pretty effective. Hitting the reporter was really stupid."

"She pissed me off and, sometimes, I have very low impulse control," I shrugged.

"I'm Tucker Rybolt," the sheriff told me.

"Aislinn Cain, but then you filled out my booking forms, so I guess you already know that.

Sheriff Rybolt broke out into a huge grin, "Did it feel good to punch her?"

"You have no idea," I beamed.

"I admit, I wish she would have punched you, then I could arrest her," Sheriff Rybolt told me.

"I know; it is much more rewarding to punish bad guys and jackasses than good guys who are just fed up with stupid jackasses."

"Yep."

"However, if there's anything useful on the tape, that will make it double worth it, and I imagine her cameraman is going to quit. She will probably be ostracized at work and eventually blackballed."

"No, she's liable to get a fucking Pulitzer for her investigative journalism."

"You do not cross the Marshals' Serial Crimes Unit without consequences," I told him. "We may not be the most likeable or personable human beings on the planet, but we keep monsters from invading bedrooms."

"Which is why I'm here," his face changed, turning grim. He set his jaw.

"I have already had that thought," I said, reading his face.

"You think it could be an inside job?"

"Yes, and I assure you, it will be pursued. Meaning if it's you, your days are very limited."

"It isn't me; I have a lot of respect for women."

"You do not strike me as a local yokel sheriff," I admitted.

"I'm not. I'm not even from Alaska. My wife is though, we met in college. I was getting my criminal justice degree, she was getting a law degree. It worked out and we moved here after we both graduated. She's a judge now. Your judge to be exact."

"Isn't that a conflict of interest?"

"Most of the time, no. She doesn't handle cases for the sheriff's department. This is a special situation. I may have issued the Miranda Rights, but it was a State Trooper that demanded you be arrested. That makes it their mess."

"Where are you from, Sheriff?"

"Miami," Sheriff Rybolt smiled. "I hate snow."

I laughed.

"I understand you want to make a phone call," Sheriff Rybolt took my cigarette butt from me and dropped both into an empty soda can.

"I would," I answered.

"Here," he handed me a cell phone. "I don't figure the rules apply to you the same way they would another prisoner. I'll give you a few minutes."

"Thanks," I dialed Nyleena's number.

"Hello?" Her voice sounded suspicious.

"I have been arrested."

"Oh my God! Do you need bail? What were you arrested for? Do I need to come . . ."

"Whoa, hold up," I interrupted her. "I was just calling to let you know that I was arrested. I punched a reporter, she decided to press charges. The sheriff is married to my judge and thinks that I will be out tomorrow without needing bail. I just wanted to make sure you weren't calling my cell phone and freaking out because I wasn't answering."

"I would feel better if you got a lawyer."

"They read me my rights and stuck me in a cell. The sheriff just smoked a cigarette with me and is letting me use his personal cell phone. I think it's fine. Gabriel is doing what he does."

"Then what is really bothering you? You don't normally call me this often when you are working. This is my third call from you or about you in three days."

"I just needed confirmation that you were still alive."

"Don't talk in riddles."

"It's been a long week."

"You're chasing the serial killer skinning people," she didn't ask, she made it a statement. She knew I couldn't give her a yes or no.

"I dreamed you were his next victim. And I feel like I am missing something and I do not know what it is."

"So you keep calling me?"

"Something like that."

"Aislinn, what is it, really?"

179

"I feel like no one cares if we catch this one or not."

"Hence why you punched a reporter. You think that will get it the attention it needs?"

"No, I punched her because she was more worried about the story than the victims or their families."

"If I didn't know you better, I'd think you were experiencing sympathy."

"I cannot experience sympathy. Maybe that's why it is bothering me. I feel like I should feel something more and I am not feeling it."

"If you could feel what the rest of us feel, you wouldn't do what you are doing."

"The others feel sympathy, they do it."

"They are not you and they internalize all the pain and misery. It drives them. You are driven by a twisted sense of justice. This keeps you from being a vigilante."

"Like my brother," that sentence hung between us for what seemed like eternity.

"No, he turned vigilante because he couldn't cope. You would do it because you could."

"Thank you," her words brought a thought to my mind. "I will call you when I get back."

I hung up and shouted for the sheriff. He walked in.

"May I call Gabriel?"

"Sure," he sat down in the chair.

"Gabriel, I had another thought," I said as soon as he answered.

"Where'd you get a phone?"

"Who cares? So, what if this is some sort of pain reliever?"

"What?"

"We haven't been able to find a sexual angle. What if that's because it isn't sexual, it's some sort of outlet for pain. Like cutters who cut themselves to relieve the pain, only he is cutting others or rather . . ."

"Yeah, I get it. I'll talk to Lucas. I got the answer to your eyes question."

I waited for several seconds. When he said nothing, I sighed loudly.

"Well?" I nearly shouted.

"The eyes are being removed after they have ruptured. We don't know what is being done with them. They are being cut through from the optical nerve. Does that help?"

"I do not know, ask Xavier."

"You wanted to know!"

"I know, but only to get Xavier thinking about it. This isn't a clean, neat process. It's messy. What's happening to the eyes, seemed like something we needed to think about. Just like what is happening to the rest of the skin."

Gabriel made a deep noise that wasn't words, just sounds. It might be interpreted as a growl, but Nyleena made the same sound occasionally so it didn't bother me. I considered it the same as a "love bite". It wasn't as bad as it seemed when you were the receiver.

"Ok, so I also talked to Dr. Ericson about the cigar ash. He has never paid attention to what happens to his cigar ash."

"All right. Any word on when I'm getting out of here?"

The line was very quiet. For several moments I wondered if Gabriel had gotten disconnected.

"Hey, Ace," Xavier's voice came over the line.

"Hey, so when am I getting out?"

"At the moment, I'd just sit tight, Gabriel looks like his head is going to explode."

"He needs less stress in his life. He should take up yoga or let Trevor make him an appointment for a massage."

"I'll tell him that when his blood pressure drops."

"We should catch this killer before Gabriel has a stroke and we lose another leader."

"I agree," Xavier laughed. I took a moment to wonder what he was laughing at and figured it probably had something to do with Lucas.

"So, about the eyes. Does cutting them out mean anything to you?"

"Not really. Best guess, when the eyes fell out as shriveled dried gelatinous globs, he cut them off just so they won't be hanging as he works on scalping the victim," Xavier answered.

"What if it is like the ankle thing and there's a purpose?"

"I don't know the significance of removing dehydrated and possibly exploded eyes."

"Me either. I will think on it." I hung up and handed the phone back to the sheriff.

"Done?" He asked.

"Well, I could call my friend in the FBI, but I imagine he is already laughing at me for being arrested."

"Why would he be laughing?" Sheriff Rybolt looked confused.

"Because he's like that," I shrugged. "Have you guys turned over everything you know?"

"You have everything I have," he answered.

"Ok, then I am going to have to work on this in my own head."

Eighteen

The following morning, I was released by Sheriff Rybolt with a handshake and a ride back to my motel. My phone had seventeen missed calls. All of them from Malachi Blake. I ignored them by deleting the missed calls and sat down at the table in Gabriel's room. He was seemingly more composed than he had been yesterday on the phone.

"How was jail?" Lucas asked as he handed me a soda and a bagel.

"Not bad. The sheriff was nice enough to get me vegetarian Mexican for dinner last night and it didn't seem to come from a microwave. There were no other prisoners in my area and he even let me smoke in the jail."

"You realize those things can get him fired, right?" Gabriel asked.

"I am pretty sure he doesn't care," I answered. "He cares about catching the serial killer. I thought all night long and did not find anything to tie the eyes and the ankles together."

"That might not be the most useful thing you've ever said," Xavier answered.

"Sorry, I'm blank on it. The ankle flesh might have significance to the killer, but I literally cannot come up with anything other than Achilles," I shrugged. "However, I did think about the cigar ash. Maybe the snow is why it flattened out. I don't know what sort of weight and pressure is required to crush cigar ash, but snow falling on it, especially wet snow, might do it."

"I'm having serious issues with your theories," Gabriel said.

"Why?" I asked.

"Because they seem, farfetched. I understand the thought that it's a cop and it has been known to happen, but this seems extreme. Also, it could be very simple why he leaves the ankle skin. Xavier said the ropes would cause the ankles to bleed and the victim to bleed out if he skinned them. Then there was the eye thing," Gabriel grunted after his sentence.

"Ah, you're irritated that I asked and didn't seem to have a reason for asking. Like I sent you on a wild goose chase," I finally got his frustration.

"Something like that," Gabriel answered.

"If the eyes were removed before the face was burnt, it might have significance. Lots of cultures have theories about what the eyes can tell after death; however, finding that they were removed after they were burned just sounds like convenience. He removed them so they wouldn't hang and slap against the forehead while he was doing the rest of his work," I said.

"That is a visual I could have done without," Gabriel frowned.

"Me too," Michael also frowned.

"Well," I gave them a look. "I don't know what to tell you, it was an image I had in my brain all night long."

"You have seriously gruesome thoughts," Lucas said.

"That's true, but it makes the answers easier. If the ankles and eyes are just because it's convenient, that says something. It means they may not be significant except in keeping the victim alive," I said.

"You can live without your eyes," Xavier answered.

"I know, but when you put it together . . ."

"We get it," Lucas assured me.

"That brings me back to the medical training," Xavier said. His face screwed up into a strange expression.

Gabriel's phone rang. He spoke quickly. When he hung up, he put his head on the table.

"They just found another body," he said, keeping his head on the table.

"One of ours?" I asked.

"They don't call us for drive-bys, Ace," Gabriel's neck was red.

"Are you ok?" I asked him.

"I'm just irritated. I mean seriously, where is all this getting us? I think we have finally found a killer smarter than us, and he just killed the fucking reporter."

"Really? That's interesting," I frowned.

"What?" Gabriel asked.

"I was thinking he tipped her off the two times she found the victims, now I'm thinking that he liked her about as much as me. Sheriff Rybolt asked me how it felt to punch her."

"Do you think it's the sheriff?" Gabriel asked.

"Not really," I remembered his hands, the newly formed scars that had crisscrossed them. I hadn't asked about them, just made a note of it as he had handed me the cigarette. "I don't think he can hold a gun anymore, let alone a knife."

"Why?" Gabriel asked.

"He wears gloves when we see him, but I saw his hands in the jail. I don't know what happened to them, but I would be willing to bet they don't function properly anymore."

"We'll mark him off after I talk to him," Gabriel stood.

"Did we learn anything from the tape?" I asked.

"The blank tape that the cameraman gave you?" Gabriel started towards the door.

"We think a switch was made. The tape we got was blank," Michael said.

"Which is why we are going to the crime scene and you and Lucas are going to go talk to the cameraman," Gabriel said as we exited.

Lucas knocked on the door; I stood to one side on the porch, my eyes drawn to the window. There was no movement from inside. Lucas beat on it again, this time with more determination. The window rattled slightly in the frame from the force of his fist on the front door. We waited a few more seconds.

"Try the back," I suggested.

Lucas walked around the house. I listened to his footfalls as they stepped on the crunchy snow. I hated snow and was ready to get the hell out of Alaska. If this guy could do that for me, I was determined to find him and get the video. I dialed his cell phone. It rang once, there was an echo. I pulled my phone from my ear. It was ringing inside the house.

I hung up. No more footfalls. I listened, straining to hear any sounds of the mountain that was with me. There was something, panting, I turned to find a dog had snuck up on me. He had blood on him.

"Lucas!" I shouted. No response. I drew my gun and stared at the dog. The blood was a bad sign, but I didn't know of what. I stepped off the porch, cursing the sounds of my feet on the wooden planks.

In the backyard, Lucas was face down in the snow. His breathing was regular. There was no trickles of red in the snow. Just footsteps. They led off the back steps, up to Lucas, and then through the backyard to a fence.

I hit a button on my cell phone. It crackled and static came over the air.

"Marshal down," I said, keeping my gun drawn, I knelt down in the snow. Lucas was alive. The back door stood open, I was betting the same was not true of our cameraman. And we had been that close.

Something slammed into me from behind. I went into the snow, sprawling. The weight on top of me was strong. I slipped into the calm.

The world slowed down. I felt the weight shift, something stabbed into my neck. I jerked, felt it tear through the skin and break. The weight lost its balance and fell to the side. I was ready. I flipped over onto him. My brain suddenly feeling foggy. Warm blood began to run into my fleece hoodie. The material soaked it up.

The man had on a mask, gloves, and everything was duct taped together at the seams. His eyes were a deep brown. They widened as I slipped the boot knife from my leg and brought it forward.

"Don't move," I told him. Something hit my back and it burned. The pain surged through me, but in the calm, it didn't hurt like it should. I fought against the hot steel, felt it scrape bone inside my body, and plunged my own knife into my attacker.

He twisted, the blade entering his arm instead of his chest. He tried to pull the knife out of my back. I fought him, determined to keep the blade for evidence. I moved to a crouching position, using my weight to keep him pinned. One knee found his elbow and I put all my weight on it. The other found his chest.

Something snapped, a loud cracking noise that echoed off the trees. The fog was getting thicker. I had to work quick. I grabbed my Taser and fired it at him. It hit his shirt, the prongs failed to penetrate, they slipped off his chest. Another snapping sound, he screamed.

"Help me!" I yelled to Lucas, forgetting he was unconscious on the ground. The calm was still upon me, but it was being forced aside by the fog. I didn't know what the fog was, but it was threatening to kill me. That thought pushed it away. My survival instincts kicked into overdrive. The calm was replaced by darkness.

The pain disappeared. My strength returned. I grabbed hold of the knife and pulled it from his arm. I stabbed him again, sinking the blade in until the hilt slammed against metal. The shirt was tightly woven and for the first time I realized he was wearing chainmail under it. The chainmail was no match for my knife. It broke the soldered rings as it sunk in deeper at his shoulder.

There was an odd noise as it hit his bone. He screamed again. He pulled out a syringe and stuck it into me. I jerked and felt the tip break off in my skin. Blood began pouring from it.

His other hand was still free and he was fighting me with it. It found my chin and pushed my head back to the point I thought it would snap my spine. I fell backwards, driving the blade deeper into my back, but escaping the force on my chin.

He used the moment to grab me. His fist balled in my shirt and he pulled me into him, driving his forehead into my face. I felt my cheekbone crack. Blood began oozing from my nose and dripping down my lips and chin.

He crawled on top of me. I reached for my knife in his shoulder, he batted my hands away. His hands went around my throat.

"Time to sleep," he whispered. There was something familiar in his voice.

"Fuck you," I whispered back and brought my knee up into his spine. It caught his tailbone. He yelped and moved, I drove the knee further up, putting it between his legs and pressed up with all my strength. He screamed, primal and terror-filled.

Sirens in the distance. He got off of me. I had no fight left to follow him. I struggled to stand up and found my legs wouldn't work. I watched as he got to the fence, pushed aside a board and slipped through. Blood drops left a trail.

"Help me," I whispered.

"Oh God," Sheriff Rybolt was there suddenly.

"He got away," I whispered again.

"Marshal, we have an ambulance on the way," Sheriff Rybolt yanked off his gloves and took hold of my hand. He rolled me onto my side.

"Hands?" I asked.

"What?" He asked.

"Your hands? What happened?" I had to stay awake. If I didn't, I would die. My body was screaming this at me. Whatever was in my blood stream mixed with blood loss would kill me.

"A dog," he answered.

"A dog did that?" I felt my eyes want to close.

"Stay with me. Keep talking, Aislinn."

"A dog did that?" I repeated.

"We busted a dog fighting ring and they let one of the dogs loose. It attacked. I have scars all over."

"One day, soon, we will compare scars," I said, rolling my eyes up to him. "Where's Xavier?"

"On his way. I was headed to the crime scene when I heard your call. I was only a few minutes away."

"I have a metal allergy. There is a needle tip in my arm. Possibly another in my neck. I need to get them out."

"I don't know how to do that."

"I have a knife in my back. I need that out too."

"We'll let the paramedics handle that."

"I do not know if we can. Do you have an EpiPen?"

"Yes, in my first aid bag."

"Get it, I need the adrenaline."

"It will . . ."

"Get it!" I said as forcefully as I could manage. The darkness was still there; I was swimming in it.

There was no fear, no pain, nothing except the will to survive. I needed the adrenaline to stay awake. It was going to make me bleed faster.

The sheriff returned. He held the pen like it was a snake.

"Jab me in the leg," I told him.

"You'll bleed more," he told me.

"I know. Once you jab me, start applying pressure to my neck wound. I don't know how bad it is. As long as the knife doesn't move, the wound should suck closed around it."

My eyes fluttered and rolled into the top of my head as the adrenaline hit my blood stream. The fog lifted completely. My heartbeat increased. I felt the blood begin to flow heavier at my neck and back. Sheriff Rybolt immediately put his gloves over the wound, his bare hands forcing the material to suck against the hole and slow the bleeding.

"Do not let me pass out," I told him. "If you think I am about to pass out, hit me or something."

"Talk about something then," he told me and began shouting.

"My brother is a mass murderer. He opened fire with a sniper rifle into a yard full of convicted felons. Took out sixty-three of them before they found his hiding spot. He was a hell of a shot, managed to not hit a single bystander or non-convict. I still don't know how he did it. My family is cursed with violence. I have survived a handful of serial killers and now, I am going to have even more scars. I killed my first serial killer when I was eight years old. I killed him with a plastic spoon to the eye or from beating his head on the floor of the room he kept me in. I'm not sure which. At the time, my only thought was that I had to kill him; I had to kill him so he couldn't torture another little girl. I was the only one strong enough. That was my thought. I wanted to kill him. I have never told anyone that."

"They're coming, Aislinn, just hang on and keep talking to me," Sheriff Rybolt said.

"I'm not good at talking about myself. If I wasn't working with the Marshals, I would probably be with my brother," I paused, remembering the conversation with Nyleena. She was not going to take my death very well. Neither would my mother. I wasn't sure how it would affect Malachi, he might be indifferent or it might the stressor that sent him over the edge. The adrenaline was wearing off. The effects of blood loss sinking in, my brain was feeling slow. My body was feeling heavy. I was going to die in the fucking Alaskan snow.

Another surge ran through me.

"What the fuck?" Sheriff Rybolt said and pressed harder on my neck.

"My own survival instincts," I told him. "I'm a sociopath with a strong desire to live. My body will fight for survival until it exhausts itself. How long have we been waiting?"

"Three minutes," Sheriff Rybolt answered.

"I fought for maybe six minutes. I have another five or so before my body gives out depending on how fast I'm bleeding."

"Your back has stopped. Your arm isn't bad. Your neck wound though," Sheriff Rybolt looked at my face.

"I tore the vein when I jerked from him. Probably the jugular. Under normal conditions, I would already be dead, but I'm a fast clotter and the hole isn't that big. If I'm lucky, I will clot the hole closed, that means I cannot have any more adrenaline spikes though."

"How do you know that?"

"This isn't the first time I have come very close to death," I thought for a moment. "First time I've ever had my veins opened though. Guess there's a first time for everything."

"Aislinn, are you going into shock?"

"Unlikely, I won't go into shock when I die," I told him. The calm kept me alive, kept me rational and thinking, even as I bled to death. "There was something about the voice that I recognized. It was familiar. Since I only know but a handful of people in Alaska, that narrows the suspect pool. How the hell did he get the drop on Lucas?"

"I don't know, he isn't awake yet."

"If I die here, yell at Xavier," I told him.

"You aren't going to die," Xavier's voice came to me.

"And you can prove this?" I asked him.

"Well, your back is bad, but it will heal," Xavier said as the sheriff moved his hands.

"The neck is worse, but not life threatening," Xavier began doing something to it. It was hot as hell. "It is going to leave a nasty scar."

"How did you beat the ambulance?" I asked.

"My favorite sociopath and best friend are both in need of help, I made Gabriel drive like the devil was chasing him," Xavier answered. "That will stop the bleeding temporarily."

"Great, can I move?"

"Absolutely not," Sheriff Rybolt answered.

"Fine," I lay on the ground. "Can I sleep?"

"No, we don't know what was in the syringe," Xavier answered. He flashed a light in my eyes. "You've lost a lot of blood. By the looks of this yard, you aren't the only one."

"Good, maybe you will find him dead in the next yard over."

"No, they are checking now. He left a blood trail that disappears at a side street. We are guessing he got in a car."

"I am bleeding to death and you're chasing serial killers?" I asked.

"We all have priorities," Xavier shrugged.

"I'm going to be stuck in the hospital, aren't I?"

"For a day or two. You may need surgery. And we'll have to watch you for a severe allergic reaction," Xavier answered. "You have a needle in your neck. I'm leaving it in for now and burning the area closed. If I pull it out here, you'll start bleeding and there will be nothing I can do about it. You may need to have the vein stitched along with the skin."

"I have one in my arm as well. He was prepared. He had multiple syringes."

"He injected Lucas with something as well," Xavier answered.

"I hate hospitals."

"And they hate you," Xavier smiled as a paramedic came into view.

Nineteen

I have never been a fan of hospitals. My current situation was doing nothing to improve my opinion of them. Since they didn't know what I had been injected with a doctor had given me a local and was now removing the blade from my back.

The local wasn't doing much. The skin was numb, but the muscles and nerves under it were not. It hurt like hell.

The blade hadn't damaged anything. It had hit a rib and lodged on it. I was going to have a scar on the bone, but that was it. It hadn't even been plunged in with enough force to break the rib.

"Just a little more," the doctor informed me. A string of responses came to mind, but I bit my lip as Xavier squeezed my hand.

Suddenly, the knife gave and slipped out. I felt every movement of it. If I were a weaker person, I probably would have been sick. Since things like that didn't bother my stomach, I consoled myself by swearing at the doctor in my head.

I felt the pressure as he stitched me up. When he finished, he moved to my arm. I put my face into the pillow as he stuck the needle into me to numb my arm. We still had two more to go. It seemed like it had been hours since he had started.

The medication went to work and there was no pain as he sliced into my arm and removed the needle remnants from the muscle. More pressure as I was stitched closed. Three more scars, two were going to be nasty looking. One was going to be noticeable.

"Ok, we're going to need you to lay on your side to do your neck. Think your arm can take it?" He asked.

With help, I rolled up on my side. There was some pain, but not enough to make me flinch. Someone removed the pillow and put something else under my head. This new thing was not soft and it put my head at an awkward angle, my scalp down further than my chin. My neck was stretched to the limits. Making the skin taut and exposing the wound that Xavier had cauterized on the scene.

"I'm going to give you a couple of shots, but it may still hurt. I need you to remain really still," the doctor told me.

I grunted at him. Xavier held my gaze, squatting down to make eye contact easier. His face said it all.

This was going to be dangerous. If I moved, there was a good chance I would start bleeding again. They were already running a transfusion IV into me.

I was feeling better though, even without the new blood. The searing pain that Xavier had pressed into my neck had made me feel better, brought me back into survival mode. My heart rate was steady and strong. My breathing regular and my O2 saturation levels normal. Even my hemoglobin count was good, despite the loss of blood. They had done a count when they drew it for analysis of whatever had been injected into Lucas and I.

"Tell me his hands are steady," I said to Xavier.

"They are," Xavier answered.

"Just remember, if he frucks up, you have to deal with Nyleena," I smiled.

"He isn't going to mess up. I'm sure he's dealt with worse."

"You realize I can hear you?" The doctor asked.

"Yes," I said.

"Just checking, now hold very still," the doctor's hand moved some of the skin on my neck.

An X-Ray had shown that the needle was beneath the burnt flesh. It hadn't moved or entered my blood stream. However, it also showed that most of the burnt flesh was going to need to be removed to get at it. The vein it had nicked would need to be stitched. I didn't know if the doctor had ever done that before, but Xavier had assured me he was the best in the hospital.

Pressure. The local was doing its job, keeping the pain from washing over me. But the feeling of pressure was disturbing. My brain searched for a way to deal with it and came up with nothing. If it had been somewhere that I could see the doctor working, it might have helped.

"Just relax," Xavier said to soothe me. I had a few choice words that I could respond with, but talking would be moving. Instead I closed my eyes and remembered the encounter.

Dark brown eyes had stared at me and were surprised when I retaliated. Even more surprised when I fought against the effects of the drugs and won. The voice had been familiar. I couldn't place the whisper, just knew I had heard the voice before. Chainmail, where had it come from? Why did he have it? It had been poorly constructed given the tip of my dagger had been enough to start breaking the links.

Were there links found at the scene? Did they look for them?

The snapping sounds. Two of them, but only one had made him scream. The first one had been something else, something unrelated maybe, something the dog had stepped on or movement of our bodies on the ground breaking something. The second one had been significant. He had screamed. Had it been a break or a dislocation?

More pressure on my neck. I felt fingers moving around inside the skin. What the hell was he doing? I opened my eyes. Xavier must have read my mind. He dug out a small mirror and held it at an angle.

I could see the doctor working on the vessel in my neck. That was the fingers. My attacker would need a doctor, possibly two or three. He still had my dagger. It had been shoved into his shoulder. Why hadn't he removed it? That is the instinct, to yank it out. He hadn't.

"All done," the doctor announced.

"Great," Xavier stood up and began inspecting the work. He took my mirror with him. "That is definitely going to leave a nasty looking scar."

"Ah well," I croaked.

"You alright?" He looked at me concerned.

"I have a million questions."

"We'll get to those later. For now, they have your results. You were injected with triazolam," Xavier said.

"Ok?" I asked.

"I'm sort of surprised. It knocked Lucas on his ass. You got two doses and stayed conscious the entire time. That shows either serious willpower or it means you are immune to the drug. Did you feel dizzy, sleepy, unsteady?"

"Yes," I told him.

"Then it was willpower. Impressive," Xavier stepped back from me. "You should take a nap. We are checking the hospitals for your attacker. You got some good blows in on him. Do you want me to set your nose now?"

"Is it broken?"

"Because I would offer to set it if it wasn't," Xavier said.

"Sure, might as well get it all over with," I said.

"Are you sure you don't want a plastic surgeon or an otologist to do it?" The doctor asked me.

"My nose was crooked long before today. I think it's been broken seven or eight times before. One day, the cartilage will completely detach and then I'll go see an ENT or plastic surgeon," I answered.

Xavier grabbed hold of my nose. He did something complicated and I felt it slide back into place. I smacked his stomach because it was the only place I could reach.

"I know, it hurt, you didn't have to hit me," Xavier said.

"It made me feel better," I smiled at him.

"I could have made it more painful," he smiled back.

"I could have made you a eunuch."

"Point taken," he turned away from me. "Let's get her into the room with Marshal McMichaels."

"They keeping Lucas?"

"He has a severe concussion from face-planting on concrete. Ironically, he also got a broken nose and needed stitches on his forehead."

"He's always been too perfect," I yawned and let them put the sides up on the bed.

"Do you want something for the pain? When the local wears off you are going to experience some serious pain. Dr. Reece says you have to be careful about painkillers though," the doctor whose name I had never heard asked.

"No, I'm ok," I told him.

"When you change your mind," he said it with emphasis.

I closed my eyes. The bed continued to be wheeled down the hall. The wheels squeaked ever so slightly.

We turned left and continued down another hall. I didn't need to open my eyes to know. My body felt every movement. We crossed a metal door brace in the floor and took a right turn followed immediately by another, sharper right turn.

"You look pretty good, considering," Lucas's voice came to me.

"Thanks, now Trevor is going to have a reason to put me in scarves and turtlenecks," I answered without opening my eyes.

"He jumped me from behind and jabbed me in the ass with a hypodermic needle. It had some sort of sedative that worked really fast. I pretty much fell where I stood."

"That seems like an extreme reaction," Xavier said.

"I know," Lucas said. "I just went down like a sack of potatoes."

"No benzodiazepine tolerance," I chided.

"Lucas has no tolerance to anything. An Advil makes him need a two hour nap. If I hadn't made them remove the Demerol drip, he'd be sleeping like the dead now," Xavier answered. "You on the other hand, should opt for a Demerol drip."

"You say that like I am staying," I finally opened my eyes.

"You are, at least overnight," Gabriel answered.

"I have already spent a night in jail, now I have to spend the night in the hospital?"

"Yes, and no disconnecting your monitor wires or driving the nurses up the walls," Gabriel glared at me.

"Xavier, please give him valium so he'll chill," I said. "You can wheel him in another bed and hook him up to monitor. He needs an EKG anyway. His blood pressure might be causing heart arrhythmia or something."

"Three in a room is a little crowded," Lucas said.

"It'd be like an orgy with Ace as the filling," Xavier chuckled.

"Ew, I don't want them. One's a redhead and one is gay. How does that help me?" I whined.

"Ok, we'll stick Lucas . . .," Xavier started.

"That's enough," Lucas interrupted.

"I'm serious, Aislinn," Gabriel brought our attention back to him. "I've had nurses threaten to kill you every time you've been hospitalized. The last time, they asked if they could put you in a coma until you healed. You have got to be nice to them."

"Yes, dear," I said.

"Why do I bother?" Gabriel flopped into a chair and took out a real cigarette.

"If you light that, the nurses will be threatening to kill you," Xavier said. Gabriel looked at it as if it had appeared by magic.

"Do I really stress you out that much?" I asked.

"At times, yes, you do. Like when you punch reporters and get arrested or have to spend the night in the hospital."

"I promise not to be an asshat while I'm here tonight, but it had better just be for tonight. I can feel the vile hands of disease scurrying around the floors and hear them scratching at the walls."

"I didn't think you feared death?" Gabriel asked.

"I don't, but it does not mean I want to press my luck. I kind of enjoy living. My life expectancy is short enough chasing serial killers, why add contagious flesh-eating diseases to the mix?"

"That being said, do you want to give your statement now?" Gabriel asked.

"Sure," I went through the sequence of events. I included the details about the eyes, the chainmail, the voice, and the snapping sound.

"Well, here's a bombshell for you, the blood on the dog belongs to the reporter. It's the cameraman's dog though. The cameraman was dead and his camera smashed, but Michael is in the process of salvaging anything he can from it. We think he went to the cameraman's house and found the reporter so took advantage of the situation. Unfortunately, we haven't turned up your boot knife or the attacker, which means he either died or found medical attention somewhere else. Xavier thinks this is proof that he has medical training," Gabriel said.

"That explains why he didn't pull out the knife," I said.

"What?" Gabriel asked.

"He did not pull out my knife. He ran away with it in his shoulder. Most people instinctively pull them out. He didn't," I said.

"We are searching through databases looking for people with military and medical training who currently work in law enforcement," Gabriel said.

"And why did he come back?" I asked.

"We don't know yet. I have autopsies to do and you two need your rest. Sheriff Rybolt is going to help with guarding your room. You seem to have made an impression on him," Xavier gave me a quick flash of a smile and left.

"We have about two hundred photos of the house and another hundred of the crime scene for you to look through," Gabriel handed me an iPad. "Michael loaded them on there for the two of you. Look over them; I'm going to go help Xavier."

"He left something," Lucas finally said after Gabriel left.

"What?" I asked.

"I don't know what he left, but when he was riding me to the ground, he had something in his hand. I think he came back to get it," Lucas shrugged. "That's about all I remember."

"He held nothing but his knife when he attacked me."

"Why'd he come back and attack you? He'd gotten away at that point."

"Need to dominate. You and Gabriel made the distinction earlier that I was sort of his type."

"That wouldn't make me come back. I'd wait and fight that battle another day. Killing you right that second wouldn't have been very satisfying."

"I know." I closed my eyes as the nurse came in with a Demerol drip. The local hadn't worn off yet.

She hooked me up to it. I sat with my eyes closed until after I felt her leave the room.

"Because we are getting close and it was a good opportunity to kidnap me. He stabbed me with the syringe first. He wasn't trying to kill me. I brought the fight and my survival instincts overcame the medication. That's why he stayed for me. I was supposed to be hanging from a tree right now. Not lying in a hospital bed. We are getting close. If I had not done the damage I did, I imagine he would be ramping up his timetable."

"Killing the ones that he has to kill before he gets caught," Lucas said.

"Yep."

"Good thing you stabbed him."

"Yep."

"Pity he got away."

"Shit happens," I felt the Demerol enter my body. I didn't fight. I let it flow into me and relaxed into sleep.

Twenty

I didn't torture the nurses or tell them my thoughts on the fact that they didn't let me sleep through the night. The bed had been more comfortable than my cot in the jail, but I had slept better in the jail. Now it was morning and Michael was booting up a computer and a projection screen. The nurses had been warned not to interrupt for a while.

The screen flickered just once as the video began. It was dark, but the clearing was bathed in an ominous glow. There were three halogen lights, on poles, set up in the snow, pointing towards the victim.

They bathed the victim in an eerie and surreal light. Making her seem even more horrifically posed. Her lack of movement and skin showed that she was already dead. Our killer was standing with his back to us. He had a cigar in one gloved hand. His head was covered with a mask, hiding his hair and skin. At his thigh was what appeared to be a large filet knife. Xavier took a deep breath, loud enough for us all to hear.

The killer walked over to a large duffle bag on the ground. Out came a large bottle of Pinesol. He used a remote and the winch began to lower the victim. Her head was only a few inches from the ground when he stopped it. He flicked ash onto the ground and stared at the spot below her head.

He went back to his bag and pulled out something that looked like a tarp but crinkled like plastic. He set it on the ground under the victim, covering the cigar ash. He stood up and began pouring the Pinesol on the victim.

It ran down from her feet, coating her body in the oily, smelly stuff. He stood for another several minutes and finished his cigar.

He stubbed it out on his Pinesol soaked glove and put it in his pocket. He checked the area and picked up any ash that had fallen. Then he rolled the black thing up carefully. The winch motor began again. It whirred and hummed as it pulled the victim to his desired height. She now towered over him.

The body in place, he went to the spike in the ground and tied the cable up. Once tied, he cut it. He walked to his winch and wrestled it from the hard, frozen ground. Something popped on the tape. He looked up, noticed something, tossed the winch onto the black thing, picked them both up, and left. There was no motion for several minutes.

Then the reporter came into frame. She picked up the halogen lights. I nearly yelled at the TV.

"That's what he was getting," Lucas said.

"Damn," Xavier sighed. Michael shut it off.

"Is that the guy that attacked you?" Gabriel asked me.

"Yeah, he looked a little stockier in person but, otherwise, he seemed the same."

"And we know what crushed the ash," Xavier said. "And why he missed it."

"He was sloppy this time," Gabriel said. "What the tape doesn't show is the reporter covering up the spots where the lights had stood. They wouldn't have left much of a mark, a small tripod of holes, but she walked over them when she pulled up the lights and they aren't mentioned in any of the other reports, except once. I went back and checked, the Sheriff reported them at one scene, but when he asked they be photographed, they were gone. I called and he said he thought someone on scene had done it deliberately."

"Much sloppier. Did the body have any differences?" Lucas asked.

"A few, not many," Xavier said.

"Maybe Agent Gentry put up more of a fight than he expected," I suggested.

"That is a good possibility," Gabriel said. "She was well trained and should have been given a medal, not a post in Alaska. But the higher ups decided to send her here to get her out of the limelight."

"Everyone has a story," I said, feeling a moment of nostalgia. She had been curious about ours. I hadn't thought to ask about hers.

"The knife mean anything?" Michael asked.

"Not really, it's pretty common except the handle, but I'd need to see it up close and personal to get any details off of it," Gabriel said.

"How do you know?" I asked.

"I hunt and fish," Gabriel answered. "It's a specialty knife, but you can order them from anywhere with a credit card."

"We came up with a few hits on the background search. Agent Arons among them," Michael said.

"He has hazel eyes. I was looking at dark brown. They were a rich, deep brown, not hazel," I dismissed the suggestion.

"Dr. Ericson was in the military and is a doctor and smokes cigars," Michael said.

"His eyes are blue," I answered in unison with Xavier.

"There's a state trooper that fits the description and smokes cigars. His name is Henry Small," Michael suggested.

"What color are his eyes?" I asked.

"Brown," Michael said.

"Let's go pay him a visit," I got out of the bed, yanking off wires and pulling out IVs. I was dressed by the time the nurses arrived. "I am checking out."

"Uh, Marshal Cain, we can't . . .," a nurse stammered at me.

"Bring me the forms, I will waive all your liability," I said as I helped Lucas find his pants. The other Marshals were trying not to laugh. I wasn't sure if it was at me or the nurses.

"As an added bonus, he is the one that had you arrested," Michael said as Lucas pulled his jeans on.

"Most excellent," I narrowed my eyes at them. The thought of revenge was a beautiful thing.

An hour later, we were parked down the road from Henry Small's house. We had seen him enter a few minutes earlier. Gabriel was handing out directions. I was practically bouncing in my seat.

It was time to catch our serial killer. I was waiting for the adrenaline surge that would bring on the calm. Or bring on the darkness, if it seemed my life was in mortal peril. I had begun to distinguish between the two. The calm was a place of functional disconnect. The darkness was a place of complete disconnect. I equated it with what Malachi felt every day. The only emotion was rage.

We spilled from the car, guns drawn. We crouched and ran towards the house. Under the Serial Crimes law, we did not have to knock or even announce ourselves. I stood on the porch with Gabriel. Michael, Lucas, and Xavier were taking the other points of the house.

However, the man inside was law enforcement and had a gun. I hit the door once with my fist. It vibrated under the force.

"US Marshals!" I shouted through the closed door. Someone inside screamed. Someone else shouted. Gabriel hit the door with his foot.

I snaked inside, half crouched, gun moving with my eyes. The living room was empty except for a couple of beer cans and a moose head mounted on the wall. My eyes adjusted to the darkness. I entered another room.

This one was brighter. The kitchen was done in yellows and browns. It reminded me of 70's sitcoms. It was also clear. I could now hear movement over my head. I reentered the living room, found the stairs and started up them. Gabriel was now moving with me. He watched the bottom of the stairs as we moved upwards into more darkness.

There was a tangy smell in the air. The smell of copper and iron and something darker, it made my nostrils flare. The darkness washed over me. The smell of blood triggering it.

"US Marshals!" Lucas bellowed below. I heard another door crash in. He'd entered the house and was now sweeping the downstairs. Xavier would be watching the back door, Michael the front. They would stand at opposite corners to watch the sides. They would come in only if gunfire erupted.

Gabriel motioned me towards a door when we reached the stairway landing. It was the only one closed on the floor. I took position to one side and knelt down. Gabriel mimicked me.

"Open the door!" Gabriel shouted.

Another scream. Definitely female, definitely from the other side of the door. She sounded like a wounded animal. I imagined the tortures he was inflicting on her at the sound of our voices. Lucas moved up the stairs and joined us.

"Break it down," Gabriel said. Lucas was the only one wearing a bulletproof vest. Not that I thought he needed one. I wouldn't fire a gun at him and I was crazy.

The door shattered. The hinges screeched as they pulled away from the wall. On the other side, the handle came loose and little bits of metal and wood tinkled as they hit the floor. The frame was torn from the wall, breaking the drywall, sending cracks down either side. It fell to the floor in two pieces with a terrible thunking noise.

I looked in. Henry Small held a woman in front of him. He had a knife to her throat and blood was dripping onto the floor from different cuts he'd made on her. Her body was a roadmap of scars and new wounds. He'd been slicing on her for a long time by the looks of it.

"Fruck," I whispered. "He's not our killer."

"No, but he's an asshole," Gabriel stood up. "Let her go, Henry, and we can talk about this."

"No one can talk to you, you're all fucked up. A bunch of psychos pretending to be cops," he spat at Gabriel.

"And what are you?" I asked, motioning towards his hostage. "A normal, happy family man?"

"She likes it," he spat at me.

"It didn't sound like it," I entered the room.

"Don't come any closer."

"Or what? You'll kill her? I think not. If you kill her, I kill you. It's that easy," I said.

"No you won't."

"You just called me a psycho with a badge and then doubt that the moment she's dead, I will put a bullet in your brain?" I shook my head. "Your logic has serious holes in it."

Gabriel gave me a slight nod. I rushed forward, tucking my gun; I wrapped one arm around his hostage and the other around him. He tried to push me away, but his arms were pinned between us. Lucas came forward. He grabbed the girl, jerked her from Small's grasp. I grabbed the wrist with the knife and heard a satisfying pop as he dropped the weapon. His teeth dug into my cheek.

"Son of a bitch!" I kneed him in the groin, his teeth let go. I jerked away from him. Gabriel came up, put his gun to Small's head.

"Don't even think about getting up," Gabriel told him. "You are under arrest."

I sat in an ambulance with a paramedic applying crap to my cheek. It smelled bad but they told me it would prevent infection and highly recommended I go to the hospital. I declined.

"How'd you know it wasn't him?" Gabriel walked up to me.

"He would not have been holding the victim the way he was if it had been him. I stabbed him in the shoulder and at least dislocated some joint on that side of the body. I also stabbed him in that arm. He wouldn't have been able to control her if he had attacked me."

"You realize that when I nodded to you, I didn't expect you to rush him," Gabriel continued.

"I know, but it was the best case scenario. He was not expecting me to be dangerous; he was expecting problems from the two of you. He might have said we were all psychos, but he gave away that he wasn't including me when he told me I wouldn't shoot him."

"He's still claiming it was consensual."

"What's she claiming?"

"Nothing, she isn't talking. Lucas is trying to get through to her, but I think she's been pretty traumatized. No one in the State Troopers office knew he was married."

"Well I guess we can mark that up as a win then," I sighed.

"It is, just because he isn't our killer, doesn't mean he wouldn't have been eventually. He'll be charged even if she says it was consensual based on the degree of trauma she seems to have sustained."

"Great, now if only we could find our killer. Why do we always find the wackos?"

"What do you mean?" Gabriel looked at me.

"We found Norman Bates' family and a sadistic state trooper, and I am sure if we looked a little harder, we could find a few more nuts in that stack of seventeen we had earlier. But we cannot find the psycho that is skinning our victims. Where the hell is he? And what the hell is he doing?" I asked.

Healing

Henry couldn't believe Marshal Cain had fought him that hard. She was feisty. It would make killing her that much sweeter, if he made it that long. He was currently in bed. He'd called work to say he was sick. He was waiting for his wife to leave so he could slip downstairs to his office and check the wounds.

He'd come home yesterday claiming to be ill. He'd used pneumonia as his excuse. He'd caught it from the Marshals. Everyone had believed it, even the Marshals.

The first task had been to relocate his elbow. Once that was done, he had passed out. When he came around, he removed the knife with half a bottle of whiskey and serious willpower. He didn't have anything that would work as a local anesthetic at his house. The knife had really hurt. She'd plunged it all the way in, until the hilt had bruised the skin. His shark suit had lost lots of rings; he'd had to dig a few of them out of the wound before stitching it up. Then he'd set to work stitching up his arm.

It had been grueling work. His hands had shook. Sweat had poured from his forehead. His entire body had felt like it was being electrified. The stitching wasn't very even, but it worked. He'd stopped bleeding.

Today he was hoping to redo the stitches, make them look more professional. Scars were easier to explain when they looked like they'd been fixed by a professional. He had hoped he had at least caught her lung.

No luck, the worst damage had been done with the hypodermic needle tear in her neck. She'd never gone into shock, never seemed to react to the medication. He didn't know why. It had worked on everyone else, but not her.

However, he had gotten the halogen lights and his spare key for the morgue back. He didn't even realize he'd dropped the key until he'd gotten home. Luckily, the bitch reporter hadn't turned it over to the police.

Henry finally heard the door downstairs close. Of course his wife didn't come check on him, she was afraid she'd catch something. He got up and crept downstairs.

He unlocked and entered his office. Bandages and bloody water and rubbing alcohol were sitting on the desk. It was a good thing his wife demanded it stayed locked. One more rule for him to live by, but at least it was a good rule.

He took out the contacts that he'd been wearing for the last day. It had been too much of a bother to take them out earlier. No one had come in to check on him. Grace had tried, but she'd been stopped by her mother at the door. Grace didn't need to catch what Henry had.

With all his effort, he snipped the stitches and replaced them. The pain came back and brought a wave of nausea with it. He waited for it to pass. He'd gotten sloppy, and this was the price he was paying.

It took him over an hour to get the stitches redone. They announced over the radio that the Marshals had raided a State Trooper's house during that time. Cain was with them so, obviously, he had gotten the worst damage.

She'd set his plan back, or rather he had, by getting greedy. The opportunity to kidnap her had seemed perfect. His son would have done it. And then it had gone all wrong in just a matter of seconds.

Henry knew he'd been sloppy with Gentry. He had expected to enjoy it, but he hadn't. Despite her appearance and her sometimes snippy attitude, she was always nice to him. It had been a fluke, a spur of the moment decision. One that he regretted. In some ways, Gentry had reminded him of Grace.

He ignored his wife's rule and lit a cigar in the house, his mind flowing backwards to the chance encounter that night. He'd stopped to get cigars and Gentry had been in there grabbing a bottle of booze. The good stuff too. She'd invited him over for a glass. He'd accepted. At that time, he hadn't intended to kill her, just have a glass of Scotch with a colleague.

Then Gentry had told him about the encounter with Cain the night before. The migraine, the vomiting, the sorrow, and sympathy Gentry had for Cain, doing that work day after day with the threat of a migraine always looming. Something in what she said had made him snap. She had said "I wish I had her determination."

In that moment, he had pictured her as Grace and the words leaving Grace's lips. There was no way Grace could grow up like that. He had lost it and he had killed Gentry as a result. The moment she was in the tree, he knew he had to go forward with his plan. She'd tell everyone and he'd be arrested earlier than he planned. So he killed her as he had all the others, but he hadn't savored it. He'd come home and checked on Grace and cried.

His eyes flashed over his son's picture. The women in their lives had broken them. Beaten them down into nothingness and then left them broken wrecks of their former selves. He blamed himself for this. He had let his son grow up with that monster he called his wife. He'd let Henry Junior get involved with the whore from the wrong side of town who shattered his heart while he was away fighting for her.

Now, he would finish what his son had started, but not today. He'd need another day of rest before he could use his arm properly. He'd need another day before he could move without groaning. He cleaned up his mess and put it in a hazmat bag. He put the hazmat bag in a black garbage bag and took it outside to the trash can.

The kitchen was brightly lit with track lighting recessed into the ceiling. All stainless steel appliances of the highest quality furnished the inside. Marble counter tops and marble tiles completed the ensemble. It was a complete waste of money. His wife could burn mac and cheese. She was many things but a cook wasn't one of them.

It took a while, but he finally got breakfast cooked and eaten. He set the dishes in the sink, realized he'd be yelled at for it later, and moved them to the dishwasher.

He considered going back into his office, but there was nothing there except memories. Memories he didn't need at the moment. He shambled back upstairs to his bedroom.

The room was dark and not just because the lights were off. The curtains were heavy drapes with thick backing that blocked out most of the light. The walls were covered in a dark paneled wood. The floor carpet was darker brown, almost black. It smelled of musk and cigar smoke. The musk was his aftershave. The cigar smoke was on his coats that hung up here because his wife refused to let them hang with hers in the hall closet downstairs.

He climbed into bed and closed his eyes. US Marshal Aislinn Cain jumped out at him from behind the closet door and screamed, "Boo!" He woke covered in sweat and fumbled for the lights. He'd never had nightmares before, not even as a child, but this one definitely qualified as a nightmare. The light illuminated the room and provided no sign of the Marshal. He slumped against his pillow. They were close. He popped a Percocet and decided that pain or not, his wife had to die tonight. He'd send Grace to stay with a friend for her own protection from his pneumonia. He texted both his wife and Grace.

The reply from his wife said, "fine. am eating dinner with friend. make soup for urself."

He thought about that. A loving wife would come home and make soup for him. His made him make it for himself when he had pneumonia. He wondered which of her chums from the FBI she'd be with tonight. Would it be Agent Arons? Or someone else? He suspected Arons and his wife were having an affair but he couldn't prove it. Maybe he could catch them together tonight.

That thought put a smile on his face. His wife was a forensic accountant during the day and his own personal overlord at night. That's why she kept the books at his office. To make sure he didn't have any money. It was one more way to control him.

He napped for a while. When he woke, it was nearly quitting time at the FBI offices. He got up, got dressed, grabbed a Taser, and a couple of syringes filled with triazolam and headed downtown. If he was lucky, he'd miss the heaviest traffic.

He arrived just in time to see his wife's car pull out of the garage. Another car pulled out behind it. He wondered whose it was and decided to follow both.

The cars pulled into Agent Arons garage. Slowly, the doors snaked closed, they would help conceal his crime. Henry parked down the street some ways. Here was his proof and his chance to exact revenge. He sat in the car and smoked a cigar. He should have brought a gun. That would have been better, but he felt fully enraged by Agent Arons being with his wife. They knew each other. Arons was always so chummy at the morgue when he needed his help. Now Arons was inside, fucking Henry's wife.

Henry grabbed one of the halogen lights from the back of the SUV and crept up to the house. He rang the bell. Fred Arons answered the door with a look of shock and surprise on his face. He was shirtless, shoeless, and covered in oil. Henry's bitch wife was giving him a massage while she thought he was home with pneumonia fixing his own fucking soup. Henry tasered Arons and watched the body slump to the ground. He hit the button again and again and again.

His wife came around the corner wearing a skimpy piece of lingerie. Henry swung the light with the one good arm and caught her in the face. She fell into a heap on the ground.

The Taser made noise again as it zapped Arons. Arons was now drooling uncontrollably and he'd pissed himself. Henry hit the button again and the smell of Arons bowels opening hit him. He didn't gag, he was used to it. He hit the button again and again and again. Finally, Arons stopped moving. His chest didn't rise or fall. Burn marks at least an inch wide radiated over his chest where the prongs were stuck.

Henry moved to his wife and injected her with the hypodermic full of triazolam. As his wife struggled not to fall asleep, Henry went out to his car and got a large box and a dolly. She was out when he returned, he muscled her into the box with as little noise as he could manage. At least he managed not to scream as his arm protested against the usage. When she was safely tucked away, he took and slid the dolly under her and left the house, making sure to hit all he bumps along the way to the car.

A neighbor looked out at him. He waved and continued on. The curtain closed. At the SUV he had some trouble maneuvering the box into the SUV hatch space, but another neighbor, who knew him, helped. They talked for a moment, Henry explaining that he was picking up some used stuff for a charity drive. The box was heavier than Fred had said it would be. As proof, he even produced a key to Fred's house. He gave it to the neighbor and said when Fred came home to give it to him. The neighbor agreed.

Dr. Henry Erickson knew that it was just a matter of time now, the Marshals might not be knocking down his door yet, but they were close. This would be his last victim, but at least he had got her.

Twenty-One

"We have another problem," Gabriel announced as we stood clustered in the Marshals' conference room. The lights were out and floor lamps had been brought in at Xavier's insistence.

"A few hours ago, the FBI notified us that one of their employees had gone missing. Dr. Ericson reported to them that his wife, Hilary, who is a forensic accountant, had not come home. He currently has pneumonia and is laid up. However, when he woke up around two in the morning, his wife had not returned home. He tried to call her phone and got no answer. She was last seen talking to Special Agent Fred Arons who is also not answering his phone. Someone has been to his house and he and his car are both missing," Gabriel continued. "We have units canvassing the neighborhood for any witnesses, but so far they haven't come up with anything. No one saw him leave this morning or come home. Now we know that both were at work until five last night, but their whereabouts after that are unknown."

"Do we think this could be another double?" Lucas asked.

"We don't think anything at the moment. There is some indication that Arons and Hilary Ericson might have been having an affair," Gabriel said. "If that's the case, we are hoping to find them asleep in a motel room and they'll have to sort that out themselves. We will be coordinating all the search efforts, but the FBI and the Marshals will be lending us agents. I'm going to sort them out and then figure out where to stick you guys. You aren't exactly good at playing with others."

Gabriel left the room.

"I'm almost offended by that," Xavier said. "It's hard to play well with others, when everyone is out to kill you."

"Some indication? Wonder what they have that says the two of them are having an affair?" I picked up a photo from a file on the table, ignoring Xavier. I wasn't sure if he was really talking about all of us or just me. "Is it me or does Hilary have blue eyes?"

"She does," Lucas said.

"Dr. Ericson showed me a picture of his daughter, she has brown eyes," I said.

"How do you remember that?" Michael asked.

"Never know when eye color is going to be important," I responded.

"Maybe she's adopted," Xavier said.

"She looks like her mother," I said. "Remember?"

"Dr. Ericson even said she looked like her mother," Xavier said.

"What are you two getting at?" Michael asked.

"Two blue eyed parents cannot have a brown eyed child," Xavier said. "It is genetically impossible. Blue eyes are a recessive gene. Brown eyes is a dominant gene. If one of them had brown eyes or hazel eyes, she could have brown, but they don't. So she isn't Dr. Ericson's child, even if she is Hilary Ericson's."

"He's a doctor," Lucas said.

"He would know that his daughter was not actually his daughter," I said.

"Do you think Dr. Ericson is our serial killer or that he just made his wife disappear?" Lucas asked.

"I don't know," I said. "If he is our serial killer, it is hard to believe that he could kill his wife or Agent

Arons. I am not at 100% and I was not injured nearly as badly."

"If he's our serial killer, he's suffering. Could be why he wasn't at work yesterday. I checked on him while you were in the hospital yesterday morning. The morning you and Lucas were attacked, he came down with pneumonia and missed work that day. So, I called him yesterday morning, he still had pneumonia, wasn't feeling much better, but said he was taking antibiotics and would be back today or tomorrow," Xavier said.

"But how does he kill his wife with those injuries?" I asked.

"Because they weren't as bad as you thought?" Xavier countered.

"He was. I know he was. I felt the knife strike bone in his shoulder. He screamed when the second pop happened. On top of that, I ground my knee into his testicles. The man is hurting," I said.

"Maybe he's a true psychopath," Lucas offered.

"Even Malachi would have some issues lifting a body like Arons after being stabbed in the shoulder with my boot knife," I said. The knife in question was five inches long, double edged, and wicked sharp. It was also forged specifically for me. It had been a gift from the Marshals when I officially joined. The middle section was just a fraction wider than the end of the area around the hilt. It also got thicker near the hilt, but had a taper just before the forged steel entered the handle. It was hard to get out of the skin and it would make a mess coming out. The tapered area grabbed hold of the skin or whatever it went through so that when it was pulled out it had a tendency to pull stuff out with it.

Lucas gave me a look.

"Ok, maybe Malachi is a bad example," I said. Malachi had taken six bullets to the chest and still brought down a bad guy. He'd spent three weeks at home after surgery and then returned to full duty at work because he was bored at his house.

"I can't think of a good example," Xavier said.

"Me either," I admitted. "But Ericson doesn't strike me as a psychopath."

"And you have a built in psychopath radar," Lucas mocked.

"No, but they usually are aggressive towards me," I reminded him.

"Dr. Ericson is not aggressive towards you," Xavier said.

"My point exactly, he is courteous, not malicious," I said.

"Maybe he's the exception, not the rule," Lucas said.

"Ok, who's telling Gabriel?" I asked.

After a round of rock, paper, scissors, Michael got saddled with the task. I abstained with the excuse that I stressed Gabriel out. The others agreed and Xavier said something about a stroke, so I sat on one of the tables while they roshamboed for it.

Gabriel came back in and hit the back of the table. It catapulted me forward, giving under the force of the hit. My feet hit the ground with a jarring thud that traveled up my legs.

"Feel better?" Xavier asked.

"A little, yeah," Gabriel smirked at me.

"Good, try to hold on to that," Michael said as he began explaining the theory of Dr. Ericson being a murderer and possibly a serial killer.

"Except our serial killer has brown eyes, according to Ace," Gabriel said.

"I don't think he's our serial. Our serial would be in a world of pain and unable to kill a trained special agent and make the body disappear," I piped up. "That does not mean Ericson didn't kill his wife and her lover, it just means he is not our serial killer."

"Unless he is a true psychopath," Lucas added.

"You keep coming back to that, but you said it yourself, our serial is a borderline personality disorder psychopath not an anti-social personality disorder psychopath," I said.

"Because there is a difference," Xavier said.

"Unfortunately, there is," Lucas sighed. "Malachi Blake is an ASPD Psychopath. He is witty, charming, easy to get along with, adventurous, and functional. He can also take six bullets to the chest and keep on coming, until he runs out of blood, because he doesn't feel pain. It is part of the physical component of ASPD. That is why Ace's pain tolerance is so high. She is an ASPD Sociopath but less functional than Malachi. Borderlines don't have that particular physical component. Yes, they are more pain tolerant and can still do things that normal people can't, but Ace and Malachi don't have the pain receptors because of their ASPD. Borderlines do, they just ignore them."

"That is very strange," Xavier said.

"It is and it isn't. The separation is a new one and we are still working to understand it completely, but the working theory is that ASPD is genetic and borderlines are created," Lucas said. "Ace outruns me not because she is in better physical condition but because her brain doesn't receive the message from her muscles that they are pushing as hard as they can. That's why she doesn't go into shock. Same for Malachi. But they were most likely born that way. Borderlines have been beaten and subjugated into becoming socio or psychopaths. They have all Malachi and Ace's personality issues, but they do not have the benefit of the physical component. In this case, receptors in the brain that receive pain information and tell the body to stop. They have something like an override button, where they can push through a lot of pain, but they still feel every bit of it. They just process it different. Most of them like it."

"Sorry, I think I fell asleep," Michael teased.

"Yeah, yeah," Gabriel waved his hand at the geek. Michael stuck out his tongue. "So our sociopath would be stronger than a borderline psychopath?"

"Our sociopath is just barely a sociopath," Lucas answered. "I don't know why she isn't a full blown ASPD Psychopath, I just know that she isn't, but she's close. In a battle between her and most psychopaths, I'd put money on her. There is a level of violence in her that is rarely seen in women, sociopaths, or any other severe personality disorder. She wouldn't string an innocent in a tree and filet them, but she'd gut a bad guy without a second thought and dance on his entrails as he bled to death."

"Thanks," I quipped.

"It was meant to be a compliment," Lucas assured me.

"That's all well and good, but if we are going to run at Dr. Ericson for killing his wife, I want something tangible before we do it. I don't want to smear his name just because Ace thinks it's possible. She's never been married and I've fantasized about killing my ex before," Gabriel said.

"Maybe you need a few minutes on the doctor's couch," I quipped. "I just think we need to look at him. I agree that Hilary Ericson falls into our killer's parameters, but I do not want to be wrong again and chase down another dead end. We have something tangible here, a cuckolded husband. I think we check that first."

"Who uses the word cuckolded anymore?" Xavier asked.

"Who starts sentences with the word 'because'?" I returned.

"Point taken," Xavier smiled.

"Fine, Ace and Xavier visit Dr. Ericson. You two have the best rapport with him. We'll join the search parties in the woods," Gabriel stood up.

The three of them left. Xavier and I were alone in the room. I sighed.

"What?" He asked.

"I'm just thinking about Lucas' comment."

"Ace, you may be a monster, but you're one of the good monsters. There's a lot to be said for that."

"Do you think I'm a monster?"

"Yes and I'm glad I'm your friend because of it. Sometimes, we forget that you are not a normal sociopath. You lack empathy, sympathy, guilt, and remorse but have somehow managed to find a way or force your way into feeling outrage, sadness, happiness, and the rest of the human range of emotions. That doesn't stop you from being a monster, it just makes you a different kind of monster. And even Gabriel likes the monster that lurks inside you, relies on it to keep him alive. Because when he goes to breech a door, he has you at his side. Not the mountain, not the doctor, but the monster, because he knows that if anyone can keep him alive, it's you."

"In other words, I'm a good monster."

"Like Sully from *Monsters, Inc.*," Xavier giggled.

"Thanks, Xavier."

"No problem, do you want to let me in on the sudden interest in your own humanity?"

"I'm missing my touch stone. I have not seen Nyleena in weeks. She keeps me grounded, reminds me of my humanity. Plus, I kind of liked Gentry, but I can't mourn for her. Her gung-ho attitude and nerve, standing up to me when I had that migraine. I liked her. But I didn't know her well or at all really, so my mind says I should be sad, but I get nothing."

"For you, she was a moment, she was background noise. I know that doesn't make you feel better, if you had experienced the same flash with her that you felt with Lucas and I, you'd mourn. Since you didn't, it's very hard to be sad."

"Does that increase the size of the monster?"

"Nope, that just proves you are still you," Xavier shrugged. "Come on, we have a doctor to talk to and bad guys to hunt down. Then we can head home, you can see Nyleena and your mom."

"And my brother," I said as we stood up.

My brother lived in The Fortress. He was a mass murderer. I hadn't seen him since his incarceration. When I became a member of the Serial Crimes Tracking Unit, I was granted access to all prisoners inside the massive prison for the not so insane. It had been nearly six months and I had never forced my way into an interview room with him. I was thinking it might be about time.

Twenty-Two

A teenage girl with brown curly hair and deep brown eyes opened the door for Xavier and I. We identified ourselves and she handed us masks that were sitting next to the door. They looked like the type we wore in the morgue. I slipped the elastic straps over my ears and pinched the metal piece down around my nose. The lower half of my face was now fully covered. Xavier did the same and we were led into the living room.

In a recliner, knees drawn up under him, sat Dr. Ericson. He also wore a mask, but his forehead and cheeks were flushed where we could see them. His eyes were blue and bloodshot with dark rings around them. He didn't look like a man in pain; he looked like a man with a serious infection raging through him.

"Dr. Ericson," Xavier sat down on the couch. I sat next to him. The girl, who I assumed was his daughter, sat in a chair across from us.

"Dr. Reece," his voice sounded congested and abnormal. I tried not to sigh.

"We just need you to answer a few more questions. The rest of our team is out looking for your wife," Xavier assured him.

"Whatever you need," Dr. Ericson answered.

"You said you woke up around two this morning and she wasn't home?" Xavier started.

"Yes. We agreed that Grace, that's my daughter, should go to her friend's house tonight. I'm getting better and I'm unlikely to be contagious at this point, but it never hurts to be careful. Hilary then sent me a text that said she was having dinner out with a co-worker. So I had some soup and went to bed. I woke about two and got up to see if Hilary had remembered to pick up some more soup and she wasn't home."

"Do you know what co-worker she had dinner with?" Xavier asked.

"No, I didn't ask, but she has several co-workers that we go out with."

"Where did Grace spend the night?" I asked.

"With my family," Sheriff Rybolt came out of the kitchen carrying a tray of coffees and teas. He set them all out, giving them to everyone but me. He pulled a can of soda out of his pocket and handed it to me. "We thought it'd be you two that would come for the interview."

"Thank you," I told him. "So she spent the night with your family?"

"Emily and Grace are on the basketball team together," Sheriff Rybolt told me.

"What happened to your neck?" Dr. Ericson asked.

"Run in with a bad guy," I told him, since I was the only one wearing a bandage on my neck. "Tore a hole in it. No big deal, just another scar."

"Daddy," Grace looked at Dr. Ericson with wide eyes. "You should tell them."

"Tell them what, honey?" Dr. Ericson replied.

"About mom," Grace pressed. "I know already. It's basic biology information."

Dr. Ericson visibly changed. His composure fell some, his face seemed to age. The disgraced man closed his eyes and took a deep breath.

"My wife may be having an affair," Dr. Ericson finally said. "I don't know who with, but it wouldn't be the first time. However, she has always come home at a decent hour. Her lateness tonight has never happened before."

"We'll make note of it," I said.

"How did you know?" Dr. Ericson asked his daughter.

"I have brown eyes, so did Henry. You and mom both have blue," she frowned. "When we started doing biology this year we had a class on genetics. The teacher assured me that it couldn't happen. So I talked to Henry about it."

At this point, she broke down crying, deep sorrowful sobs that shook her small body and made her curls bounce. I didn't know who Henry was, but it was something to look into.

"I asked Henry if I was adopted and he told me that no, he'd been at my birth. There was no way I was adopted. Then I told him what my teacher said about the eye colors. He confronted mom after Thanksgiving dinner," the sobs got worse and snot began to drip from her nose. I turned away from the scene. It was obvious her pain was great.

This brought Dr. Ericson into full view. He too was crying, gentle tears that ran down his face and dripped onto his shirt. He wiped at them right handed and shook his head.

"Grace, you weren't supposed to know. I'm so sorry," he finally told his daughter.

"Why are you sorry? It's her that should be sorry," his daughter told him, anger suddenly flashing in her eyes. I watched as the anger continued to smolder even though she dropped her father's gaze.

"Grace, why don't you come help me with some stuff in the kitchen," Sheriff Rybolt said.

Grace got up and left the room. Xavier looked at me for a moment. He had seen the anger too.

"Who is Henry?" I asked.

"My son, he died in December, killed himself a few weeks after Thanksgiving actually," Dr. Ericson looked older still.

"Do you know who fathered either child if it wasn't you?" Xavier asked.

"My brother," Dr. Ericson answered. "He's quite a bit younger than I am. He got married a few years after Grace was born. His family doesn't know, but he and I have talked about it."

I remembered a Tolstoy quote about dysfunctional families and tried not to smile. Dr. Ericson was proof that no matter how perfect your life seems to be, there is always something. Dr. Ericson relaxed a little with Grace out of the room.

"I'm sterile, accident when I was a kid. My brother and I agreed that at least this way, I got to have children. There were hard feelings in the beginning, but both of them were a blessing. Henry graduated valedictorian from high school, joined the military. He came back after his second tour a changed man. At twenty, he was no longer the son I knew. He was distant; his discharge papers said he had PTSD. I think there was more going on, but he wouldn't talk to me about it. The serial killer case we are working on had just started. Sheriff Rybolt and lots of others were patrolling the woods as much as possible. Tucker found him. He'd slaughtered a moose, decapitated it, removed the eyes, and then turned the knife on himself and slit his own throat. As far as the vet could find, he caught the moose off guard. He hadn't shot him with a bow or a gun, just stabbed him in the leg and severed one of the tendons the moose needed to run. When the moose collapsed, well, we can only guess what he was thinking at the time. As I said, he was changed by what he saw over there.

"Now, there's just Grace and she's following in her brother's footsteps. She's an overachiever with big dreams of becoming a researcher and curing diseases. She's already started taking college classes through correspondence courses in association with her high school. She plays basketball, volleyball, and softball. Has tons of friends. Even when the rest of us were at our worst, sick with Henry's death and the grief, Grace managed to put on a smile and help me get through it."

"And you have no idea who your wife might have been having an affair with now?" Xavier pressed him again.

"Oh, I'm sure I could point a finger at a few people, but it would just be speculation," Dr. Ericson took a cigar from the table next to him, clipped off the end and lit it. I watched the smoke curl up from it.

"Well, we won't keep you," Xavier stood up. "We'll go join the search. I'll let you know as soon as we have something."

"Thank you," I said, standing and looking at Xavier.

Outside was freezing, dawn was just over the horizon. We climbed into the SUV. Xavier started the motor and we sat for several minutes in the cold silence.

Anchorage has the same problem as other cities, too much light pollution to see anything but the brightest stars. The moon seemed far away. It was waning to just a sliver of silver in the darkened sky. Two or three nights and there would be no moon.

"Dr. Ericson is left handed," Xavier said finally. He pulled away from the curb.

"So?" I asked.

"So, he lit his cigar right handed and he wiped his face with his right hand. Why?"

"Because he could."

"We unconsciously use our dominant hand for almost everything, unless we can't. Then we become conscious of our lack of ability to use it and use the opposing hand with more difficulty."

"I eat left handed, but I'm right handed."

"You eat with a knife and fork, knife in your dominant hand. Unless you don't have one, without a knife, you eat with your right hand."

"I still don't see your point. Maybe he's ambidextrous."

"No, I've seen him work, Ace. He's not. He's clumsy right handed. When you smoke, you smoke right handed. You lit your cigarette lighter with your right hand. You hold the cigarette with the right hand. I can tell which hand is dominant based on the nicotine stains."

"Get there already."

"If you were on top of him or vice versa when you stabbed, you would have hit his left arm and left shoulder. He wouldn't be using them because of the pain."

"So now you think he is our serial killer."

"It would clear up a lot of questions. The killings started just after Thanksgiving. What if it wasn't a partner but a son? Henry Ericson Junior kills himself and his father takes over, that's why the skill improves. Dr. Ericson would have more experience with the tools of the trade."

"Henry Junior confronts his mother about her infidelities. He's already broken. She brushes him off or worse, becomes aggressive and he turns into a serial killer. Then he's in the woods, doing whatever and slaughters the moose. Seeing what he's done to the moose, he realizes what he has become and slits his own throat. Dr. Henry Ericson takes a few weeks and then starts going through his son's stuff and finds what? Souvenirs from the kills? Realizes his son is who we are looking for and just to throw things off, he kills thirty-eight, well forty women, now?"

"Maybe he was only going to kill one or two so that the killings didn't end with Henry Junior's death, but finds he likes it. He ups the age of the victims to match his wife and starts killing surrogates of her."

"Then he runs into Lucas and I, we tussle, he realizes just how close we are and with a severely damaged shoulder, he manages to kill Agent Arons and his wife?" I asked.

"I haven't gotten that far in the thought process of it, but essentially, that's what I'm getting at," Xavier answered.

"That's thin," I said. "But it does fill all the necessary holes."

"The sheriff's wife is a judge, right?"

"Yeah, she dropped the charges against me," I answered.

"We'll never get a warrant," Xavier sighed. "We need to talk to Gabriel."

"Why would he kill Agent Gentry? They seemed pretty buddy-buddy."

"Because he could," Xavier said.

Twenty-Three

"Good news, we think we know who our serial killer is," I said as I walked up to Gabriel and Lucas. They were standing against the SUV in the parking lot of another state park. "Bad news, he's pretty deeply involved in the case."

"Since you consider him to be our serial killer, I'd say that does make him deeply involved in the case," Gabriel turned to look at me.

"Point taken, but this is different. We are pretty sure it's Dr. Henry Ericson based on Xavier's analysis of his hand behaviors and his wife's infidelities," I said.

"I'm going to find this explanation annoying, aren't I?" Gabriel asked.

"Most likely. Do you want a chair? A Valium? An ambulance on standby?" I asked.

"Just tell me," Gabriel sighed heavily and looked at Xavier.

"Around Thanksgiving, Dr. Ericson's son found out his mother was cheating and had been cheating on his father for decades, literally. We think he did the first three victims. Then he killed himself and Dr. Ericson took over. It explains why they never found anything in the toxicology reports, Dr. Ericson would know what not to look for. It also explains the increased skill level of the replacement killer. And the timing is perfect. Also, whoever attacked Lucas and Ace was stabbed in the left arm. Dr. Ericson is left handed, but this morning, as we talked with him, he did everything right handed, even things we normally do unconsciously. Like he began crying but wiped his tears away with his right hand."

"What about the eye color?" Gabriel asked.

"Contacts," I offered. "You can do anything with colored contacts. I still cannot figure out how he killed his wife and Arons, but I am pretty sure he did."

"Ericson is the right build for the guy on film," Lucas said. "The death of a son could have sent him into a dissociative situation and in order to keep the son's name from being smeared by the press when it came to light, he continued the killings. He probably only planned one or two, but found he liked it. Parents do amazing things for their children."

"Can you prove it?" Gabriel asked.

"No, which is where we have a problem. I don't think, even using our special status, we are going to get a warrant from any judge in this town based on what our gut is telling us. My guess, between Hilary's ties to the FBI and Ericson working as a coroner part time, he knows all of them. They aren't going to be happy if we come to them wanting a warrant for a fishing expedition," I said.

"Great," Gabriel sighed and closed his eyes. "Is there any way to use Ace to get to him?"

"That is a possibility," Xavier said. "If we are right, then Ace attacking him back was probably a surprise. I told him once she was not your average woman, and I don't think he believed me. I imagine he does now. He'll come for her if he thinks he can get away with it."

"If I was a serial killer and wanted to attack me, I'd wait for me to get a migraine," I told them my deep dark fear. "I have always worried about that. But once the migraine hits, death looks better and better."

"How do you feel when you have a fake migraine?" Gabriel asked. I frowned at him.

"Not keen on the idea of being bait?" Michael snickered at me.

"Sometimes, it's fine. This one," I shrugged. "I'm not bothered by Dr. Ericson, him I can take. I think it's his daughter that bothers me. She's a sociopath in the making, and finding out daddy and brother were serial killers and that daddy then murdered mommy, might be the proverbial straw. If we trap him using me as bait, in ten years, she might come looking for revenge."

"Why do you think she's a sociopath in the making?" Lucas asked.

"Because of her anger. I saw it flash across her face. She is one angry teenager who almost worships her father. I foresee bad things in her future. Especially if she figures out who her biological father really is," I said.

"Yeah, I noticed it too," Xavier said. "It's not uncommon for teens to be angry, but she has a lot of it pent up. If we arrest her father, Lucas might want to sit her down and talk to her. I don't think it will do any good, but it might help."

"Who is her real father?" Lucas asked.

"Her uncle, Dr. Ericson's brother. I didn't get any more details," I said.

"Well, Cain, how about it? Ready to take one for the team? I'll radio to say you are headed back to the motel with another migraine. I'll send Lucas with you; he can hide in the other room. He's the stealthiest and he'll be good back up," Gabriel said.

"If I say no, what happens?" I asked.

"You get to go back to the motel and fake a migraine anyway," Gabriel said.

"Well then, I guess I don't have anything better to do," I said and started walking to the car.

"At least you get out of the cold!" Xavier yelled to my back.

"There is that," I shouted giving a wave.

I was in the SUV again. It was still warm from our trip over. Lucas started the engine.

"You really don't want to do this, do you?"

"I didn't kill him the first time. I have questions about a second encounter," I admitted. "Then there is this nagging thing in the back of my mind about him getting the drop on you last time."

"It was a onetime thing," Lucas said. I doubted that. Lucas might be the stealthiest, which was odd in and of itself, but he also managed to get sucked into his own mind at the wrong time. It didn't happen often, but it only took once. I don't know what went through the big man's mind when it happened.

His face would change, contort just a bit, almost as if he were in pain. I didn't know if that was the case when our killer had jumped him from behind, but I had a suspicion that it was a contributing factor. Even after six months, we didn't know all of each other's secrets. And Lucas, like me, had many.

The world flashed by the window. There was still snow everywhere. The roads were cleared, tearing black lines through the blinding whiteness. It was getting lighter, but was still dark enough that the street lights were on. Sodium arc lights and fluorescents dotted the landscape, offering orbs of light to stand in. They made the snow look worse as if it were an illusion waiting to suck an unsuspecting bypasser into an off-colored abyss.

The windows of the shops were not yet lit up. The darkened panes reflected the poor outside lighting, holding in the secrets of what was inside. They seemed to stare at our car, cursing us for being interlopers.

The parking lot of the motel was bleak. A few sodium arc lights lit the front of the building. The lights turned the beige paint into a yellowish-tan. The building looked sickly. Only the office had lights on, and they just added to the sickly glow. A feeling of dread overcame me.

I wanted nothing more than to stay in the warm car or go back to the search scene.

"Tell Xavier to find out where Henry Junior killed himself and look there," I told Lucas as he stopped in front of the motel. He was going to park on the backside of the building and come in through another door. The motel had exterior and interior room doors.

"Will do," Lucas stared at me. "How badly do you not want to go in?"

"There's just something about this one, I have felt it since I got here. I'll be fine," I gave him a wink as I exited the SUV.

The room was dark. I hadn't bothered to leave a light on; I knew my way around without it. I locked the front door and stopped. I took a deep breath. Something twitched near the bathroom, a jerk in the dark. I pulled my gun, but didn't turn the lights on.

"US Marshal, I'm armed," I said to the dark. Another twitch, I realized the bathroom door was closed and the light was on. The twitch was a moving shadow.

It moved rhythmically in the light, swaying slightly back and forth. I listened for sounds and found only the whirring of the heater and normal noises that I associate with motels. Then I heard a small, faint noise. Since the rooms next to me were empty, I wasn't expecting anyone to be snoring and was surprised to hear a gentle snoring sound coming from Lucas' room.

I was at an impasse. I couldn't check the bathroom and the bedroom with the adjacent door. I could wait for Lucas and hope that whatever was in my bathroom came out peacefully and that Sleeping Beauty remained sleeping. Or I could try to sneak back out the front door and call for more backup.

Footsteps made the decision for me. They were fainter than the snoring. They stopped at my door and I rapped once on the table next to me. The footsteps didn't move. There was a soft clicking noise and my door opened.

Light spilled in around the huge dark figure. It obscured his features and made the short cut hair appear to glow. He did something with his hands. I pointed at the bathroom then at his bedroom door. He turned his head to the side, listening.

He heard the noise, the snoring from his room. He stepped inside, closing the door quietly behind him. The latch catching was terrifyingly loud. We both waited, holding our breath.

Nothing changed. The shadow continued to sway. The snoring continued, unbroken.

I moved next to the bedroom door and peeked inside. There lay Sleeping Beauty, curled up in Xavier's bed. I wondered if she'd had her tetanus shots. The dark brown curls spilled out over the top of the blanket and cascaded down the pillow. I sighed.

Lucas gave me a look. I shook my head at him. We approached the bathroom. Lucas suddenly kicked in the door.

The sound was deafening. Wood slivers flew through the air, raining down on the carpet. The door hit the sink, causing even more damage to it. The smell hit me, overwhelmed me. The decomposition process was already in full force. The smells emanating from the bathroom forced me to take a step back to keep from gagging.

We'd found Agent Arons. His body was hanging from the shower rod. The thing creating the movement darted out between my legs.

"That was a rat," Lucas said to me.

"Yeah, got that," I told him, breathing shallowly through my mouth. I raced to shut the adjoining door. The curls continued to sleep. I didn't know what drug she had in her system, but it was strong.

"Ace, you might want to come here," Lucas said.

I was pretty sure I didn't. I had only caught a glimpse of the dead body, but it had been enough. I opened the front door and called Gabriel.

"I think Dr. Ericson knows we suspect him," I said.

"Why?"

"His daughter is asleep in Lucas' room. Agent Arons is dead in mine."

The rat, seeing outdoors, scurried past me. I watched it continue its strange running through the parking lot and then it disappeared into the snow and darkness.

"Are you sure he's dead?"

"Oh yeah, he's dead."

"On the way," Gabriel hung up.

Phone call made, I reluctantly approached the bathroom again. On the wall, written in black sharpie "Take care of my daughter".

"I already figured that was Grace," I told Lucas.

"And this?" He pointed at Agent Arons.

He'd been gutted; the entrails lay on the floor and draped over the bathtub like party streamer from hell. His eyes were clouding over, staring blankly at the mirror. The rat had been chewing on his bare feet. His manhood lay in the sink. Strangely, there was almost no blood and what was there, was black and clotted.

"He was dead when he was hung up," I left the bathroom.

"How long were you gone?" He asked.

"Not long enough for all this. We were at the Marshals office for two hours, then at Dr. Ericson's, but Grace was there. It took us twenty minutes to get to the search area, we talked for maybe ten minutes, then fifteen minutes back here," I told him.

"How'd he do it then?" Lucas asked.

"I don't know. Forty-five minutes to drug your child, drive here, slip her into bed, then gut the body, find a rat, and throw it in with it. That seems pretty close to impossible."

"Not if you killed Arons while we were at the Marshals," Lucas said. "He doesn't expect to bring Grace here. He leaves Arons for us to find. You and Xavier pay him a visit and he realizes he's done. So he brings Grace here, under sedation, and leaves her. He must really love the girl."

"How'd he get him up there?"

"Are you sure you actually stabbed him in the shoulder as opposed to just thinking you did? You had been drugged and were in the middle of a hectic situation."

"I did not imagine stabbing him, Lucas. I don't have that kind of imagination."

Something nagged at me. Something terrible was forming in my mind.

"How did he have time to put Arons in here before Xavier and I showed up at his house?"

"What do you mean?"

"I mean he couldn't have hung the body before calling to report his wife missing. I was here, trying to sleep. So he does it after the call. When? Someone had to go interview him. Then when Xavier and I showed up, Sheriff Rybolt was there with Grace. When did he have time to hang the body?"

"Are you implying that maybe he didn't?" Lucas narrowed his eyes at me.

"I don't know. Maybe, maybe not. The timeline just isn't making sense to me."

"I'm going to go back with he's a psychopath."

"Yes, but a borderline personality. He isn't Malachi."

"Maybe he is and we just missed the clue for it?" Lucas frowned at me. "It's easy, he calls in the missing wife. We instantly get notified and head to the Marshals. At that time, Arons is already dead, it takes maybe thirty minutes to get here, string up Arons and return to his house. He returns, a few minutes later, someone comes by to get his statement. That gets relayed to us. The sheriff and Grace show up. Then you and Xavier go to his house. Hell, they took most of his statement over the phone on a return call, he could have been here during the follow-up on his cell phone."

"Ok, well, we'll go with that for now," I sat down on the bed. The smell of death was filling the entire room. "Why did you get a sleeping child in your room and I got a hanging body in mine?"

"I'm not a sociopath," Lucas said like it answered everything.

Twenty-Four

Lucas and I were ushered into another room. Someone was trying to decontaminate us. We both smelled of death.

"Well, he's been dead for a while," Xavier said. "Nice scar."

"Thanks," I said.

"I'll know more when I get him to the morgue. He was tasered, probably multiple times. There are burn marks on his chest. They are taking Grace Ericson to the hospital to let her wake up there. A psychologist is waiting and we've called Dr. Ericson's brother," Xavier continued. "She was drugged, but we don't know what with."

"Not triazolam?" Lucas asked.

"She'd be awake by now. This was something stronger," Xavier answered.

"As soon as the HAZMAT folks get done with us, I say we go to where his son's body was found," I hooked my finger at someone who had a scrub brush and a hose. They were encased in a white suit that covered everything from head to toe. I didn't even know if the person scrubbing me was male or female. They kept pouring a chemical on me. It didn't burn, but it smelled almost as bad.

"Consider yourselves lucky, he could have found something predatory to shove in there," Xavier said.

"Rats are predatory, but in this case, I think it was just scavenging a meal. We might want to change hotels, considering Lucas' phobia," I said.

"Nothing makes sense at the moment," Xavier shrugged. "We will be checking Arons for pathogens and toxins during the autopsy. Ericson could have put anything on the body. I'd like to get the rat, but I'd say it is long gone. To answer your question about when he put Arons in your room, it took over an hour for a uniformed officer to stop by Ericson's house after he made the call. Sheriff Rybolt showed up maybe half an hour later."

"I am starting to feel like Alice after she entered the looking glass," I said.

"Good news, we can get a warrant. Him leaving Grace in Lucas' room convinced Judge Penelope Rybolt to give us carte blanche to search his house," Gabriel was holding up a piece of paper.

"This is not a peep show," Lucas said. I looked over at him. "I would hate for them to become insecure over sizes."

Until that moment, I don't think any of us had thought about the nudity of myself or Lucas. We all looked down, including the white-suited scrubber working to make me smell better.

"You smell good enough, let's get a move on," Gabriel grabbed a robe and tossed it to me.

"It isn't for the smell," Xavier said. "It's for the exposure to unknown chemical agents. Decomposition has been sped up by something, hence the black blood clots everywhere."

"What?" I frowned.

"His skin is starting to fall off too. That's not normal. I don't know what it is, so you are being decontaminated so that it doesn't happen to you," Xavier said.

"Ugh," I groaned.

"My thoughts exactly," Gabriel said. "How much longer?"

"Almost done," the scrubber went back to work. It was female judging by the voice.

"Did you touch anything?" Xavier asked.

"I am not really in the habit of touching things I know to be dead," I told him.

"Me either," Lucas said.

"Then you should be good. If you feel any tightness in the chest or start wheezing, let me know," Xavier left.

"My mother would abhor the person I have become, if she knew," I said.

"What?" Lucas asked.

"You can never tell her that I lack modesty and stood in a room with three men and two unknowns being scrubbed down while talking about dead bodies," I told him.

"Your secret is safe with me," Gabriel answered.

"It could be worse, we could all be nude," Lucas offered.

"If you say," the scrubber stopped and didn't finish the sentence. She took off the hood. Sweat was running down her forehead.

"I've dealt with a lot of things, I have never seen a person with as many scars as you," she said.

"Thanks," I answered.

"Really?" She looked at me, eyes narrowed.

"Each one is a badge of honor. It means I survived," I turned my full attention to her. She took a step back.

"I think you're done," she turned and left.

"Don't freak out the help, Ace," Gabriel said.

"I don't know what you're talking about," I said.

"Oh please, you know exactly what I'm talking about. You just went all dark and creepy on her," Gabriel scolded.

"Maybe a little, I just do not like people judging me by the scars I bear," I told him.

"You have to admit, you have lots, some of them weird. Like the brand on your side and the road rash on your leg," Gabriel said.

"Life's little hazards," I told him.

"For you, yes, for others, not so much," Gabriel handed me a towel. I dried and got dressed. Lucas finished up.

"Shall we go search the good doctor's home?" Lucas asked as he tied a pair of boots.

Dr. Ericson's house was blue with gray accents on the outside. It was an old-style Victorian that had been built in the last twenty years. Gabriel beat on the front door. We waited. No sounds wafted out to us.

After a few more seconds, Gabriel used a breech key and opened the door. It popped open, revealing a dark interior. He found a light switch and nailed one of the copies of the search warrant to the door. I heard the backdoor open.

"We'll sweep the place, then begin searching," Gabriel said into a collared microphone. It echoed in my ear. I hated using the radios when we were standing next to each other. The millisecond delay was enough to cause me some disorientation.

Gun out in front of me, I moved quietly through the house. Gabriel and Lucas were also searching. I entered an upstairs room. The smell was overwhelming. Pinesol hit me full in the face. I gagged and backed out of the room.

"Something upstairs," I said into the microphone. I didn't have a HEPA-Mask, but I did have access to a crappy little face mask. They had been positioned by the front door when you walked in. "Grab me a mask, they are by the door."

"On the way," Lucas was capable of moving very quickly, very quietly. I didn't understand how he did it. He weighed over three hundred pounds, yet moved like a ballet dancer.

His whispering footsteps came up the stairs and joined me. After handing me the mask, he trained a flashlight into the room. It fell on the mutilated remains of something.

"Think we found the wife," Lucas said.

Sensing nothing moving, I flipped on the lights. The body lay on the bed. The skin was tacked to the walls. There was a bow and arrow drawn on the wall in blood.

There was a second body in the room, slumped in the corner. Blood had ran down from the hairline and onto the face. The eyes stared at me.

"Fruck!" I yelled and slammed my fist into the wall with enough force to break a hole in it.

I was staring at Sheriff Rybolt. Gabriel came up next to me. His eyes searched the room and found the sheriff. He exhaled loudly.

Gabriel turned and pulled out his phone. I heard him talking to Xavier. I walked into the room. Lucas following me.

I stopped and stared at the bow and arrow. Something in my head clicked. I looked at Lucas.

"His son killed himself after slitting the throat of a moose. The bow has always been the sign of the hunter," I said.

"So?"

"So, that's what this is about. The son was the great hunter, but after he killed himself Dr. Ericson kept the symbol for himself. He's fulfilling his son's mission."

"That's bizarre," Lucas said.

"You said yourself that parents will do almost anything for their children," I reminded him.

"I remember, I wish I didn't," Lucas pulled me from the room. "Find his office, go through it, and see what's in it."

"On it," I went back downstairs.

Half way down there was a squeaky board. I briefly wondered how Lucas had missed it. I began to search the rooms on floor level. I moved through each slowly and methodically. Finally, I found the door set into the back of the stairs. I expected it to open onto a basement staircase. Instead, I found it locked.

I kicked it and it didn't budge. I tried to pick it and found that I didn't have the skill. I sighed and shouted for Lucas.

Even walking over my head, he didn't make much noise. I waited for him to hit the squeaky step but he was beside me in just a moment. I looked at him like he was made of magic.

"Someday, I'll teach you about stealth," Lucas said before ramming the door with his shoulder.

It gave under his weight, splintering the frame and taking the hinges out of the wall. Lucas' secret to breaking down doors, if they opened inwards, he always hit the hinges. For a moment, it seemed suspended in time, then it danced and spun before crashing to the floor. He flipped the light switch.

The room was filled with bookcases, a large desk, an old style office chair, several lamps, and a painting. The painting was gruesome, dead figures danced under the moon. I had never seen it before and didn't see a name on the canvas. I moved to the desk.

Lucas was searching through the bookshelves already. He took out a book, thumbed through it and put it back. He repeated the gesture several times as I opened drawers.

The middle one was locked. I jerked on it hard and got nothing. Lucas frowned at me.

"What?" I gave him a look and took a knife off the table. It had good weight, feeling almost perfectly balanced. I slid it between the drawer and the desk until it hit the latch. For a second, it did nothing, then the lock clicked and the drawer opened. I set the knife back down and took a step back.

The knife was my knife. It had been cleaned, but it was definitely my boot knife. I looked at Lucas. He walked over.

"You'll get it back, eventually," he said, taking a bag out of his back pocket and putting the knife into it.

There was a box inside the drawer. Lucas handed me a pair of gloves. I took them and slipped them on. I'd screwed up grabbing the knife to open the drawer, but I wasn't a crime scene tech, so I'd get yelled at and then the breech of protocol would be forgotten.

Noises came from the front of the house. I was guessing the cavalry had arrived. Ignoring them, I took the box out and opened it.

There was a large photo album, a journal, and a single sheet of paper. I handed the journal to Lucas and took the photo album.

Skin, perfect patches of it, cut with extreme precision were carefully put into the photo holder spots. There was a slip of paper with neatly printed words containing names under them. Amazed, I flipped through the pages. The last spot was wet with something that I imagined came from the human body when you removed skin. The writing was slightly smeared on the slip of paper, but still legible: Hilary Ericson.

"Holy hell," Lucas said. He had moved and was looking inside a hope chest. I walked over to join him. Strips and swatches and patches of skin filled it almost to the top. It didn't smell. Something had stopped it from decomposing.

"Tanning?" I asked.

"Most likely," Lucas gave a loud whistle. Several people in jumpsuits came into the room. They looked into the trunk. A few gasped. A few others turned from the scene. It was gruesome to see the skins stacked together like they were.

I went back to the desk. The piece of paper was still sitting on top. I bent over, making sure not to touch it and read the words aloud.

"The great warriors left this earth for a more divine realm. They frolicked and danced and feasted all the daylong in their kingdoms in the Elysium Fields." I finished and read them to myself again and again. They seemed foreign to me and yet, not so foreign.

"He and his son were both soldiers, right?" Lucas asked, jarring me from my thoughts.

"Yes, and good soldiers go to the Elysium Fields in Greek Mythology," I told him.

"So you were right and wrong at the same time. How do you do that?" He asked.

"How do you manage to walk around like you weigh no more than a mouse?" I quipped.

"He's going to kill himself," Lucas said.

"In the spot where they found his son," I added.

Endings

Henry Ericson sat in his SUV and smoked a cigar. Almost an hour earlier, Dr. Xavier Reece had entered the morgue with Agent Arons body. He put the car into gear and pulled into traffic. The city had become busy with the dawn.

Cars and SUVs moved along the streets. They zigzagged in and out of lanes, doing a dance that had been perfected over years of driving on the highways. The city might not be big by most standards, but it was big enough. No one seemed to realize that with the FBI and US Marshals both having staging areas in Anchorage, the population signs were wrong.

He drove past his street. It was cordoned off. Police cruisers kept traffic from turning down the road. Onlookers were standing, gawking. He knew they were staring at his house.

This would have been easier if he hadn't let himself be stabbed, but he had. Now he would make the best of it. He had his knife under a newspaper on the front seat next to him.

He turned on the radio, trying to find a news station. Finally, one tuned in and he listened to see if he heard his name. After thirty minutes of aimless driving, he didn't.

Henry still had a few things to take care of. He pulled the SUV into a driveway. For a few seconds, he just sat inside it. Then he got out and walked to the front door. His finger found the doorbell.

It was a pretty one story house. Painted green with white shutters, it had a large covered porch. The woman that answered looked at him, surprised.

"Henry? What is it?" She asked.

"It's your sister, I'm afraid Hilary was kidnapped last night by the serial killer the newspapers are calling the Flesh Hunter. They found her body about an hour ago. I thought I should tell you in person," Henry answered.

"Oh my God. Come in," Bell Turner said. She was Hilary's younger sister by four years. They had never been close.

"We have to talk, Bell," he said. He was holding a newspaper. "I know that Grace and Henry were not my kids, not biologically. But I found her diary this morning. Hilary had an affair with your husband."

"What?" Bell shook like someone had turned on a cold stream of air.

"I'm sorry, Bell, I just wanted you to know. Henry was actually your husband's son. I thought he was my brother's until I read the diary."

"Henry," Bell sat down suddenly. Her body seemed to collapse. Henry tried not to smile. He was going to make the bitch's entire family suffer for saddling him with the monster. She was directly responsible for Henry Junior killing himself. The bitch thought only of herself, never of their children.

"Let me make coffee," Henry slipped into the kitchen. He found the coffee and began brewing a pot. He was desperate for a cup. He hadn't had a cup since he'd been stabbed. The coffee smelled like heaven as it brewed. He shoved the folded newspaper into his back pocket. Taking his time, he fixed two cups of the strong black liquid, added cream and sugar to Bell's, and headed back into the living room.

He handed her a cup and took a sip of his own. It tasted wonderfully bitter as it warmed his mouth and throat. The steam felt refreshing on his face. He sipped it gently a few more times. Bell just held her cup, her hands shaking. Henry knew she was thinking about this mind-blowing information. Her husband, Ed Turner, was a state trooper. He wondered if she was considering what to do to him when he got home.

The phone rang. She looked at it and threw it across the room. It hit the wall and shattered. The action seemed to break her even more. She set down the cup and began to sob.

"Was that Ed?" Henry asked.

"Yes," Bell wiped at the tears and tried to compose herself. "Probably calling to tell me that Hilary was dead."

"We all knew she was like this, Bell, I don't think we should hold it against her now," he said, trying to soothe his sister-in-law.

"I knew, but my own husband. How could she do that?"

That was the confirmation Henry was waiting for. Bell had known about the plethora of affairs. She had known and never said anything, just smiled when they saw each other.

Bell began to cry again. Henry wrapped an arm around her. With the other, he drew the knife. Bell was just as responsible for Henry Junior's death as Hilary had been. The knife entered between her ribs, puncturing her lung. Her eyes grew wide. Her mouth opened and an odd gurgling noise escaped her lips.

Henry drew the knife out and leaned Bell back against the couch. She was trying to reach for the wound. He knew he only had a few minutes to finish. He lifted her shirt and plunged the blade into her stomach. He closed his eyes, relishing the feeling of the blood flowing over his hands, then moved it upwards.

The knife hit Bell's sternum. Henry jerked it out and watched as the woman's insides spilled out onto the floor. Her eyes stared for a few more seconds. Her last breath escaped her lips.

Blood and intestines dribbled from her abdomen, filling the room with the smell of copper and shit. Death was always messy. He wanted to take a patch of her skin, but knew he didn't have time. Instead, he moved up to her, put the knife in her cheek and removed the entire section, skin, fat, everything. The hole in her face oozed bloody mucus.

Henry used the kitchen to clean up. Once his hands and arms were blood free, he wrapped the knife back into the newspaper and dug out his cell phone.

"Henry?" Ed's voice was filled with concern.

"I guess you've heard. Well, Bell got to know me up close and personal," Henry laughed and hung up.

Henry left. His SUV took him away from the scene of death, closer to another destination and another woman that needed to die. He drove up to the morgue. The police radio crackled to life. It was Ed reporting that he thought Henry was at his house. Ed was very slow with the report, Henry thought as the car idled.

A black SUV with tinted windows pulled into the parking lot. A coroner's van arrived at the same time. They unloaded two black bags from the van. Marshal Cain stared at them, waited for the attendants to take them inside. She spent a few moments speaking with the people in the SUV before climbing back into it. He'd have to wait a little longer.

When the parking lot was empty, he used the fire escape to climb to the roof. He took several things from a bag and set them up around him. Carefully, he put a tube into the ventilation system.

Twenty-Five

Gun drawn, I walked through the snow. The whiteness seemed wrong in this place of death. It symbolized innocence and this place was anything but innocent. It had seen butchery, slaughter, and death. In my mind, they were not associated with whiteness.

Around me, I could hear Gabriel and Lucas moving. We had taken different routes, unsure what we would find. Their boots crunched on the snow. The crisp, cold layer on top had not yet started to thaw.

The trees threw long shadows on the ground. The branches grabbed at me, trying to tear at my face and hair, reminding me that I was an interloper, an unwanted guest. I pressed forward.

The woods were silent except our footsteps. No birds, no small mammals, nothing moved. The world seemed to have stopped. We had stepped into a vacuum that defied space and time. It felt as if the world were holding its breath, waiting for us to find the dead doctor.

There was nothing in the clearing. I entered it and lowered my gun. I had expected to find him, alive or dead. I checked the map as Gabriel and Lucas came into view. We all looked around.

Lucas frowned. Gabriel pulled out his own map. Together we compared them. We were in the right spot, but there was no sign of Dr. Henry Ericson. Not even footprints in the snow.

"Fruck!" I crumpled up the map.

"Chill," Gabriel said. "We just guessed wrong."

"That is the problem. We didn't find him," I said. "If he's not here, where is he and what is he doing?"

"I see your point," Gabriel said.

"Is he out killing more?" I asked.

"If he is, he could be anywhere," Lucas said.

Together we hiked back to the car. Gabriel started the engine. I stamped my feet, shaking snow into the floorboard.

"We've got him on a most wanted list, he can't get far," Gabriel said.

"Yeah he can, he has all of northern Alaska to hide in," I countered.

"It would be very hard to search all of Alaska for him," Lucas answered.

I shook my head, "Drop me at the morgue. Xavier will need some help, I am sure."

"You really aren't that much help in an autopsy," Gabriel told me.

"Oh, I know; he likes me there for living company, and he bounces crazy ideas off of me," I told him.

"Is that why he keeps taking you there?" Lucas asked.

"Yes, I know just enough about anatomy to be very dangerous," I said.

We arrived at the same time as the coroner's van. They unloaded the bodies of Hilary Ericson and Tucker Rybolt. I waited on them.

"We have another possible victim," Lucas said, rolling down the window to talk to me as I stood in the parking lot.

"Who?" I asked.

"Hilary's sister, Bell. Her husband just reported that Henry called him and threatened her. We're going to go check on it," Lucas said.

"Xavier can wait," I climbed back into the SUV.

We drove to the address. Police squad cars were already there. They were marking off the area. Near one of the cars, there was a state trooper shaking from head to foot.

The house was pretty, painted a light green with white shutters and wide front windows that let in tons of light or filled the yard at night from the inside. The front door had a window in it and showed no signs of being forced open. We entered the living room.

"What the hell?" Gabriel said.

The pretty pastel pink carpet was sucking in the drying brownish blood. Black spots dotted the floor around her feet. She wore pink house shoes, lined with fleece that made them look soft and fluffy. They too had suffered from the blood, soaking it in, tinting them with brownish streaks.

Her body was leaning back on the couch. Blood was pooled around her, filling the cushions. Like Arons, she'd been gutted. I breathed through my mouth.

"She has three wounds, one in back, two in front," someone said to Gabriel.

That's when I noticed her face. The cheek was turned away from me, but I could tell that the skin had been removed. The wound was deep enough that it had punctured the sinus cavity. There was a hole, almost perfectly round, in Bell Turner's face. Something that wasn't blood dripped from it. I forced myself not to gag. I could deal with blood, snot was a completely different story.

"He couldn't skin her, so he took her cheek as a souvenir," Lucas said.

"That's just wrong," Michael was still in the doorway, refusing to enter.

"Great, we know Ericson isn't still here, so where is he?" I asked.

"Watching?" Lucas suggested.

"No, too obvious. He's wanted and everyone knows what he looks like and what he's driving," Gabriel said.

"I should have just stayed at the morgue," I said.

"Well, you can ride back with the attendants," Gabriel told me.

"Ok," I waited outside. I lit a cigarette, the smoke burned in my throat.

"Xavier is going to be livid when you show up smelling like smoke," Lucas took the cigarette and took a drag.

"I keep telling him that I am not going to live long enough to get cancer," I said.

"Shit happens," Lucas shrugged.

The attendants began wheeling out the body. One of them looked at me. I had finished my cigarette, so I crushed it out on my boot and shoved the butt into my pocket.

The ride was quiet. I was stuck in the back with the dead Bell Turner. If I believed in zombies or any other form of undead, it would have been terrifying. Since I didn't, it was just disturbing. If I was going to be forced to deal with people, I preferred the living. This seemed to be in direct contrast to my personality, dead people didn't talk or make stupid statements. However, they made other noises, noises associated with living but were part of the decomposition process, like sighing. I found dead people creepy.

The van stopped. After a few seconds, the back doors were pulled open. I nearly rushed out the door. This time, I didn't wait for the attendants. I went in before them.

"Got another one," I said to Xavier, entering the room that said "Occupied".

"Killing spree?" Xavier asked, not looking up.

"Looking like it," I said.

"Was she skinned?"

"No, but she is Hilary's sister, and her cheek is missing. Finding anything?"

"Yeah, toxicology reports. The answers were there, they were just ignored because our serial killer was the attending coroner." Xavier sounded irritated.

"Here?" I asked.

"Yes, shoved in a drawer. I finally got curious about my surroundings and found them. The real ones, not the ones given to the police departments. He was scanning for it, but the results weren't being sent to the agents in charge or the police departments, they were being sent to him. Then he'd create a fake report and submit it to the police."

"Take a deep breath or you are going to blow a gasket," I told him. "Why would he scan for what he was using?"

"I don't know, my guess, he couldn't order it to not be tested for, it is standard in most tox screens to test for sedatives and illegal drugs," Xavier said.

"Seems careless to leave them lying around here," I frowned.

"Why? Who is going to search a morgue? Any of the other coroners would have just thought they were sending copies to the police departments. The police certainly weren't going to start opening drawers," Xavier huffed.

I walked over to the table where Hilary Ericson lay. Vacant holes where her eyes should have been, she was also missing lips, ears, and a nose. But then she was missing her hair and everything else as well.

"Are you alright?" I asked him.

"I'm fine, just tired," Xavier finally moved back from the body. He leaned against a desk. "I'm doing a little better with Hilary. She died around 8 p.m. This is going to disturb you, but my theory is she and Arons were both killed in the Ericson house. He butchered both of them in his bedroom. After he finished with Hilary, he reported her missing and then took Arons to your hotel room. That's where I hit a dead end. I know how she died, I don't know how he died."

"Well, we aren't having any luck either. He's disappeared."

"You'd think since everyone is searching for his car . . ."

"Oh, shit," I interrupted. "We're looking for the wrong car."

I dug out my cell phone and called Gabriel. He answered on the third ring.

"Stop looking for Ericson's car, start looking for Sheriff Rybolt's car," I told him.

"Yeah, we just found Ericson's. It's on fire in a city park, with another body. This one looks like it's been dead longer than the sister-in-law. Judge Rybolt had a cell phone call coming in about an hour and a half ago from Sheriff Rybolt's phone. And we confirmed that no one had informed her yet that her husband was dead. She drives here to meet her husband and Ericson, no idea why, he kills her and steals her car."

"From serial killer to spree killer?" I asked.

"Seems to be and the car swapping ensured that we were not going to find either his car or the sheriff's. The judge was killed simply for her car."

"Stop sending Xavier bodies, he's getting tired," I said and hung up.

"Another?"

"Sheriff Rybolt's wife, the judge that released me."

"Damn, they had a daughter, young daughter."

"Yep."

"I don't know what I'm looking for anymore. We know it's him, we have a mountain of evidence. I think I'll leave these for someone else," Xavier took off his mask and tossed it on a desk.

259

"I'll do it," the voice came through the door, ahead of the body. "Easier to make the evidence disappear."

I pulled my gun at the approaching figure.

"I wouldn't do that. I used ether on Arons, he's combustible," Dr. Ericson entered the room.

I looked at Xavier. He shrugged. I fired.

The room filled with fire. It exploded around us, turning the very air into flames. My lungs hurt as I left my feet. Xavier landed next to me.

The ceiling overhead was made of drop tiles. They instantly caught fire. I heard someone swear. It wasn't Xavier. I hadn't killed him, yet again.

"We need to get out of here," Xavier whispered to me.

"Is there a back exit?" I whispered back. He grabbed hold of me and began pulling me forward. We crawled across the floor. Smoke was filling the room. My eyes stung and watered. My nose was running. My throat hurt. Xavier passed something back to me. I took the cloth mask and put it on.

We reached a second door. Xavier knelt and opened it. We entered a freezer area. There were drawers lining the walls. The entire room was made of stainless steel, except the ceiling. It was also well sealed. The smoke didn't follow and an air system sucked the smoke that had gotten in up through a vent.

"You've been burned," I said as I gasped for air.

"So have you," he responded.

"Are we safe in here?"

"For a while, unless Ericson comes at us directly," outside there was an explosion and something slammed into the door. "Or we get buried alive."

"Told you I wouldn't live long enough to get cancer."

"This wouldn't have happened with just ether on a body. He's been slowly filling the place," Xavier shook his head.

"Might be why you are tired and cranky," I said. "When would he have time?"

"It's very easy to fill a room with ether," Xavier frowned, "especially if you arrange it ahead of time. He has full access to the morgue, it could be in the ventilation system."

The door might have been steel, but the ceiling wasn't. Smoke began to seep in through the ceiling area. It was quickly followed by fire.

"Help me find the empty drawers," Xavier said.

"I am not climbing onto a slab in a morgue," I told him.

"Would you rather burn to death?"

"I hate fire," I looked around. There was another option. I pushed on the steel door; it was warm to the touch, but not yet hot. I dropped to my knees. Behind me, Xavier swore, but I heard him following.

"You realize if the ceiling comes down, we die, right?" He yelled.

"Don't think negative thoughts," I yelled back.

We crawled to the hallway on our bellies. Both of us coughing and gasping with the effort. The hallway was engulfed in smoke. We continued crawling.

The glass entry door came into view. The glass was already broken out of it. I didn't bother to push it open; I crawled across the broken glass.

Outside, someone grabbed me and pulled me away from the building. I looked up and saw the morgue attendant. He frowned at me.

"Get the other," I coughed.

"I'm here," Xavier was trying to stand in front of me. He doubled over with a coughing fit. He spat black stuff onto the concrete. I looked at him. He was missing his eyebrows and his face was black.

"Do I look that bad?" I asked.

"No," the attendant told me. "Dr. Ericson did, but he got in a car and drove off anyway."

"Oh, you have got to be kidding me," I groaned.

"Fucking hell," Xavier spat again.

"Chances are good that if I have to shoot or stab him again, I am going to start enjoying it," I told Xavier.

"Get in line, girly," Xavier coughed some more.

Twenty-Six

Quite impolitely, I told the doctor what he could do with his recommendation that I stay in the hospital. Xavier did the same. They had cleaned us and dressed our wounds. It was now time to hunt down our serial killer.

Gabriel was frowning as we exited our new motel rooms. I had strapped on an extra knife at my wrist. Gabriel could see it.

"There's been another murder," Gabriel said. "This time, he killed some waitress that worked at a pizzeria. She was walking into the pizza place when he walked up and gutted her in the parking lot. No one stopped him."

"This is definitely devolution," Lucas said.

"Of humanity? Because six people watched as he cut off her cheek," Gabriel said.

"People don't want to get involved," Lucas responded. "Although, that seems extreme."

Gabriel's cell phone rang. He spoke into it quickly. He hung up and screamed. His face screwed up in rage like I had never seen from Gabriel.

"Another?" Lucas asked.

"Another FBI agent. We have his picture up everywhere," Gabriel was shouting.

"It will not matter," I said. "He's on the hunt, moving ahead, and moving faster than us. But not for long."

"Why?" Gabriel asked.

"Because he really wants to kill me," I said. "I bring out the worst in him. Or at least I will."

We talked for a few minutes and a press conference was arranged at the Marshals office. Gabriel drove at break neck speed to get us there. The press was already assembled.

I gave the usual speech but used adjectives like "small", "pathetic", and "unmemorable". Lucas gave me a thumbs up from the crowd. I was bound to rattle him into action with the speech.

Press conference concluded, I stood on the steps of the Marshals office and thought. I thought about the woods where his son had been found. It was still nagging at me.

"I want to go to the woods," I told Gabriel after a few more minutes.

"Which woods?"

"The one where the son was found," I answered.

"Fine, get in," he pointed towards the car.

The two of us drove in silence. We pulled into the parking lot. There was a dark patch where snow had melted and the concrete could be seen.

"This is where he burned the cars?" I frowned.

"Sort of," Gabriel answered. "There is more than one entrance into the park. I'm told this is the least used and the remotest section of Anchorage."

"That's interesting," I responded. I stared out the window for a moment, getting a feel for the place. The parking lot was maybe big enough for five cars. The trees were much denser, closer to the road. We had missed the smoke of the burning cars earlier. I could see why.

"I am not letting you go in alone."

"I don't expect you to," I answered getting out of the car.

I examined the scorched parking lot. The snow had melted and ran, cutting odd valleys through the unmelted snow. I stood and shook my head.

"What?" Gabriel rolled down the window.

"He isn't coming back here; the fire was either cleansing or desecration. I'm not sure which," I got back in the SUV.

"So where is he?" Gabriel asked.

"Probably killing someone," I told him.

"Where do we go?"

"I do not know," I shook my head again and thought some more. If I was a serial killer where would I be? I'd be trying to kill me.

"Let's just hang out for a few minutes," I finally said.

Gabriel left the car running. He scooted his seat back, closed his eyes and in minutes, he was catnapping next to me. My mind was too busy for a catnap. It was going through a list of places Dr. Ericson was familiar with.

My cell phone rang. Xavier's name flashed on the screen.

"What's up?"

"Hello, Marshal Cain," Dr. Ericson's voice came over the line. I slapped Gabriel so hard he coughed. I put the phone on speaker, motioning for Gabriel to keep silent.

"And what did you give Xavier, Lucas, and Michael to put them all to sleep?" I asked.

"Nothing, Xavier went back to the motel alone, I merely hit him in the head. Do you want to come save him?"

I thought for a moment. Yes, I did, but Dr. Ericson was obviously crazier than I had estimated. I took that into consideration a moment longer.

"Where?" I asked.

"Where what?"

"Where am I supposed to meet you?" I made sure he heard the exasperation in my voice, emphasizing that he might not be as smart as me.

"How about the spot where my son died?" He told me.

"Sure, race you there," I hung up. "Go find a tree and scurry up it quickly."

"I'm the boss," Gabriel protested.

"Ok, what are you going to do?"

"I'm going to find a tree and climb it before he gets here. You stay in my view at all times, Aislinn."

"How are you going to get there without leaving footprints?" I asked. Gabriel seemed to think about this a moment.

"I'll manage," he got out of the car.

My feet hurt from the cold. It had finally seeped into my boots. My bones felt like they were breaking. I was too old and too broken down, even at twenty-eight to enjoy cold weather. Plus, I had new injuries. The cold air soothed my lungs and throat. It was the only good thing.

I had been standing for at least thirty minutes. However, it beat Gabriel's position. He was blended pretty well. He had found a pine tree to hide in. When he came down, he'd be covered in sap and pine needles.

Finally, I heard the crunching sound of feet in snow. It seemed to be coming from all directions at once. I felt very exposed. Yet, I knew that shooting me from the safety of the trees was not in his plans. It would be too easy.

"Marshal Henders, why don't you climb down from that tree and make yourself scarce," a voice suddenly called out. Gabriel didn't move. My eyes finally found Dr. Ericson. He was standing near Gabriel's tree, gun pointed up.

He fired six shots. There was a noise and Gabriel came crashing down to the ground. I hoped he was wearing his vest. I drew my gun and fired. Dr. Ericson laughed. He pointed the handgun at Gabriel's head.

"He's still alive, you should drop that," Dr. Ericson said to me.

"And Xavier?" I asked.

"Also alive for now," Dr. Ericson said. "That depends though on how fast Marshal Henders can get to him."

Gabriel groaned. I tossed my gun about fifteen feet away. I added my cell phone before he could comment on it. Gabriel groaned again.

"Let's talk," I said.

"No, I don't want to talk, Marshal Cain. I'm going to finish you off while Marshal Henders goes to save Dr. Reece, then I'm going to kill myself. I had planned to put my wife in this spot, but you screwed that up when you stabbed me."

"You stabbed me first," I reminded him.

"You'd better get a move on, Marshal, or Dr. Reece isn't going to make it out of this alive. His address is on your dash," Dr. Ericson reached down and took Gabriel's gun.

"Go, Gabriel, I got this," I told him. Gabriel struggled to his feet. He gave me one last look and took off through the trees. The look said it all. I'd better come out alive.

"I understand you are a sociopath. I've never skinned one of those; it will be a new experience for me."

"You think you are going to have time for all that?" I asked. The darkness was washing over me.

"Oh, that is a neat trick. It's like your humanity just disappeared."

"It did."

He walked into the clearing. His eyes traveled up and down my smaller frame. He wasn't checking me out. He was summing me up, trying to decide if I was going to be as much of a challenge as he thought. Most nut jobs did this to me, I was used to it.

He growled and rushed me. His shoulder caught me in the stomach and we rolled into the snow. Momentarily, he had the upper hand. I kicked my leg up, wrapped it around his neck and pulled him backwards. He lost his leverage and rolled over, off of me. I drew the knife at my wrist.

This was shorter than my boot knife, only three inches, but I kept it sharpened. Instead of a standard hilt, it had a flattened handle with two holes. The holes slid over my fingers, allowing the knife to stand over my fist.

My fingers were already in the holes. I lunged at him, jumped on top of him and plunged the knife into his face. It pierced his cheek, went through the skin and hit teeth. Blood instantly began to pour from the wound. I twisted the blade as I pulled it out, making the wound a gaping hole.

His other hand clipped me, slamming into my cheek, drawing blood as the skin against my cheekbone split. I didn't feel it. I drew back for another attack, my blade drove home again, my fist hitting his shirt, as it slipped through the skin at his side. I had aimed for a kidney and missed. He laughed at me.

I smiled back.

"You know the problem with most people," I told him. "They always underestimate me."

I let go of the small wrist knife and dug out a second boot knife. His eyes widened. It was a matched set. One I hoped to get reunited soon. He fired a small gun. It tore through my shoulder. I hadn't seen him pull it. It didn't matter.

I sunk the knife in to the hilt, felt it hit bone, break through it. Blood began to trickle from his chest. His fingers flexed, firing again, but the shot went wide. I twisted the blade and yanked out as hard as I could. Bone splintered from his chest. He gurgled and blood gushed from his mouth and his chest. The chest wound pulsed in time with his heart.

It slowed. He gurgled again. I wiped blood from my cheek.

"You should have worn your shark suit. I may be just a lowly sociopath, but I am just as much of a monster as you," I whispered to him like a lover telling a secret. "I hope hell hurts."

Epilogue

My living room was completed when we returned from Alaska. I sat on the couch, drinking a soda. Nyleena sat with me, not talking. We'd just finished watching *Monty Python and the Holy Grail*. I hadn't left my house in over a week. We were officially on leave while we all healed. Gabriel hadn't left. He'd videoed with his cell phone my encounter with Dr. Ericson.

Lucas had saved Xavier before Gabriel had even been found in the tree. Dr. Ericson had injected him with blood thinner and sliced open his leg. By the time I killed Dr. Ericson, Xavier had been at the hospital getting treatment. It had come out over the police channel in the car.

Ericson had been smart enough to cut the microphone off, but not smart enough to destroy the radio.

Gabriel had sustained a gunshot wound to the leg and five to his vest. His chest looked like he had slept on quarters that had left bruises.

"How do you feel?" Nyleena asked.

"Like hell," I told her.

"No, I mean," she paused. "Lucas and Xavier talked to me about you having issues on the case."

"I am a monster," I told her. "But a good monster. I can live with that."

"What are your plans for the rest of the week?"

"Well, they say the stitches will come out at the end of the week. After that, I will have a few new scars. Otherwise, I do not really have plans."

"Why don't you come out with us on Friday night? We're all going to dinner. I'll even consider inviting Malachi," Nyleena said trying to sound playful. Her and Malachi didn't exactly like each other. While they trusted each other, they only tolerated one another when necessary.

"I do not know who would suffer worse through that dinner, you or Malachi," I said. "Probably you, Malachi does not have a huge range of emotions. You really are a masochist."

"We all have our faults," Nyleena wiggled her eyebrows. "Come on, we can make a weekend out of it. Dinner Friday and then away for the weekend, we jump in the car and just drive. We could be in Nebraska by Saturday afternoon, go to Ash Falls Archeological Site or somewhere equally historic and dull."

"You know," I frowned. "I do have something to do actually. Mind if I ditch you for the day?"

"Sure, but what?"

"I have to go see an old friend," I walked into my garage. The door whirred open as the car roared to life. I dug out my cell phone and made a call.

I drove in a daze, eventually pulling into the maximum security facility, but not remembering how I got there.

A guard led me down a hallway into an interview room. Across the table, chained at the feet and ankles, sat my brother. I sat down in the opposite chair.

"Hi," I said.

"What happened to your face?" He asked.

"Serial killer."

"I read the article."

"So did I," I sighed.

"What is it, Aislinn?"

"I have come to realize something about both of us."

"What's that?"

"We are both monsters, but good monsters. The only difference is that I sit on this side and you sit on that side."

"You are not a monster."

"Yeah, yeah I am. I'm ok with it. I just want you to know that I'm doing good in my new job. I know how you used to worry."

"I worry even more now. The killers in here have created a fan club for you."

"It's nice to have fans," I smiled. For the first time in ages, I heard my brother laugh. The sound tugged at my heart. Yes, I was a sociopath, but I was also human.

~~~~~~

Gabriel sat in a large office with windows that looked out across the city. The Sprint Center could even be seen. Technically, this was not a federal building, but there was a floor of federal offices, hidden in plain sight. He was not nervous, but irritated as he waited.

"Marshal Henders," the deep voice of the speaker came into the room.

"Sir," he said.

When the man walked around and came into Gabriel's view, it was obvious that he had never been in uniform. Never attempted to apprehend a bad guy. Had probably never seen one up close and personal either. Gabriel's irritation grew.

"I have the report from retired US Marshal Alejandro Gui who states that Marshal Aislinn Cain is extraneous and places the entire team at unnecessary risk. Do you have anything to say to that?" The smaller man asked.

"Loads, sir," Gabriel responded. "Have you seen the video?"

"I have and that brings me to another issue we have. Why did you go off and leave a fellow US Marshal to face down a serial killer alone?"

"Ever since Alejandro Gui turned in that report a month ago, you guys have been busting my balls about Aislinn Cain. You've read all of Lucas McMichaels' reports. You've read Xavier Reece's reports. Yet, you still question it. I think the video speaks for itself. I didn't leave a fellow US Marshal with a serial killer. I left a sociopath to take care of business. Which, she did, with distinction. Reece might have been able to do it. McMichaels probably could have done it. Giovanni and I would not have survived it. Aislinn Cain did, that's what she does, survives. Even if I had really left that clearing, it would have been Cain getting into a car and the serial killer being put in the coroner's van. Now, I realize that our methods aren't by the book. And I realize that we have a higher than normal death rate for suspects we are taking into custody. You need to realize that it is a side effect of what we do and having a genius sociopath who is functional and forces herself to feel something, is not only terribly rare, but very useful to us, sir." Gabriel was working not to grind his teeth. This man, in his expensive suit, who surveyed the city from above, without getting his hands dirty, was just another example of how much the system was broken.

"Gui says she is unstable and a time-bomb," the man pressed.

"Gui is an alcoholic and a steroid user with paranoia issues, sir," Gabriel replied.

"You think his assessment is wrong?"

"I think Alejandro Gui is just one stressor away from being on the wrong side of the Serial Crimes Tracking Unit. Cain is not a danger to this team in any way, shape, or form and has proven herself on every hunt she's participated in. She has a vast library of information available in her head. She isn't afraid of the monsters we have to catch. And she is quite capable of taking care of herself. I know that we may coddle her sometimes, but this is not because she isn't capable, it's because we need her in ways that you cannot imagine. She is the one that told me to put on a bulletproof vest to climb a tree. She is the one that told me to go to Reece and not to worry about her. And she was right on both occasions. Without the vest, I wouldn't be here and she handled Henry Ericson just fine, sir."

"Which brings us back to the unstable part of Gui's report."

"She is not unstable or at least, not any more unstable than the rest of them. But I believe that is exactly how this team was constructed; you took the most unstable good guys and tossed them together. I have seen her when she goes all creepy. I have heard her talk about the lack of emotions in that state. I agree with Lucas's assessment. She's a sociopath, but not in the traditional sense. She's something new, something much scarier. She faced down a psychopath and survived in Alaska. She's done it time and time again. She puts the team before herself. And she's good at catching the monsters, sir."

"What should I do with Gui's report then?"

"Honestly? I think you should crumple it up and find a trash can. His report was written solely because he didn't like her when he was in charge and he likes her even less now. Mark my words, one day, he's going to snap and end up being hunted by us. He doesn't want her around for that because he knows he can't outsmart her or manhandle her the way he does other women. He's the one you need to be watching, sir. Not Aislinn Cain."

"Fine, Marshal Henders, for now, she remains your problem. If you are correct in all your accusations against Gui, then I will of course, file the report in the appropriate trash bin. Until then, keep a tighter leash on her. I do not want her face flashing up on news reports. There is no need to glorify a monster."

Gabriel chuckled. It didn't lighten the mood.

"We glorify monsters every day, Cain is at least worth the glorification. You know, you really want to understand her place on my team, you should visit the prison. Go take a survey or something of them about US Marshal Aislinn Cain and look at the results very carefully. Most of the bad-asses inside that place will tell you what I'm about to tell you, they wouldn't want to fuck with her. Most agree she'd kill them, sir. Those that are smart enough fear and respect her. Those that don't, never make it inside The Fortress."

"Are you done with the theatrics?"

"It isn't theatrics. You don't get a fan club of serial killers behind bars without a reason. Marshal Cain has a fan club there and they are all sending in requests to be interviewed by her and McMichaels. The Tallahassee Terror described his encounter with Cain as enlightening and of Cain herself, he said 'she is the boogeyman of serial killers. When we have nightmares, we dream of her.' But then you have that report, maybe you should re-read it, sir."

"You're excused."

Gabriel left the office shaking. The small man in the expensive suit smiled. He took Alejandro Gui's report and shredded it. He'd been right to go with his gut. Aislinn Cain was going to be just fine hunting down serial killers. Gabriel Henders was right, she knew how to survive. He stood, adjusted the stack of papers on his desk, and picked up the phone.

"I'd like to be connected to Special Agent Malachi Blake," he told the woman who answered the phone.

"This is Blake," someone said after a few moments.

"I've just heard from US Marshal Henders about their last case. I thought you'd be interested to know that Aislinn Cain killed another serial killer."

"Imagine that," Blake gave a short bark of laughter. "With reason I hope."

"Oh lots of reasons, he was trying to kill her. Henders trusts her survival instincts enough to leave her in the woods with a serial killer and expect her to walk out."

"I told you she'd be a good fit, once Alejandro was gone. I didn't expect his demise to come as it did, but, then, shit happens and he should have been more careful."

"Are you still worried about her?"

"I will always be worried about her," Malachi answered. "But she's going to attract them to her regardless of whether she has a badge or not, so she might as well be a Marshal. Besides, Lucas and Xavier have become attached to her, so they will help her when it's needed."

"You know she has a fan club inside The Fortress?"

"Yes, serial killers think she's great."

"Malachi, I know it's none of my business, but do you love her?"

"I am incapable of such a thing, but if I weren't, then yes, I'd love her. As it is, she is the only person that fills the void for me."

"Do you want me to continue to watch her?"

"No, it's not necessary, I'm sure you're busy with whatever it is you do."

"I sit on the board that controls the Serial Crimes Tracking Unit. I get all the reports."

"It's fine Uncle, I just wanted to make sure that Gabriel didn't feel the same way as Alejandro."

"All right, I have to go. I'll see you later." The man hung up. He motioned his secretary who was frantically waving her arms through the window, into the room.

"You have to be in court in thirty minutes," she said as she came in.

"I had business to attend to," he answered.

"Judge Greer, I know that the Serial Crimes Tracking Unit takes up some of your time, but it's a board, some of the others could help more."

"Barb, one day, you will understand why I let it take up so much of my time. What am I dealing with today again?"

"You have a tough one, the prosecutor is Nyleena Clachan. The defendant is Ramon Vega, suspected spree killer out of New York. The FBI handled the case and someone bungled something, so Clachan is out for blood and you know how brutal she can be."

"Bungled how?"

"They missed catching him for six hours because an FBI agent didn't check in when he went for lunch. Clachan is demanding his badge. She's going to crucify him on the stand."

"And rightly so," Judge Greer grabbed his briefcase. "Barb, go home for the rest of the day, you look tired."

"I was up all night sorting through paperwork," his secretary admitted. "We had seventeen reports filed on the Alaska case."

"And?"

"And most were favorable. One from a state trooper said that if the team had worked harder, they would have caught him faster, but he was the husband of a victim during the end. His sister-in-law was also a victim and the killer's wife."

"File it with the rest of the complaints," Judge Greer told her.

"Will do, I'll shred it and make sure that it makes it to the incinerator today."

"Good, see you tomorrow." Judge Greer left his office and met his driver in the parking lot.

"I see you are in a good mood today, Judge," the driver said to him.

"I am. I love it when things work. To court, driver, and make it snappy," the judge laughed.

"On it," the driver slipped into the car.

About the Author

I've been writing for over two decades and before that, I was creating my own bedtime stories to tell myself. I penned my first short story at the ripe old age of 8. It was a fable about how the raccoon got its eye-mask and was roughly three pages of handwritten, 8 year old scrawl. My mother still has it and occasionally, I still dig it out and admire it.

When I got my first computer, I took all my handwritten stories and typed them in. Afterwards, I tossed the originals. In my early twenties, I had a bit of a writer's meltdown and deleted everything. So, with the exception of the story about the raccoon, I actually have none of my writings from before I was 23. Which is sad, because I had a half dozen other novels and well over two hundred short stories. It has all been offered up to the computer and writing gods as a sacrifice and show of humility or some such nonsense that makes me feel less like an idiot about it.

I have been offered contracts with publishing houses in the past and always turned them down. Now that I have experimented with being an Indie Author, I really like it and I'm really glad I turned them down. However, if you had asked me this in the early years of 2000, I would have told you that I was an idiot (and it was a huge contributing factor to my deleting all my work).

When I'm not writing, I play in a steel-tip dart league and enjoy going to dart tournaments. I enjoy renaissance festivals and sanitized pirates who sing sea shanties. My appetite for reading is ferocious and I consume two to three books a week as well as writing my own. Aside from introducing me to darts, my SO has introduced me to camping, which I, surprisingly, enjoy. We can often be found in the summer at Mark Twain Lake in Missouri, where his parents own a campground.

I am a native of Columbia, Missouri, which I will probably call home for the rest of my life, but I love to travel. Day trips, week trips, vacations on other continents, wherever the path takes me is where I want to be and I'm hoping to be able to travel more in the future.

http://www.facebook.com/hadenajames

hadenajames.wordpress.com

@hadenajames

Printed in Great Britain
by Amazon